"*IS* IT CASt?" GRISSOM ASKED.

Catherine came back in from the kitchen, kit in one latex-gloved hand, gesturing behind her with the other. "I didn't find anything except dirty dishes. . . ." Seeing Brass, she froze and blinked. "Aren't you on vacation?"

Brass nodded to her. "I was." His sad gaze fixed on Grissom. "Well, it sure *looks* like CASt's handi-work. . . ."

"Cast?" Catherine asked, joining them. The three had the corpse surrounded—he wasn't going anywhere.

Closing his eyes, Brass touched the thumb and middle finger of his right hand to the bridge of his nose. "You didn't work that case . . . you might even have been a lab tech still. I dunno."

Catherine looked at Grissom and tightened her eyes in a signal of *Help me out here?* Grissom, of course, merely shrugged.

Brass was saying, "I know you've heard me talk about it—my first case here? Never solved? Lot of play in the press? Worst serial killer in Vegas history? Cop in charge an incompetent New Jersey jackass? Sound familiar?"

"Taunted the PD in the papers," Catherine said, nodding, thinking out loud. "Used the initials . . . C period A period S period tee."

" 'Capture,' " Grissom said, " 'Afflict, and Strangle.' "

Original novels by Max Allan Collins in the CSI series:

CSI: Crime Scene Investigation
Double Dealer
Sin City
Cold Burn
Body of Evidence
Grave Matters

CSI: Miami
Florida Getaway
Heat Wave

CSI:
CRIME SCENE INVESTIGATION ™

BINDING TIES
a novel

Max Allan Collins

Based on the hit CBS series
"CSI: Crime Scene Investigation"
Produced by CBS Productions, a
business unit of CBS Broadcasting Inc.
and Alliance Atlantis Productions Inc.
Executive Producers: Jerry Bruckheimer,
Carol Mendelsohn, Anthony E. Zuiker, Ann Donahue,
Danny Cannon, Jonathan Littman
Co-Executive Producers:
Cynthia Chvatal & William Petersen
Series created by: Anthony E. Zuiker

POCKET
BOOKS

London · New York · Sydney · Toronto

An *Original* Publication of POCKET BOOKS

Published by
POCKET BOOKS, a division of Simon & Schuster, Ltd.,
Africa House, 64–78 Kingsway, London WC2B 6AH
www.simonsays.co.uk

ISBN-10: 1-4165-0239-4
ISBN-13: 978-1-4165-0239-5

First Pocket Books printing 2005

10 9 8 7 6

Cover design by Patrick Kang

Printed and bound in Great Britain by
Cox & Wyman Ltd, Reading, Berks

A CIP record for this book is
available from the British Library.

For Terri and Rod—
nicely bound.

I would like to acknowledge my assistant on this work, forensics researcher/co-plotter **Matthew V. Clemens.**
Further acknowledgments appear at the conclusion of this novel.

M.A.C.

"A sound thinker gives equal consideration
to the probable and the improbable."
   —R. Austin Freeman's Dr. John Thorndyke

"Nothing is simpler than to kill a man;
the difficulties arise in attempting
to avoid the consequences."
                —Rex Stout's Nero Wolfe

Like a cold harsh mountain wind wailing down across the Nevada desert, panic swept through Marvin Sandred.

Awake again finally, his first realization was of his utter helplessness, a figure behind him, straddling his ass—literally—and a rope looped around his neck, pulling back, choking. Chills shook Marvin's body, making the noose chafe harder, and he felt it tighten more and more with each passing second.

Arms flailing, Marvin tried to control and even out his breathing. He did not have the time or frame of mind to take stock of his situation; still, he knew he was home, in the livingroom of his small North Las Vegas house—on the floor, on his stomach, his bones aching, his lungs burning, his assailant sitting astride his backside, as the noose slowly squeezed against his windpipe, and no matter how hard he worked to avoid it, his breaths could only come in short, sucking gulps. The room reeked of his sweat and the rope seemed to be squeezing his bladder as much as his throat.

Somehow, the worst thing of all, the most extreme indignity, was his nakedness—his clothes had been stripped from him, and he battled the urge to piss himself. Cold yet sweating, hands swimming limply in the air, fighting suffocation even as he wondered if he should just go ahead and free his bladder to remove the only pain within his control, Marvin Sandred was experiencing the reality behind the abstraction.

This was terror.

Terror—that word so bandied about on the news every day—was not an abstraction, but a very real emotional and physical state. Sheer terror—pain and helplessness and fear and despair and, worst of all, hope. He was still alive. He'd gotten into this somehow, and he could still get out. He might still survive. . . .

Not so long ago, Marvin had responded to the doorbell, finding a well-dressed man in a black suit standing before the peephole, clean-cut enough to be a Jehovah's Witness or Mormon missionary, only those guys travelled in pairs and the man on Marvin's doorstep had been alone.

Marvin had long since learned that there is much in this life that the individual cannot control. But a man remained king of his castle, however shabby, and invasions by phone solicitors and door-knocking salesmen were indignities he did not have to suffer. Didn't he have a NO SOLICITING sign on his goddamned door?

Marvin saw the bland individual on his doorstep as representing every intrusion, every invasion of his precious privacy, and an indignant Marvin Sandred had opened the door wide, to tear this guy a new orifice and send him on his fucking way, only not a word had emerged from Marvin's mouth before things went wrong, horribly, terribly . . . wrong.

Whether he had been drugged or punched or hit with a tire iron, he did not know, perhaps never would know. Right now, all he knew for sure was that he lay naked on the floor, the rough carpeting irritating his nipples and his ample belly and his genitals, even as the noose closed ever tighter around his throat. He stopped flailing and tried to get at the rope, but couldn't get his fingers beneath the damn loop. . . .

Even though his attacker was behind and above him, Marvin kept his eyes pinched shut. On waking, finding himself under attack, that had been his first instinct—if he didn't open his eyes, he reasoned, he wouldn't see his antagonist's face.

If he did not get a good look at the man, the attacker might let him live—the intruder might be a burglar who would leave Marvin unconscious on the floor to be found later. Two facts that Marvin did not grasp made the point moot: Had he opened his eyes, sweat would have poured into them, impairing his vision; and his attacker's ride-'em-cowboy position made him impossible for Marvin to see, anyway.

The attacker controlled the situation so utterly, Marvin knew that the decision of his life or death belonged to the man in the black suit.

One tiny hope glimmered in Marvin's mind. . . .

He knew that a letter opener lay on the nearby coffee table, under the morning paper and a stack of bills, if only *he could reach it. Eyes still squeezed shut, Marvin pawed helplessly in that direction, with his left hand, but his arm felt heavy, like trying to lift a refrigerator, not his own limb.*

The attacker slapped the arm down, and Marvin couldn't find the strength to raise it again. . . .

As it got harder and harder to breathe, and surviving became more and more abstract, a thought jumped into his mind, between panic-stricken plans to somehow get loose: That thought was how stupid he had been to move to Las Vegas in the first place.

Then his wife Annie popped into his mind: her pretty, smiling face, the way she had looked at him so often, before she left him last year.

Though these thoughts lasted only a few seconds, they were profound: Marvin realized he still missed his ex-wife, and wished he'd been smart enough to stay in Eau Claire and try to patch things up with her, instead of throwing away his entire life to move to the city of dreams. . . .

He'd been an idiot. He still was an idiot. He knew as much, even with the breath being sucked out of him for what was probably the last time . . . a goddamned idiot, cashing in his retirement, driving away Annie, looking for a new life. . . .

Marvin Sandred, at the brink of death, did not have the time or luxury of acquiring a longer, more mature view of his life and where it had gone awry. Lots of people had come to this city of dreams, from Bugsy Siegel to Howard Hughes, from Liberace to Penn and Teller. Formerly an assistant plant manager at Eau Claire Steelworks, Marvin Sandred had been one of hundreds of thousands of dreamers who'd migrated to the neon oasis, not just to visit, but to live.

Marvin's dream was modest, comparatively speaking, if typically unrealistic of Vegas dreamers. Just as Annie was entering menopause, Marvin's midlife crisis kicked in, and the forty-six-year-old had felt life slipping through his fingers, opportunities and dreams betrayed by a lifetime of doing "the right thing." Marvin had started watching poker on ESPN, and then played it on the Internet, till his wife put her foot down just when he was starting to win a little; so he'd practiced on a ten-buck computer game and did very well indeed, so well that he finally decided to come to Las Vegas to play poker professionally.

His retirement settlement gave Marvin just enough money to get to Vegas and put a down payment on this little bungalow; he'd hoped his wife—they were childless—would view this as a fresh start. Actually, she saw it as a dead-end. The rest of his money he had used to fund his fantasy of becoming the next Amarillo Slim or Doyle Brunson.

The dream had indeed gone quickly south, his poker skills faring far better against his computer game than real people. After two tournaments, Sandred got a day job in the sales department of a welding equipment company. The dream began its slow death from that point on, his meager earnings winding down the spiraling hole of Texas Hold-'em, casino-style. . . .

Still, Marvin had never given up, and his sick-gambler's optimism stayed with him, right up to where his dream was swallowed by this full-fledged nightmare, the attacker applying even more pressure now. . . .

Marvin felt his head grow heavy, the weight of it trying to sag to the floor, the rope around his neck keeping his skull up, but a certain bobbing motion making his forehead occasionally brush the rough rug. Colored lights burst behind his eyelids in a tiny fireworks show, and for just a moment he was downtown in Glitter Gulch with the overhead display of Sinatra singing, "Luck be a lady," and Marvin's arms were rubbery things and tears mingled with sweat as his dream dissolved and his mind was filled with a nightmare that would end not with waking, but rather with going to sleep.

Forever.

And as the colored lights subsided and blackness fell across, Marvin Sandred saw Annie in his mind, smiling sadly, shaking her head, saying, as she had when she left, "Don't you know, Marvin? One person's dream is another's nightmare?"

ONE

The North Las Vegas neighborhood was slowly making the transition from cozy to shabby. A 420 on the radio, this homicide call—which on the Strip would be treated like a presidential assassination, every squad car rolling in with lights strobing and siren blaring—had generated only one North Las Vegas PD squad, which sat parked out front of the house as quietly as if this was the officer's home . . .

. . . and not a crime scene.

Which was what brought LVPD Crime Scene Investigation supervisor Gil Grissom to this declining residential area, and not for the first time—wasn't a habit yet, but calls in these environs were definitely on the upswing.

Seasoned veteran Grissom descended on this troubled neighborhood like the angel of death, albeit a casually attired one, such a study in black was he: sunglasses, Polo shirt, slacks, shoes. Gray was invading the dark curly hair, however, intruding as well into a beard he'd grown to save himself time, only to find trimming the thing was its own burden. He'd thought of shaving the damn thing off, at least twenty times, but that much of an expenditure of time he wasn't ready to invest.

Gil Grissom's life was his work, and his work was death.

Nick Stokes, behind the wheel, parked the black CSI Tahoe behind the NLVPD cruiser; after him, Warrick Brown pulled in a second Tahoe. Grissom and Stokes had ridden in the lead vehicle while Warrick shared his with fellow CSIs, Catherine Willows and Sara Sidle.

Muscular, former college jock Nick had dark hair cut close and an easy smile that belied how seriously he took his job. The heroic-jawed CSI wore jeans and a T-shirt with the LVPD badge embroidered over the left breast.

Green-eyed, African–American Warrick was tall and slender, and his expression seemed serious most of the time, though wry twists of humor did come through. In his untucked brown T-shirt and khaki slacks, the loose-limbed Warrick seemed more relaxed than Nick, but Grissom knew both young men were tightly wired, in a good way, excellent analysts and dedicated hard workers.

Even more intense than her two male teammates, Sara Sidle wore her dark hair to her shoulders and preferred comfortable clothes like today's tan T-shirt and brown slacks. Still, she was as striking in her way as Catherine Willows, a redhead with the chiseled features of a model and the slenderly curvaceous body of a dancer. Wearing an aqua tank top and navy slacks, Catherine still more closely resembled the exotic performer she had been to the crack scientist she'd become.

Though they worked the graveyard shift, Grissom's team—thanks to manpower shortages this week—was currently working overtime to help cover dayshift court appearances and vacations. Normally, these CSIs would have showed up at a crime scene in the middle of the night, but with the OT, they found themselves arriving at this one with the summer sun already high in a cloudless blue sky, the heat dry but not oppressive, tourist friendly.

Pulling off his sunglasses, Grissom studied the bungalow: tiny and, particularly for this neighborhood, still in decent repair. The dirt yard was small and bisected by a crumbling sidewalk that passed a steel flagpole on its way to the open front door. Two flags hung limp on the windless day, an American flag at the top and a Green Bay Packers one beneath it, while a short gravel driveway ran up the far side of the house, a dark blue early nineties Chevy parked in the middle.

Even though homes surrounded the bungalow all along the block, to Grissom, the house looked lonely, somehow. Heat shimmered off the pavement outside this house; but sadness shimmered off the house itself.

As Grissom hopped down from the Tahoe, his peripheral vision caught an unmarked Ford pulling up on the other side of the street. He paused to glance back and see the detective getting out, a lanky six-three in an ill-fitting gray suit—Bill Damon. The detective was still in his late twenties, having been with the North Las Vegas PD for five or six years, now deep into his first year as a detective. Though his pants always seemed an inch or so too short, and his jacket seemed large enough for a man twice his size, Damon fit the job nicely—if still unseasoned as a detective, this was a good cop, with his heart in the right place.

While more than a hundred thousand souls made North Las Vegas their home—and had their own police department—the Las Vegas crime scene analysts served all of Clark County, which meant occasionally the CSIs worked with detectives from departments other than their own. Grissom had run into Damon on a couple of cases before, but always as the secondary detective, never the primary.

As the detective crossed the street, he held out his hand to Grissom—long, slender fingers with big, knobby knuckles.

"Gil," he said as they shook. "Been a while."

"Yes it has," Grissom said, offering up a noncommital smile.

"Checked inside yet?"

The CSI supervisor shook his head. "Just got here. All we know is it's a 420."

Damon shrugged. "Which is what I know. Guess we better get informed. . . ."

"Always a good policy."

While Grissom's team unloaded their gear from the back of their vehicles, a stocky, sawed-off uniformed cop walked over from the front door of the bungalow to join them. He carried a click-top ballpoint pen in one hand and a notebook in the other. His nametag said LOGAN. An African-American of forty or so, he wore his hair trimmed short, which minimized the tiny patches of gray here and there. He stood just above the minimum height requirement, making the tall Damon seem towering.

Logan nodded to Grissom but gave his attention to his own department's detective.

"Hey, Henry," Damon said.

"Hey, Bill."

So much for small talk.

Logan smirked humorlessly, nodding back at the house. "Got a real ugly number for you in there. Guy murdered in his living room—but I sure don't call that living."

Grissom asked, "You've been inside?"

Logan nodded, shrugged. "Don't worry—your evidence oughta be waiting, and plenty of it. All I did was clear the place and make sure the killer was gone. One path in, one path out."

"Good," Grissom said, looking toward the house again.

No screen and the front door yawned wide.

"Did you open that door, Officer Logan?" Grissom asked.

"Hell no. Do I look like—"

"Have you done this before? Cleared a murder scene?"

"Had my fair share of bodies over the years. And this is the kind of corpse you don't trip over or anything—guy's in plain sight from the front doorway, and dead as shit."

Grissom's smile was so small it barely qualified. "Officer, I don't care how many murders you've covered, our victim deserves more respect than that."

Logan looked at Grissom like the CSI was from outer space.

Damon asked, "You're *sure* he's dead?"

Logan gave the detective a vaguely patronizing look. "Hey, I been doin' this a long time, Bill. Like I said, this guy's dead as . . . can be—or I'd have an ambulance here and we'd be wheeling him out. Take a look for yourself."

But Grissom wasn't satisfied with the background yet. "How did the call come in?"

"Next-door neighbor," Logan said, jerking a

thumb over his shoulder. "She went out to the street to get her mail . . ."

Logan pointed at the row of mailboxes running along the curb.

The cop continued: ". . . then our neighbor lady glanced over and saw the door open. The guy who lives here . . ." He checked his notebook. ". . . guy who *lived* there, Marvin Sandred, usually worked during the day. So, when the neighbor, woman named . . ." He checked his notebook again. ". . . Tammy Hinton, saw the door standing open, she went to check on the place. One gander at the body and she phoned us."

Grissom asked, "She said it was Sandred?"

"Yeah."

"We should talk to her."

"Yeah," Damon said, as if reminding everyone, including himself, that he was in charge, "we should talk to her right away."

"I can cover that," Logan said, but shook his head. "I'm just not sure it'll do any good, right now. She was pretty shook up, which is why I sent her home. Anything else you need?"

"No, Henry," Damon said. "Thank you."

Logan frowned at Grissom. "All due respect, Dr. Grissom—I know who you are, everybody does—I don't appreciate you going all self-righteous on me."

With no inflection, Grissom said, "Then don't use terms like 'dead as shit' to describe a murder victim."

Logan's indignation faded to embarrassment. "Yeah, okay. Point taken. No harm, no foul?"

"Not yet," Grissom said.

Logan headed to the neighbor's house, while Damon said, "You ready to check this out?"

"Yes."

Grissom started for the house, the CSIs and the North Las Vegas cops trailing in his wake. Over his shoulder, he said, "Nick, you take the backyard—Warrick, the front."

"You got it, Gris," Nick said.

Warrick just nodded.

While the two CSIs peeled off, Grissom, Catherine, and Sara—trailed by Detective Damon—pressed on to the front door atop a two-step stoop. At the threshold, he stopped.

"Sara," Grissom said, as he and the others snugged on their latex gloves, "let's see if there are any prints on the doorbell."

She nodded and stepped off to the side. Like the other CSIs, she had lugged along her tool-kit-style crime-scene case, which she set down on the concrete, and got to it.

Grissom led the way through the front door, Catherine right behind; Damon was lingering on the porch, watching Sara work, making conversation that she wasn't taking much part in.

The house was dark, curtains drawn, lights off. In the gloom, Grissom could nonetheless see that the living room was to the right, the kitchen through a doorway to the back and a hallway, at the rear of the living room, led to the bedrooms and bathroom.

Next to him, Catherine clicked on her mini-flash. There could be no turning on of lights until the switches and their plates had been dusted for prints. She used the beam to highlight doorways, then settled on the corpse, at right.

The living room stank of death in general; sweat, urine, and excrement, in particular. With its scant rent-to-own furnishings—a sofa, a coffee table, a TV at an angle in the far corner, and a couple of end tables—the room seemed as lonely inside as the house had from out. A lamp on one end table seemed to be the only potential light source, other than a picture window behind drawn curtains. Newspapers, some mail, a couple of carry-out containers cluttered the coffee table; otherwise, the room was clean—not counting the body sprawled in the middle of the floor.

The first detail Grissom picked up on was a pool of blood near one of the hands, where the index finger had been amputated. Grissom got his own mini-flash out and its beam looked around, but there was no sign of the digit. Perhaps the killer had taken a souvenir.

"I'll work the body," Grissom said, "while you do the rest of the house."

Catherine glanced down at the victim. "He's all yours. . . . Wasn't exactly in charge of his own destiny when he died, either."

"Might have something significant here," Grissom said, as he swept with the mini-flash around the body, not wanting to disturb any evidence when he drew nearer.

Catherine arched an eyebrow. "You think?"

She turned toward the hallway as Detective Damon finally made his way inside the house. Pulling up short, he winced, nostrils flaring before he quickly covered them. "Whoa—well, isn't *that* nasty?"

"Victim evacuated at death," Grissom said matter-of-factly.

Between the man's spread legs, feces pooled in urine. Grissom was long since used to this, but what bothered him most was that these strong odors could blot out other, subtler, more important ones.

From the corridor, Catherine said, "I'll start in the kitchen." Her crime-scene case swinging at her side, Catherine disappeared through the doorway.

Color had drained from the detective's face; perhaps the word "kitchen" had in this context given him a bad moment.

"You need me here?" he asked with an audible gulp.

"You'll just be in the way," Grissom said.

"I mean, it is *my* crime scene. . . ."

Grissom gave him a firm look. "No it's not—it's mine. Let me process it, then we'll talk . . . outside."

The detective desired to take the argument no further; he practically sprinted out the front door.

Returning his attention to the body on the floor, Grissom started by getting the big picture.

A Caucasian man between forty-five and fifty, he estimated; the victim was nude, prone, on his stomach, a rope around his neck. The index finger of his right hand had been severed and—so far, indications were—taken away. The man's head was to one side, giving Grissom a view of a telling touch by the murderer: the deceased's lips had been painted with a garish red lipstick.

A CSI always kept an eye out for *modus operandi;* but seldom was a signature so explicit. The normally detached Grissom felt a chill, but it had nothing to do with fear or even revulsion—he just knew he had to make a phone call on this one. A friend was affected by this.

But, his nature being his nature, he decided to work the scene first.

The vic had probably been asphyxiated, but Grissom knew better than to make that more than a working hypothesis, and would wait for the coroner, to make the final call on cause of death.

Grissom got his camera from his stainless steel crime-scene kit, and started taking pictures. First he did the room, then the body, then close-ups of the body. It took a while, but he had long ago learned patience, and even though thoughts flooded his mind, Grissom held himself to the standard of quick-but-not-hurried. He forced the impending phone call to the back of his mind and continued his work.

After a while, Sara came into the room. Unlike the detective, she reacted not at all to what a civilian would consider a stench, but which a professional crime scene analyst would consider par for the course. Nor did anything but the faintest trace of sadness—even pros were allowed compassion—cross her wide, pretty mouth.

Then she said, "Got a partial off the bell, couple partials off the knob."

"It's a start," Grissom said.

"What's Catherine up to?"

Grissom glanced at her, a little mischief in his faint smile. "Woman's place is in the kitchen."

She grinned, grunted a laugh. "You wish. . . . This one's . . . specific, isn't it?"

"It is that."

"Doesn't ring any of my bells, though. How about yours, Grissom?"

"They toll for him," he said, nodding toward the victim, but explained no further.

Sara didn't expect him to, and didn't press it, saying, "Okay I head over next door, to join our detective and officer? They're interviewing the neighbor, and I'd like to print her, get her eliminated. Partial on the bell might be hers, y'know."

"Might. You do that."

". . . There's never a good way, is there?"

"What?"

"To get murdered."

"No," Grissom admitted. "But this strikes me as one of the least desirable."

"I hear that," she said, and strode out.

He smiled to himself, pleased at how unfazed by the crime scene she'd been. He had picked Sara personally, when a CSI had been killed on the job and needed replacing; she'd been a student who excelled at his seminars, and he'd been impressed and sought her out and brought her in, and she had not disappointed.

On the other hand, he was disappointed in himself, sometimes, as his affection for this bright young woman had on occasion threatened to take him over the professional line.

And that was a line Gil Grissom did not wish to cross.

The supervisor returned his attention to the dead body.

Some sort of liquid pooled on the victim's back and he bent down to take a closer look.

Little sailors, he thought, as he took a photo of the semen gathered at the small of the victim's back. Setting the camera aside, he then swabbed a small portion of the fluid for DNA testing later. Something about the sample troubled him, though; this was part of the M.O. he had recognized, but it was a little . . . off.

Then he had it: The fluid on the back was meant to suggest that the killer had masturbated onto the victim, but the semen pooled neatly in that one spot on the vic's back.

It's been poured there, Grissom thought with a grim smile.

If the killer had ejaculated, in a sick frenzy attached to the murder, the result would hardly have been one tidy little pool. Most likely, other droplets would be here and there, spattered. . . .

He bagged the semen sample, finished taking his photos, swabbed the blood in the rug, and went over the body for any trace evidence. He found nothing. The last thing he did was carefully remove the rope and bag it. When he had completed his initial pass at the body, he withdrew his cell phone and punched the speed dial.

On the second ring, a brusque voice answered: "Jim Brass."

"I've got something you need to see," Grissom said, without identifying himself. "It's not in your jurisdiction, but it's right up your alley."

"Cute, Gil. But haven't you heard? I'm on vacation."

"Really kicking back, are you?"

Silence; no, not silence: Grissom, detective that he was, could detect a sigh. . . .

"You know as well as I do," Brass said. "I'm bored out of my mind."

"You know, people who live for their work should seek other outlets."

"What, like collecting bugs? Gil—what have you got?"

"An oldie but baddie—I wasn't with you on it . . . kind of before our time, together."

"What are you *talking* about?"

"The one you never forget—your first case."

The long pause that followed contained no sigh. Not even a breath. Just stony silence.

Then Brass said, "You're not talking about my first case back in Jersey, are you?"

"No. I've got a killing out here in North Las Vegas that shares a distinctive M.O. with your *other* first case."

"Christ. Where are you exactly?"

"Just getting started."

"I mean the address!"

"Oh," Grissom said, and gave it to him.

"Twenty minutes," Brass said and broke the connection.

The homicide captain made it in fifteen.

From the open doorway, Grissom watched Brass's car pull up and the detective get out, and cross the lawn like a man on a mission. Which, Grissom supposed, he was.

The compact, mournful-eyed Brass—always one to wear a jacket and tie, no matter the weather—had showed up in jeans and a blue shirt open at the neck.

The uniformed officer, Logan, went out to catch Brass at the front stoop, thinking a relative or other civilian had arrived. The detective flashed his badge, but Logan seemed unimpressed.

"What brings you to our neck of the woods, Captain?"

Leaning out the doorway, Grissom called, "He's with me, Officer. It's all right."

Logan, apparently not wishing to tangle with Grissom again, sighed and nodded and let Brass pass.

"You could've told him I was coming," Brass complained.

"Yeah, well I'm still working on my social skills," Grissom said.

"Really? How's that coming along?"

Shrugging, Grissom stepped back inside and got out of the way so Brass could see the body.

The detective took one look and shook his head. The blood had drained from his face and his eyes were large and unblinking. "Well, son of a—"

"*Is* it CASt?" Grissom asked.

Catherine came back in from the kitchen, kit in one latex-gloved hand, gesturing behind her with the other. "I didn't find anything except dirty dishes . . ." Seeing Brass, she froze and blinked. "Aren't you on vacation?"

Brass nodded to her. "I was." His sad gaze fixed on Grissom. "Well, it sure *looks* like CASt's handiwork. . . ."

"Cast?" Catherine asked, joining them. The three had the corpse surrounded—he wasn't going anywhere.

Closing his eyes, Brass touched the thumb and middle finger of his right hand to the bridge of his nose. "You didn't work that case . . . you might even have been a lab tech still. I dunno."

Catherine looked at Grissom and tightened her eyes in a signal of, *Help me out here?* Grissom, of course, merely shrugged.

Brass was saying, "I know you've heard me talk about it—my first case here? Never solved? Lot of play in the press? Worst serial killer in Vegas history? Cop in charge an incompetent New Jersey jackass? Sound familiar?"

"Taunted the PD in the papers," Catherine said, nodding, thinking out loud. "Used the initials . . . C period A period S period tee."

" 'Capture,' " Grissom said, " 'Afflict, and Strangle.' "

"I did a little lab work on the case," Catherine said. "I was nightshift then, too. And wasn't it a dayshift case?"

"Yes. This was ten, eleven years ago." Brass rubbed his forehead. "I just transferred in, from back East. Still shellshocked from my . . . my divorce. Not exactly on top of the Vegas scene, yet. . . ."

"All I remember about the case is pretty vague," Catherine admitted. "More from TV and the papers than anything in-house. . . ."

Grissom said, "Lots of media, but we were able to control it better in those days. And fortunately it never caught wide national play."

Brass said, "Yeah, we kept as much out as we could. My partner, Vince Champlain, didn't want to muddy the waters."

"Good call," Catherine said. "Wish we had better luck with that, these days."

Brass continued: "Vince was the senior detective. He figured, more we put in the paper, more crackpots we'd have to deal with. S. O. P. And yet, of course, there were plenty just the same. We must've had twenty different whack jobs try to claim those crimes."

"None of the wrongos looked right?" Catherine asked.

Brass shook his head. "Nah, standard issue nutcases. Serial confessors."

Catherine said, "What *did* you have?"

With a dark, defeated smile, Brass looked at her and said, "Victims—we had victims. Five—all male, all white, all in late middle-age, and all on the heavy side . . ."

As if it had been choreographed, the detective and the two CSIs looked as one at the dead body.

". . . and all strangled with a reverse-eight noose."

Catherine frowned. "Which is what, exactly?"

"A knot—a 'wrong' running noose," Grissom said. "It's about which end of the rope you pull to tighten the noose. This knot's backward . . . and other than yo-yos, you never see it used."

Turning back to Brass, Catherine asked, "Any real suspects back then?"

"We started with a slew, but we narrowed it to three," Brass said. "I had a guy I liked, Vince had a guy *he* liked, and there was a third one that looked good, only neither of us thought he did the killings."

Pointing at the body, Grissom said, "Here's how we do this: Run it like we would any other homicide investigation."

Brass nodded, then asked, "You want me to start with looking into our old suspects?"

Grissom gave him a long, appraising look. "First, a question."

"Second, an answer."

"Should you be working on this?"

"Shouldn't I?" Brass said, his voice rising slightly.

"Jim," Catherine said. "You've carried this one around for a long time. Objectivity—"

"Can kiss my ass," he blurted, then immediately seemed embarrassed about it.

Grissom studied his friend. "So you're Captain Ahab on this one?"

"Let's just say," Brass said, "I'm gonna catch the dick."

"Ah," Grissom said ambiguously.

"And," Brass said, swallowing, his tone softening, "we will, as you say, work it like any other homicide."

Grissom's eyes met Catherine's. Her skepticism was etched in an open-mouthed smile.

Apologetically, Brass said, "Come on, you two— you'll keep me honest on this. You'll keep me—"

"Objective?" Catherine offered. "You really think this is a good idea, Jim?" But her question was obviously intended for Grissom.

Grissom ignored that and said to Brass, "Do you see any reasonable way this could be a coincidence, looking so much like a CASt-off?"

Catherine added, "Which is what the press called his victims, right?"

"Yeah, and it's no coincidence." Brass indicated the corpse. "If this isn't the guy's real signature, it's sure as hell a copycat who knows how to commit a hell of a forgery."

Catherine asked, "How so?"

Brass shrugged. "Well, if it's a copycat, he or she knows way more than was ever in the media."

Nodding, Catherine said, "You kept things back, so you could sort through the false confessions. Of course . . ."

Grissom said, "Whether this is a blast from the past, or a latterday cover artist . . . we're going to need all the help we can get."

Catherine drew in a deep breath and let it out. "New or old—this is one vicious killer."

Grissom was watching the homicide captain. "See anything here, Jim? You're the veteran of the CASt-off crime scenes."

Brass moved closer, squatted next to the dead man, then finally rose and faced Grissom.

"Much as I'd like to have a crack at the original CASt," he said measuredly, "I think this may be a copycat."

Grissom and Catherine traded a look.

"Why?" Grissom asked.

"Appears staged. For one thing, there's not enough blood."

Catherine stared at the coagulating puddle on the rug. "How so?"

"Those five original murder scenes," Brass said, and his eyes took on a haunted cast, "spray was everywhere. Here, there's none of that."

"Blood spatter," she said with satisfaction; after all, it was her specialty. "In the other cases, were the fingers cut off *before* the victims were killed?"

Brass, pleased she was following him, said, "Yes."

"Here it would seem to be postmortem. A living victim would have considerable spray, and might wave his mutilated hand around, further spreading the blood."

"Right," Brass said with a nod. "And there's something that isn't right about how the semen is pooled on his back. . . ."

Grissom fielded that one, explaining his theory, concluding with, "It's always hard to tell with ejaculate at a crime scene—configuration of the victim's body, and how the perp's body functions; but this looks almost—poured on."

"B.Y.O.S.," Catherine said.

Brass and Grissom frowned at her in confusion.

Her eyebrows rose. "Bring your own semen? The killer brought his specimen from home. Or maybe it was a woman, who *had* to bring a specimen. . . ."

"Makes sense either way," Brass said. "A copycat is coldly staging a crime; the real crimes were driven by passion, by a killer really . . . *into* it."

"Exactly my point," Grissom said. "Still, this crime scene is close to the originals, right?"

"Yeah," Brass said. "Other than these details we've discussed . . . oh yeah."

"With a copycat, our lines of inquiry become nicely narrowed." Grissom gestured toward the body. "Who *did* know this much information about those murders?"

Thought clouded the detective's face. Then: "Well, the killer, of course . . . the cops on the case, ourselves . . . and a couple of newspaper guys."

Catherine asked, "Who, specifically?"

"Two crime beat reporters for the Las Vegas *Banner*—Perry Bell and David Paquette. They received the original taunting letters from CASt. And they even did a quickie paperback together, about the case."

"Isn't Paquette an editor at the *Banner?*" Catherine asked.

"*Now* he is—Paquette seemed to get the better end of the book notoriety. Paquette got the editor's post, but then Bell *did* get his own column."

Both CSIs nodded.

Most LVPD personnel knew of Bell and his column, *The Bell Beat*. Grissom didn't think the guy was much of a writer, but then neither were Walter Winchell or Larry King; but the columnist did have a reputation for honesty, and it was said he never betrayed a source, or any kind of trust, which was a big part of how he'd been successful for so long. When a cop shared something with Bell in confidence, it stayed that way until the officer told him he could print it.

"Guess I better go have a chat with the Fourth Estate," Brass said.

Catherine gestured to the grotesque corpse. "You think either Paquette or Bell might be capable of . . . this?"

Brass shrugged. "Gacy was a clown, Bundy a law student, Juan Corona a labor contractor who killed two dozen for fun and profit. Who's to say *what* people are capable of? One thing I do know—if we're treating this like a normal homicide, then Perry Bell and Dave Paquette are suspects . . . and I'm going to go have a talk with them."

They met with the other cops and CSIs in the yard while paramedics went inside to deal with the body.

Damon looked annoyed as he eyeballed Brass. "What are you doing here, Jim?"

Brass started to say something, but Grissom stepped up like a referee.

"I called him in," Grissom said. "As an advisor. He worked a case very similar to this years ago."

"Similar how?" Damon asked.

"Similar," Grissom said, "exactly."

"Another murder?"

"Murders," Brass said. "A serial killer."

"Oh, come on," Damon said. "What is this, the movies?"

Catherine said, "Why, do you get a lot of d.b.'s out here in North Las Vegas, men with lipstick smiles and semen on their backs?"

Damon's mouth opened but no words came out.

Grissom said, "It's a perp called CASt."

That really got Damon's attention; he took a long pause and swallowed and said, "Holy shit . . . I remember him. It was in the papers when I was in college! Damn . . . you think *he* did this?"

Grissom and Brass exchanged glances; then the CSI supervisor shrugged. "We don't know. He's been inactive for something like eleven years. We'll see."

"You'll be working with me, of course," Damon said. "I mean, it is my case."

Again, Brass started to say something and Grissom cut him off. "Certainly."

"Well . . . then . . . good." Damon nodded, put his hands on his hips and puffed up a little bit. "Glad that's understood. Good."

Turning his attention to his team, Grissom asked, "Well?"

Nick said, "Nothing that seems related in the backyard."

"Front yard looks clean too," Warrick said. "Got a partial footprint, but it could be nothing."

"Or something," Grissom said.

"Or something," Warrick said with a humorless smirk.

"I got a sample of the neighbor's prints," Sara said. "But she claims she never touched the bell or the knob. She says she just looked inside, saw the 'horrible thing,' and called 911."

Grissom began to smile—just a little. "Possible fingerprints, possible footprints, DNA evidence. . . . We've started with less. And we have an M.O. match to past crimes. What do you say, gang? Shall we cast out our line, and reel in a killer?"

TWO

One of the nice things about living in Vegas, Captain Jim Brass knew, was that if you wanted to get away from everything and everybody, and go completely unnoticed, well . . . you could.

All you had to do was head out to the Strip.

Crazy as it seemed, the busiest part of Vegas was—for locals—the easiest place to hide. Of course, some residents worked there; but the ones who didn't—and those who did, in their off-hours—generally avoided the area like an active desert nuclear test site.

The Strip's never-ending influx of cash, after all, came from visitors. If Las Vegans wanted to go out to eat or even gamble, they steered well away from that massive neon hive of tourist traps, and found places in the less trendy, and less expensive, corners of the city.

Was it Sherlock Holmes or maybe Poe's Dupin who said the best place to hide is in plain sight? That maxim made the Strip the perfect place for Brass and Grissom to hold their meeting with Perry Bell and David Paquette of the *Banner.* The detective and the CSI had little chance of running into anyone who would know all four of them, and at this point, Brass figured a low profile wasn't a bad thing.

But it did trouble him that he had to start his investigation by talking to members of the media, as the goal of keeping this a by-the-book inquiry included staying off the public radar as long as possible.

Walking down the stairs from the parking building connected to the Sphere, Brass said to the CSI, "I don't mean to keep you away from valuable time at the lab."

Grissom shrugged. "I got the feeling you wanted Catherine and me to spot you on this."

"Spot me how?"

"Keep you from prematurely throwing harpoons, Captain."

"Gimme a goddamn break, Gil. I been on this case, what? An hour, and already you're thinking I'm—"

"An hour on this case?" Grissom's smile was gentle and not at all mocking. "Isn't that more like, going on a decade or more?"

Brass felt a surge of warmth for his friend and colleague—something that wasn't a common emotion between the two, at least not one that either man allowed to enter in very often.

Still, the detective couldn't keep the real feeling out of it, when he said to Grissom, pretending to kid, "So—you're really there for me, huh, Gil?"

Without a beat, but not allowing his eyes to meet Brass's, Grissom said, "Always."

The Raw Shanks Diner huddled in a far corner of the casino, near the back. A fifties motif ran rampant through the place—everything from the Fiestaware plates to the menus to singing waiters and waitresses who served up Elvis, Little Richard, and Fats Domino tunes to the luncheon crowd.

A tiny waitress with corn rows and a big voice was belting out the Etta James classic "At Last" as Brass and Grissom took seats on opposite sides of a corner booth, getting as far away from the karaoke waitress as possible. A waiter with a pompadour haircut a sixteen-year-old Frankie Avalon would have envied brought them coffee while they waited for the newspaper men to show.

A place this relentlessly entertaining, no sane local would ever frequent.

Grissom said, "A suggestion?"

"Sure."

"Let's not pose the copycat theory."

Brass nodded. "Yeah. Good idea. Be interesting to gauge their reactions."

The detective was less than halfway through his coffee when the crime beat writer, Perry Bell, waved at him from the hostess stand. Two other men huddled behind him—David Paquette, the *Banner's* Metro editor, and Bell's research assistant, Mark Brower.

The captain had known Bell and Paquette for the better part of eleven years, and Brower he'd met not long after the man took the job as Bell's assistant, maybe seven years ago. Or was that eight? Brass sighed to himself, struck by how the years were slipping away, and yet how immediate the old CASt case still felt.

Brower had, no doubt, heard all of the stories about CASt, but hadn't been part of the original coverage. The guy was in his early thirties now, and would have still been in journalism school somewhere or even high school, when the crimes occurred.

The hostess, the diner's idea of Sandra Dee (ironically, a waiter was doing Bobby Darin's "Splish Splash" right now), spoke to Bell, who pointed at Brass, then moved past Gidget to waddle toward the table, Paquette and Brower trailing.

Bell was all smiles, but Brass wasn't: He was wondering just why the hell Brower was even along on this trip. Damn it, he had *told* Bell that he wanted to meet the two of them, Bell and Paquette, *alone.* . . .

A roly-poly man with a thick brown toupee parted on the left, Perry Bell looked like he'd been trapped in a time warp in the disco era—witness the wide-lapeled brown suit with yellow shirt, its top three buttons open to show a gold Star of David medallion on a gold, chest-hair-nestling chain. The huge open collar of the shirt extended like giant wings outside the jacket.

Bell had a concrete block of a head with a large glob of loose mortar serving as a nose. His deep-set dark eyes peeked out from under broad, heavy brows and as he approached, his wide mouth broke into an easy, if uneven and tobacco-discolored, smile.

"Got a hot lead for me, Jimbo?" Bell said, extending his hand.

Yes, Brass thought, *a real wordsmith. . . .*

"We'll get to that," Brass said, shook the moist hand, and gave it back to its owner.

"Must be big," Bell said, turning to shake Grissom's hand as well, "if you're bringin' 'round the Crime Scene Investigator's Crime Scene Investigator—great to see you, Gil."

The big build-up got a curt nod out of Grissom.

"You all know my boss and buddy, Dave, here."

Nods were granted to the editor.

Paquette had mischievous blue eyes and a ready smile; his blond hair had long ago flown south for the winter and showed no signs of coming back north. But Brass thought both the editor and his columnist seemed forced in their bonhomie, with each other as well as Brass and Grissom.

Though Paquette and Bell had been peers at the

time their book *CASt Fear* came out, their careers had taken significantly different routes. Easy-going with a ready-smile, happy in his fate, editor Paquette now supervised his old pal, whose career had hit a groove more than a decade ago only to have the needle get stuck: A crime column that had gone briefly national had flamed out in syndication, making a bumpy local landing.

Perhaps out of the grace of his old friend, Bell and his column were hanging on.

Brass and Grissom both shook hands with Paquette and Brower also. Grissom moved around to Brass's side of the booth, while Bell and Paquette sat on the opposite side, Brower pulling up a chair from a nearby table.

Solidly muscular—hardly the norm for the sedentary newspaper breed—Brower wore his dark brown hair short; his dark eyes and the thought-carved groove between his thick brows conveyed seriousness, and a narrow, nearly lipless mouth gave him a vaguely feral look, especially when he smiled. He'd been with Bell for quite a while now, and had earned from Brass the same trust as his boss.

Still, Brower remained, in Brass's mind, an uninvited guest, which was the first topic of conversation. . . .

Brass said, "Don't take this personally, Mark," he said, then turned to Bell and asked, "but what's he doing here?"

The reporter's smile faded. "Well, hell, Jim. He . . . he's my assistant. Mark goes where I go, you know that."

"Did you think this was a social call?"

Bell glanced at both Paquette and Brower. "Isn't it?"

Brass studied the crime writer for a long moment. "Your scanner broken?"

"No, why?"

"You didn't hear the 420 in North Las Vegas this morning?"

The newspapermen would all know the radio code for homicide.

Bell shrugged. "Yeah, so? There was the original radio call, then nothing. I figured there'd be more later, if it was anything worth covering. Is that what you got for me?"

"It's not like you to miss a residential murder call, Perry . . ." Brass tried to keep his voice neutral, even nonchalant. "So where were you off to, this morning?"

The reporter seemed not to notice that he was being questioned. "In the office, mostly."

"All morning?"

For the first time, Bell seemed to understand he was being interrogated.

Alarm was morphing into anger, and he was about to speak when their Teen Idol waiter came over and put a cup of coffee in front of Bell and the others, then freshened Brass's and Grissom's.

"Any food for you guys?" the waiter asked.

"No," Brass said, waving the waiter away.

Steam rose off the coffee—but the reporter was steaming, too.

"What in the hell kind of crap *is* this, Brass?"Bell caught himself—he'd almost been shouting—and looked around, but none of the other diners seemed to notice over the din of the restaurant and the singing staff. "I mean, really, Jim . . . am I some kind of suspect in something? What the hell kind of murder went down this morning, anyway?"

Brass said nothing.

Paquette leaned forward, his features intense. "Look, Captain Brass, if you're accusing one of my employees of something, you do it through proper channels, not call us out to a restaurant on some flimsy damn—"

Eyes taut, Grissom said, "There's nothing flimsy about murder. Captain Brass is making this informal, as a courtesy to you people."

Brass held up a hand and said, "No, Gil—Perry and Dave have a point."

The editor and columnist exhaled air, like twin punctured tires, and settled into a placated limbo, waiting for Brass to continue. From the sidelines Brower watched quietly but intently.

The detective gathered himself, took a long pull on his coffee and then studied Bell, considering exactly how much he wanted to tell the reporter.

Finally, he said, "I'm sorry, Perry . . . Dave. We caught one that's put me on edge, and if I've been

out of line with you guys . . . I do value our relation-
ship . . . please blame it on tension."

The two journalists shrugged, in accidental rhythm
with a waiter doing Elvis singing, "All Shook Up."

"But," Brass said, "when this case goes public,
there's going to be hell to pay."

Reaching into his inside pocket for a pen and pad,
his anger all but forgotten, Bell said, "Well, then, let's
get started. . . ."

Brass held up his hands, as if being robbed.
"That's just it—I don't *want* it to go public, just yet."

The reporter froze for a moment, then, slowly, his
hand came out of his coat—empty. "Well, Jim, why
are we here, then, if we can't talk about it?"

For the first time in a long time, Brass wished he
hadn't quit smoking. "I needed to talk to you, off the
record."

"Captain Brass," Paquette said irritably, "we're all
for cooperation with the authorities, but just like you
have a job to do, so do we. We have a responsibility
to the public."

"You have a responsibility to me," Brass said, "that
overrides that, in this instance."

The editor shook his head. "You don't have that
kind of pull."

"I don't?" Brass asked. "My cooperation on a certain case gave you two a bestselling book. Which you
both made careers out of."

"What," Bell said, "you're calling in *that* marker?"

"Yes," Brass said.

After a moment's consideration, Paquette asked, "If the story's that big . . . and you need our help, including putting the public's right-to-know on hold . . . we'll want something in return. Something more than the old news of what you did for us a long time ago."

Brass and Grissom both just looked at him.

"When the time comes," Paquette said, his hands flat on the edge of the table, "we want an exclusive."

Brass started to say something, his temper rising, but Grissom put a hand on his arm.

"Not possible," Grissom said. "Not even legal."

Everyone at the table knew that the two county employees could never consent to an exclusive on a big case; but by asking for the whole pie, Paquette clearly expected to come away with the biggest slice.

Brass relented a little. "Twenty-four-hour lead."

Paquette considered that, then nodded.

"What have you got?" Bell asked, sitting forward, the hunger in his voice obvious. Other than an exposé on crime in the rap world, when Tupac Shakur got shot, Bell hadn't had a story go national since the CASt book; and the columnist could easily see, from Brass's behavior, that this was something very big. . . .

"You gotta promise, Perry," Brass said. "Not even a hint until I give you the okay. That means all three of you. You can cover the story in a modest way, just straightforward news . . . but the key aspect, we have to downplay, even sit on."

Bell studied him, questions all over his face, even though the reporter never uttered a word, simply nodded his agreement.

"Cross me," Brass said, with a smile that wasn't friendly, "and the cooperation you've known in the past . . . will be past."

The reporter snapped, "Hey, Jim, when was the last time any of us screwed you over?"

Brass wiped a hand across his forehead. Christ, he'd been on the job forever and here he was sweating like a rookie. He'd been needlessly antagonizing these people, who had always been allies.

"You're right," Brass said. "You've always been straight-up. So let me ask a question—how long ago was it? The CASt case."

The reporter, apparently thinking this was another reference to Brass helping him and Paquette out on their book, raised a single eyebrow, then shrugged. "I don't know, ten, eleven years?"

Bell looked to Paquette for confirmation.

The editor nodded. "Eleven. When it started."

"Qualifies as ancient history in this town," Bell said. "Is that a point of reference, or . . . what?"

Three waitresses were singing, "My Boyfriend's Back (and You're Gonna Be in Trouble)."

Brass sipped his coffee, eyes travelling from Bell to Paquette and making the return trip. "We always wondered why he stopped—had he died in an automobile accident? Was he committed somewhere? Did he move, and pick up somewhere else?"

Bell said, "You know the latter isn't true—even now, I keep an eye on the national scene, looking for that M.O. to turn up again. I mean, as M.O.'s come, they don't come much more specific."

"Not hard to recognize," Brass admitted. "What would you say if that M.O. had turned up again?"

"I'd want to know where," Bell said. "What state, what city, hell, what country?"

Grissom said, "Nevada. North Las Vegas. The United States of America."

"Bull . . ." Bell began; but then he pushed away from the table a little. "You two aren't kidding, are you?"

Brass sighed. "Has this meeting struck you as hilarious so far?"

"The M.O.," Bell said. "The same M.O.—in North Las Vegas, *this morning?*"

Brass indicated Grissom with a head bob. "We just left the crime scene, and it looks very much like CASt's handiwork."

"Hard to miss," Grissom said.

Brower hadn't said anything yet, but now he leaned forward, as did Bell and Paquette. Their eyes were glued to Brass, waiting for more, coyotes catching the scent of blood.

The detective's eyes volleyed from Bell to Paquette as he said, "We wanted to talk to you two, because nobody knew as much about that case, those murders, as you guys. . . . And frankly, Mark, that's why your presence here got under my skin. No offense meant."

Brower said, "None taken."

But Bell's hackles were up. "So *that's* why you're treating me like a suspect! Because I *am* one. Listen here, Brass, you knew as much, more than either Dave or me. You and Vince Champlain were our primary sources!"

"That's fair," Paquette said.

Grissom said, "Let's hold off before we start suspecting the police, shall we, gentlemen?"

"What's this?" Bell blurted. "The great Gil Grissom making an *assumption!* I thought you were Mr. Follow-the-Evidence-Wherever-It-Goes! Unless in this case, if it goes to your pal Brass. . . ."

To his credit, Grissom kept his cool. The press annoyed the CSI, their place on his list of unfavorite things ranking just under politics and politicians.

Knowing that, Brass jumped back in. "Guys, yes, you're right—Vince Champlain, and, yes, yours truly, knew more about this case than anyone."

"The tens of thousands who read our book," Paquette said, "also knew the case inside out, from the naked vics to that distinctive knot. Mark's been subjected to Perry and me babbling over beer about this case so much, he oughta go on your suspect list, too, I suppose. And maybe that Hollywood producer who optioned our book, and—"

"The killer," Brass said, "knows more than what was in your book—he knew the handful of things you agreed never to share with the public."

Bell blinked. "How much *did* . . . this killer know?"

"Every damn detail," Brass said. "And as to adding Mr. Brower to the suspect list, hey, I'd be glad to. How much *have* you told him?"

"Hey, hold on there, Jim," Brower said. "You want to know what I know, ask me!"

Paquette held up a silencing palm, Brower's way. "Mark knows more than was in the book, but he doesn't know *everything* everything. The things that Perry and I agreed we wouldn't tell anyone until the killer was caught, we haven't told him, we haven't told *anyone.*"

Brass gazed at the editor for several seconds then turned his eyes to Bell who nodded affirmation.

Bell leaned closer again. "Did he cut off—"

But Brass cut Bell off, with a look.

The detective's eyes went to Brower, then back to Bell, who got the message.

"Mark *is* my research assistant," the reporter complained.

Shaking his head, Brass said, "You can't tell anyone about the two hold-backs. Even at this late date—*especially* at this late date."

The "hold-backs"—designed to trip up false confessors—were the semen on the victim's back, and the severed (and collected) finger. These key details both Brass and Grissom knew, and Paquette, too. The point was to keep the circle as small as possible, and that didn't include adding Mark Brower to the loop.

"I know," Bell said in embarrassed frustration, "I know . . ."

A waitress was doing Connie Francis singing, "Who's Sorry Now?"

Pointedly, Brass asked, "So neither of you has shared either hold-back with anyone?"

Paquette shook his head. "No one's even asked about that case in years. Old news."

"Now me, I've talked about the case to groups," Bell said, "even as recently as this year. See, I put our book back into print—print on demand? I have several boxes in my car trunk, and you can buy it on Amazon and . . ."

Bell, it seemed, had been out on the local lecture circuit, even travelling to towns as far away as Los Angeles, hawking his self-published reprint.

Sad, what things had come to: Paquette had used the national publication of the book to build a local celebrity that had ultimately led to the editor's chair; but short, pudgy Bell—less telegenic than Paquette—had a stalled career that his self-financed reprint was being used to help shore up.

But Brass knew this effort was far too little, far too late, to have any effect on Bell's flagging fortunes, and the reporter mining the rubber-chicken circuit, selling paperbacks out of his trunk, seeking support to help him hang onto his column, was frankly a little pathetic—Rotary Club luncheons, library chat groups, and the odd program at the museum, were not going to rekindle a flame that had never burned that brightly to begin with.

Bell was saying, ". . . but obviously, I've never spoken on the things we kept silent about."

Grissom asked, "Is the book a revision?"

"I did a new introduction, but we just used a copy of the original book to shoot from—didn't retype-set it or anything."

A nugget of ache that would eventually become a full-fledged headache throbbed just behind Brass's eyes. Such headaches had been with him for years; they'd began about the time he'd become embroiled in the CASt case. . . .

He said, "Either somebody has shared information, or CASt is back, and his M.O. is the same."

Brass studied their faces. Paquette seemed to be processing the information, while Bell appeared shellshocked. Brower was unreadable, the intense serious expression pretty much a constant with the guy. None of the men said anything for several long moments.

Paquette was the one who finally broke the silence. "Have you talked to your old pal Vince? Maybe he's been talking."

"There's a thought," Brower agreed.

Brass's words came out cold and hard: "Look, Mark, I'm going to cut you slack, because Vince was long retired before you even started at the *Banner*. Dave, *you* know better. Vince was *always* a good cop.

He never did anything to jeopardize an investigation, not on *any* case!"

Grissom said blandly, "But, of course, we'll be talking to him next. You're quite right to put him on the suspect list."

Brass turned sharply toward the CSI.

"This is a murder investigation like any other," Grissom was saying. "We'll talk to anyone and everyone we think can help us. For example, there are easily half a dozen others in the department who might have had access to the withheld information about CASt's full M.O."

"That's right!" Paquette said, with a snap of his fingers. To Jim he said, "Who did you report to, you and Champlain?"

"The sheriff at the time," Brass said. "Who is now deceased."

Bell said, "What about Conrad Ecklie? He was the dayshift CSI supervisor. He knew!"

Grissom said, "We'll talk to him."

Knowing how much Ecklie and Grissom hated each other, Brass thought to himself: *Someone will talk to Conrad, but it won't be Gil. . . .*

Brass said, "Search your memories, guys. I confided in Grissom, here—he did only incidental work on the original case. Maybe you confided in somebody, too, and it's slipped your mind. . . . Anyway, think about it."

The newspaper guys lapsed into silence.

"I can assure you," Brass said, "we're going to turn over every rock we can."

Paquette and Bell both flashed glares his way.

"Sorry . . . I didn't mean it to sound quite like that. . . . I just mean that we're going to do everything we can to catch this guy, and quick. If it is CASt, we all know what he's capable of. If he's decided to repeat his cycle, we could be looking at four more victims. . . ."

"Jesus," Brower said.

"If it's a newcomer with a similar M.O . . ." Brass let that hang in the air for a few seconds, before he added, "We don't wanna go there till we have to . . . but either way, we've got to catch this guy, and fast. Look, I know it's a big story, but we need, at the outset anyway, to control it."

Bell glanced at his two cohorts, who both gave him slight nods, the three of them somehow communicating silently.

Then the reporter said, "Whatever you need, Jim, you let us know. We'll help any way we can."

"Thanks."

"But," Paquette added, shaking a forefinger, "we get that twenty-four-hour lead, remember."

Brass nodded and Grissom said, "That much we can do."

The Elvis waiter was singing "Jailhouse Rock" when Brass and Grissom headed out.

* * *

Vince Champlain and his second wife occupied an independent living apartment at the Sunny Day Continuing Care Facility in Henderson.

A guard stopped Brass and Grissom at the gate and checked their credentials and wrote their names on his clipboard. Brass and Grissom were familiar with Sunny Day since Catherine and Warrick had worked a case recently concerning murdered patients in the continuous care wing.

Not far from Lake Mead Drive, Sunny Day offered independent living apartments in a building at the left end, and various levels of escalating care in a high-rise at the right end. For the geriatric set, Sunny Day was the living end, or the end of living, depending on which building you occupied.

Brass turned the Taurus to the left and found a parking place not far from the entrance. The Champlains were on the third floor, and—Brass having called ahead—the visit was expected. In fact, when Grissom and Brass exited the elevator and started down the hall, a petite blonde stuck her head out from a door and waved eagerly.

"Jimmy!" she practically squealed. Her expression was joyous.

Grissom gave Brass a sideways look and pointed at him. "Jimmy? You're . . . Jimmy?"

"Keep that to yourself."

"That's asking a lot."

"Don't make me shoot you."

Grissom was smiling at Brass, who was smiling at

the tiny woman who stood just outside her doorway with outstretched arms.

"Margie," Brass said, and allowed himself to be folded in a surprisingly massive hug coming from such a diminutive woman.

As slender as she was short, Margie Champlain had hardly aged since Brass had last seen her; the blonde hair had always been dyed, and she'd had at least one facelift back then—and at least another since.

Brass had first met Margie not long before her husband had retired. A bartender in a small dive off Fremont Street, Margie had been a fireball back in those days, one too powerful for Vince Champlain to resist. The affair had led to the break up of Vince's marriage, but Vince and his first wife, Sheila, were both better off today. Vince's affair with Margie had blossomed into true love and Sheila was now happily married to a retired Golden Nugget casino manager. Brass knew the two couples even went out to dinner together occasionally.

"How could you let yourself be such a stranger, Jimmy?" Margie asked, backing away to look him in the face but still hanging on and in no hurry to let go.

"It's working the damn nightshift," Brass said. "I got no social life. You were lucky you hooked up with Vince so close to retirement."

"Yeah, I missed all the *fun* of being a cop's wife, right?" She released Brass and finally noticed Grissom. "I recognize you from TV—you're the one who's always nabbing the bad guys!"

Brass glanced at Grissom, who seemed to be trying to decide whether to be confused or embarrassed.

"I like to think of him as my little helper," Brass said dryly. "This is Gil Grissom—our crime lab's answer to Sherlock Holmes."

Grissom frowned and said, "I didn't know Sherlock Holmes was a question."

Margie laughed once, then said to Brass, "Is he kidding?"

"No one knows," Brass said.

Margie stuck her hand out and Grissom took and shook it.

"Aren't you the cutie pie," she cooed to Grissom, maintaining her grip.

The CSI supervisor smiled nervously and looked down at his hand like a trapped animal wondering if he'd have to chew off his paw before he could escape.

"Did Vince get back yet?" Brass asked.

"Afraid not," Margie said, finally releasing the CSI's hand. "No, like I said on the phone, he's been gone since early this morning."

"But he will be back soon?"

"Should be any minute," she said. "You kids come on in and wait. I'm making decaf."

Margie had said on the phone that Vince ought to be back by the time Brass and Grissom arrived; but now Brass—knowing how abstract time could be to older, retired people, and how lonely for company they could be—wondered if he and Grissom should enter that apartment and risk wasting valuable time, the early hours in any murder case being the most vital.

Knowing Grissom was probably thinking something similar, Brass looked at the CSI, who shrugged in an it's-your-call manner.

Before Brass was forced into making an executive decision, a tall, athletic, silver-haired man strode into view up the hallway.

The well-tanned Vince Champlain wore light gray sweat pants, a dark gray-and-black striped Polo shirt, and tennies. He moved toward them with no sign of weakness or age in his gait.

His wide silver-mustached mouth broke into a smile, his teeth a little too white, too straight to be nature's work.

"Jim! Why you dirty son of a—"

Margie shushed him loudly and said, "Vince, please . . . the neighbors." Then she whispered to Brass and Grissom, "We have goddamn prudes on either side of us, and then here's Vince, with that fuggin' cop's mouth of his!"

Grissom's eyes were wide and Brass had to smile; Margie had worked as a barmaid for a long, long time. . . .

Champlain was patting Brass on the shoulder, then nodded and grinned at Grissom and said,

"Been seeing your name in the papers, your shining face on the tube, Gilbert. Making a mark, making a mark."

Grissom shrugged a shoulder and gave up a shy smile.

"Let's go inside," Champlain said, waving them toward the open door, "where I can say 'son of a bitch' without Margie having heart failure."

"Vin-cent," Margie scolded, but she was smiling.

Margie went in first, Champlain followed, and Brass looked at Grissom and said, "After you, Gilbert . . ."

"No, no—you first . . . Jimmy."

Brass smiled and Grissom chuckled, and the homicide captain wondered if the CSI shared his relief at even being able to smile, considering the circumstances of this day.

Champlain closed the door after them, and Brass and Grissom took in the living room, which wasn't terribly large, but had a nice homey feel to it, particularly considering the Champlains were essentially in the least-assisted wing of a nursing home.

A big-screen TV dominated one corner while a well-worn lounge chair angled into another corner and a floral sofa took up the wall near the door. Another chair sat at an angle to the sofa, and the tiny, magazine-covered island of a coffee table floated. Champlain gestured easily for them to sit. Brass and Grissom took the sofa while Champlain fell into his lounge chair.

"Beer, gents?" their host asked.

"No, thanks," Brass said. "We're actually on duty."

"Thought you guys were strictly graveyard . . . ?"

Grissom said, "Dayshift's got sick leave and court time."

Brass said, "Pulling more than our share of double shifts."

"Don't bitch," Champlain said. He'd been the kind of career cop who had not looked forward to his last day on the job. "I miss what you got . . . though retirement does have its bennies."

Hovering, Margie asked, "How about some of that decaf?"

"Please," Brass said.

"Yes, thank you," Grissom said.

"Bottle of water, honey, please," Champlain said.

Margie disappeared through a doorway into the kitchen.

"Two under par today," Champlain said, only the merest trace of gloating in his voice. "Golf's one of those bennies I was talking about."

"Where at?" Brass asked dutifully.

"Rio Secco," Champlain said, as if that would mean something to the cops.

Brass nodded like he understood and the expression on Grissom's face said that he suspected Champlain was speaking Esperanto.

"Now," Champlain said with a glance toward the kitchen, "surely a couple of on-duty coppers like you two didn't come all the way out here to the old fart's home to hear me brag about my golf game. . . . What's up?"

"I think we may have a ghost," Brass said.

Champlain sat forward, eyes slitted. "The past rattling its chains, is it? Some old pal of ours resurface?"

Margie brought in a tray with cups of coffee for herself, Grissom, and Brass, and a cold-sweating bottle of Evian for her husband.

Again she hovered, clearly wondering if she should alight and join the party—but was she wanted?

"To what do we owe this pleasure?" Margie asked tentatively.

"Business, dear," Champlain said.

"Oh," Margie said, her disappointment not well hidden. "I just remembered—I have some straightening to do in the bedroom."

Champlain gave his wife a warm smile. "Thank you, babydoll."

After the "babydoll" in her early seventies walked down a hallway and slipped into a doorway on the right, Champlain turned his attention back to Brass and the CSI.

The detective said, "This morning, Gil had a murder call out in North Las Vegas. The M.O. was too damn familiar—Vince, it reminded me whole a lot of CASt."

Some of the color managed to drain from Champlain's deeply tanned face. "You have got to be shitting me. . . ."

Brass said nothing.

Champlain blew out air, as if an invisible birthday cake with every candle he'd earned sat in front of him. "Okay, Jim—let's have it . . . chapter and verse."

Brass did—leaving nothing out this time, including the copycat notion.

Then, with another huge sigh, Champlain shook his head. "But if this kill had the earmarks of the real CASt, like you say—how could any copycat pull that off? We kept a lid on everything."

Grissom fielded the question. "Certain aspects of the scene do suggest a staged crime, as opposed to the more spontaneous activity of our original killer. But we're not ruling anything out yet—certainly not the idea that our original CASt is back."

"What can an old retiree like me do to help?" Champlain asked.

Right now, the "old retiree" looked more fit than Brass had ever felt.

Brass said, "Have you spoken to anyone about the case? Anyone at all?"

"Not since the newspaper coverage died away years ago. And you know how careful we were back at the time—only the sheriff, rest his soul, and the dayshift CSI supervisor knew our hold-backs."

"How about lately?" Brass asked. "I mean, you might sit around with some of your new friends here, and swap war stories about your various professions."

Champlain waved that off. "Come off it, Jim—you, too, Gil. You *both* know we don't go around bragging about our failures . . . and CASt was my biggest."

Nodding, Brass asked, "How about Margie?"

"No. She's got a tough hide, but the rougher aspects of what I used to do . . . she's squeamish. And I don't remember ever getting into the case much with Sheila, either. Of course, that was a long time ago," Champlain said, brow furrowed. Then he shrugged, rather elaborately. "Guys—I'm afraid I got nothing for you. God knows I'd like to help. CASt was the big fish that got away."

"I know how you feel, Vince," Brass said. "We just had to check."

Champlain said, "Be honest with you? . . . If I can avoid it, I try to not even think about that goddamn case. We were so close to catching that bastard. So close. Jim, I was always pretty good at leaving the job behind, when I got home at night. But that case . . . those poor S. O. B.s who got humiliated and strangled . . . the mental pictures of those crime scenes . . . late at night. . . ."

Champlain shivered.

Brass and Grissom got to their feet.

"If it is him," Brass said, "we'll get him. Don't worry about that, Vince."

"And if it's not him?"

"If it's not him, if it's some other sick bastard,

we'll catch his ass, too. Either way—this killer goes down."

Champlain rose and walked them to the door. He laid a hand on Brass's shoulder. "You sure as hell aren't the young guy that filled my shoes when I left."

"Those were big shoes," Brass said. "And I don't remember *ever* being young."

"You will," Champlain assured him. "You will."

"Lot of miles since then," Brass said distantly. "A lot of miles and a lot of death. . . ."

Out of nowhere, Grissom chimed in: " 'The condition upon which God hath given liberty to man is eternal vigilance.' "

Brass smirked and asked Grissom, "Who said that?"

But it was Champlain who answered: "Judge John Philpot Curran."

Grissom, impressed, bowed his head and smiled at the retired cop.

"But," Champlain said, "I kinda doubt that judge was talking about Las Vegas Homicide."

With a little shrug, Grissom said, "Well, there's always that other old saying, Vince."

"Yes?"

"If the shoe fits . . ."

THREE

Almost every black leather chair around the large rectangular table in the CSI conference room was filled, although the one at its head remained vacant. The X-ray box on one wall, and the whiteboard running the length of another, were not in use. Fluorescent lighting gave the assembly a deathly pallor, as they sat like relatives gathered to hear the reading of a wealthy patriarch's will, each with the expectation of not getting one red cent.

Catherine Willows, leaning back, arms folded, unobtrusively gauged the other faces around the table. To her left, Warrick Brown studied some papers, his eyes half-lidded, his face a grim mask. Across the way, Nick Stokes slouched in his seat, uncharacteristically down, staring at nothing, his mouth a tight line. Opposite Catherine, Sara Sidle fiddled with a pen, spinning it on the table in front of her, her forehead free of thought, her eyes hollow.

The crack CSI nightshift team—who prided themselves on not only their expertise and energy, but their patience—seemed beaten down by a dreary week of dead ends.

Left of Sara, Greg Sanders, their spiky-haired top-notch DNA lab tech—whose inexplicable aspirations for the lesser pay of CSI field work Grissom had been humoring of late—sat and rocked back and forth, his head bobbing to some rhythm playing in the iPod of his mind as he read a report. The energetic Greg alone seemed happy with where he was in the current investigation. Perhaps this was due to Grissom recently granting his request to leave the lab for the field, even though Greg's apprentice CSI status was not yet full-time.

Across from Greg, immediately to Catherine's right, sat Dr. Al Robbins, his metal crutch propped next to him, his eyes riveted to autopsy photos spread out on the table in front of him, like a losing hand of cards he was trying to assemble into some kind of winning order. His salt-and-pepper beard was merely flecked with pepper now, its sodium count long since out of control. The doctor's normally cheerful eyes seemed clouded as he looked from one stark picture in the pile to the next. The gravity of the situation was apparent in the coroner's rare public appearance outside of the autopsy room.

To Catherine's left, beyond Warrick, at the far end

of the table, Brass stared into space, as if seeking an opinion on whether he should remain pissed off or give in to despair. He had been the last one to walk in, carrying a large cardboard box that now sat on the floor next to him.

Supervisor Gil Grissom, who had called this meeting, wasn't here yet, and his disheartened troops were getting antsy. They had been on the Marvin Sandred murder for a week and had little more to go on than the victim's name. The only thing working in their favor was the press coverage—no one in the media had thus far connected Sandred with CASt.

While Grissom had kept tabs on what each individual CSI (as well as Greg and Robbins) had been up to, this would be their first group meeting, to present, contrast, and compare what they'd all learned, and have a look at the lab results that were just coming in.

Grissom entered quickly, his demeanor just as serious as the rest but minus any overt sign of frustration. Catherine admired quite a few things about Gil, but not the least of them was the chief CSI's ability to remain objectively professional no matter how fast and hard the brown rain was coming down. Oh, there'd been exceptions; even Grissom had his weak spots—violence against children brought the human side out, in spades—but generally he maintained a high standard of scientific detachment that Catherine could esteem without really striving toward.

Catherine's process necessitated maintaining her humanity, and even subjectivity. Different strokes.

A light-blue lab coat was draped over Grissom's standard black attire; his wireframed glasses were on. Unceremoniously, he dropped a stack of folders onto the table with a dull thud. The CSI's upper lip formed a subtle sneer, which was the equivalent of anybody else tearing the room up and throwing things out windows.

Sitting up, Catherine said, "Let me guess—somebody up there hates us. . . ." She'd gone for a light-hearted tone but fell just short.

"Nicely deduced, Catherine," Grissom said tightly.

Nick groaned. "Atwater?"

"Atwater," Grissom affirmed, the word sounding more like an epithet than the name of a human being—specifically, their boss, the sheriff. "He's starting to get calls . . . about CASt."

"Ah hell," Warrick said, pawing the air.

Grissom continued, "Our esteemed sheriff wanted my assurance that no one at CSI was leaking anything to the press."

Brass said, an edge in his voice, "Who is it, bugging the sheriff? Our pal Perry Bell?"

"No," Grissom said. "It's from the broadcast side—a local TV station."

Catherine considered that for a moment, then asked, "Do we trust our North Las Vegas brothers? Bill Damon and Henry Logan? You gave Logan kind of a hard time."

"I did?" He seemed genuinely not to know what Catherine was referring to.

Brass said, "I'd be more inclined to think it was one of our 'friends' from the *Banner,* feeding info to the TV guys—tips get traded, you know."

"Once the CASt aspect is public knowledge," Nick said to the detective, "any gentlemen's agreement you had with the *Banner* boys becomes moot—and they'd be free to run with it."

"If those clowns sold us out," Brass said, his voice as hard as the table his hands rested on, "they'll never get cooperation out of this department again . . . Gil, do you know *which* TV reporter?"

Grissom's shrug indicated that to him, these reporters were interchangeable, but he said, "Jill Ganine."

"Maybe we ought to go have a chat with her," Brass said.

"I have no intention of wasting my time with the media," Grissom said. "If we've been betrayed by the *Banner*, finding out exactly who leaked it does not put us any closer to our killer."

Brass grimaced, but said, "Right. You're right."

Grissom's eyebrows flicked up and down. "We had a week without press pressure, and that luxury helped us get a good start on this thing."

Warrick looked at Grissom like his boss was cutting out paper airplanes, but said nothing.

"Now," Grissom said, finally sitting, "we work the case and worry about the media in our spare time . . . and if any of you *have* any spare time, please let me know. So . . . what have we got?"

He looked around the table, but no one volunteered to get things going.

Not a good sign, Catherine thought. But she didn't feel like being the first in class to raise a hand. . . .

Grissom turned to Greg, sitting immediately to his right; apparently the supervisor sensed the only positive attitude in the room and honed in on it. "Make me happy, Greg."

Greg said, "All the blood belongs to the victim."

Grissom looked no happier. "Anything else?"

"The semen on his back did not belong to the victim. CODIS is still working on finding a match."

While the Combined DNA Index System was growing, Catherine knew all too well that getting a hit off CODIS was far from a sure thing.

"Catherine," Grissom said, turning her way, his face passive, any tension from the sheriff and media a distant memory now, "what do we know about the victim?"

Without referring to the report before her, Catherine said, "Marvin Sandred, forty-seven, lived in Vegas a little over a year. Worked for a welding supply company where he'd been for six months."

She glanced at Brass to pick up her thread, which he did: "I talked to Sandred's boss, and half a dozen coworkers, too. Nobody had anything bad to say about him. No one had much good to say about him, either—he was still the newbie, never really integrated with his coworkers. They thought of him as kind of a sad guy, oddly distracted, like work was something he was just putting up with till he could get back to . . . what really interested him."

Taking over again, Catherine said, "He was originally from Eau Claire, Wisconsin. Ex-wife back there. Her name's Andrea Dean, Annie for short, remarried after Marvin moved to Vegas."

Grissom winced in thought. "You found this out how?"

But it was Brass who explained: "I asked Catherine to make the call for me—I know it's not really CSI work, but I felt, woman to woman we'd get more."

Catherine picked up: "She really broke down bigtime when I told her . . . cried so much, she asked me to call back in five minutes. I did, and she had composed herself, and answered all my questions. But she couldn't help us much, either."

"Had she kept in touch with her ex?" Grissom asked. "Ever visited him here?"

"They talked on the phone a few times. They were a childless couple, who broke up acrimoniously, over his cashing in his retirement and moving here . . . to be closer to his gambling habit."

Warrick said, "So that's what he was preoccupied about at work."

Both Catherine and Brass nodded.

"By the way," Brass said, "the neighborhood canvass was a bust—what few people were home didn't notice anybody strange in the area, much less actually see our killer go to the front door."

"So much for talk," Grissom said. "What about actual evidence?"

"The partial footprint is from a current Stasis M658 running shoe," Warrick said. "There weren't any of those in Sandred's closet, or anywhere on his property for that matter . . . and the next door neighbors don't own any either. Could belong to the killer."

"Good, Warrick," Grissom said.

Sara said, "Partial prints on the bell and front doorknob? Didn't belong to Sandred."

"Do we know whose they are?" Grissom asked.

Nick said, "I ran them through AFIS and got a goose egg."

Sara added, "I went through the Gaming Commission, the military . . . came up empty."

"Any trace?" Grissom asked.

"Just those black threads you found," Nick said. "Polyester."

Grissom turned to the coroner.

Dr. Robbins said, "Victim died of asphyxiation due to the ligature around his neck. Quite a bit of struggle. I'm afraid I don't have a lot more than that to offer."

"You've gone over the original CASt files?"

"Yes—this death is consistent with those."

Grissom nodded and the coroner did the same, then rose, slipped the cuff of his crutch over his arm, and headed out, but then paused at the doorway, file of photos under one arm.

"It wasn't a pleasant death," Robbins said. "It'd be nice not to have to add any more pictures to my collection."

Catherine said, "See what we can do, Doc."

Robbins nodded somberly, then exited.

"Takes one sick perp," Nick said, "to bum out a coroner."

Grissom turned to Nick. "You were working the lipstick database . . ."

"Yes—this one's called Bright Rose, made by Ile De France. Similar to, but not the same as, the Limerick Rose that was CASt's preference years ago."

Catherine said, "Limerick Rose was also an Ile De France."

Nick found a meager grin. "Ask an expert. . . . Problem with the Bright Rose is, it's sold everywhere, from the cosmetics counter at a Fashion Mall department store to Walgreens. We'd have about as much chance as tracking a bottle of soda."

"The rope?" Warrick said. "Same deal—sold in every hardware store. But I did get epidermal cells off both sides and both ends of the rope."

"I'm still testing them," Greg said. "Trying to figure out which are the vic's, which the killer's. Where the rope was around the vic's neck, that was easy— but the rest of the rope, well, key is trying to find where the vic fought *against* it, and where the killer might have been *pulling* it. Then we can determine whose cells are whose."

Grissom's head tilted to one side. "Matter of time?"

"Matter of time—not much of that, really."

"All right, Greg. Keep me in the loop."

"In this case," Greg said, "you might not want to be in a loop."

Grissom said, "I'll do the gallows humor, Greg—and I'm not in the mood."

The lab tech lifted his eyebrows and set them down and looked anywhere but at Grissom.

"Come to think of it, Greg," Grissom said with a ghastly smile, "don't you have work to do?"

"Yes. Yes I do." Greg rose, his smile one of the most strained in the history of man. "Work. To do. 'Bye. Everybody. . . ."

And Greg took his files and went.

So much for the only upbeat attitude at the table.

Travelling from face to face of his CSI team, Grissom said, "All right—here's what we're going to do."

Brass said, "You're going to tell *me* what to do, Gil?"

Grissom said, "Yes."

Brass thought about that; then said, "Okay."

"You want to talk to that reporter, Jim, be my guest. But first, sit down with Catherine and Nick."

Brass gave Grissom a tentative nod.

Grissom said, "Cath, I want you and Nick to go through the old case file, all five kills, all the old suspects, find out everything you can, cross-reference and collate and stay alert. Sit down with Jim. Find out where our suspects are . . . here in town, moved away, in the ground, but find their whereabouts. And keeping in mind what the files have told you, develop theories about whether any of them might be back in business with an adjusted M.O."

"Theories?" Catherine said, wondering if she'd heard him right.

"That's right. Not wild guesses."

"Glad to."

"Warrick, Sara, and I will continue to work the evidence from the Sandred house and see if we can turn something we've missed. Call it the first of the theories if you want. But I'm on record: This guy is just getting started."

Not a wild hunch, Catherine knew, as they all recognized the mark of a serial killer when they saw it, and there could be no question: This creep was just amping up.

"And another troubling aspect," Grissom said. "If, as with our would-be Jack the Ripper a while back, we have a copycat who's following the pattern of an original, then we might have a finite number of victims . . . five in this case . . . after which our homicidal performance artist stops, and fades into the night."

"Like the original Ripper," Nick said.

"Hell," Warrick said, "like the original CASt!"

Grissom, Warrick, and Sara surrendered the conference room to Brass, Nick, and Catherine, who huddled around one end while Brass pulled the large cardboard box closer to him, to lift items out.

Businesslike, nearly robotic, Brass withdrew the first file. "First vic was November 1994. Guy's name was Todd Henry. He lived in an apartment downtown. No family, no friends. He'd been dead better part of a week before we got the call."

"Who found him?" Nick asked.

"Smell got so bad one of the neighbors called in a public-nuisance complaint, and we went in. Guy was on the living-room floor, rope still around his neck."

Catherine asked, "Was the full M.O. established from the start? Lipstick, semen, noose?"

"Yeah," Brass said. "This perp had either been setting this up, planning it out, for a long time, fantasizing maybe . . . or he'd been doing it somewhere else. However you look at it, when the killings started in Vegas, the M.O. was full blown and never deviated."

Nick said, "Obviously you and Vince checked other jurisdictions."

"Nationwide, but nobody ever matched up. We checked out Canada, too, and finally Europe. Anyway, after Todd Henry, John Jarvis showed up dead a month later. Everything was exactly the same as the previous case."

Catherine asked, "Jarvis have any connection to Henry?"

"Other than a basic physical similarity? No." Brass tapped a forefinger in a palm. "Henry was a transplant, Jarvis a lifelong Vegas resident. Henry did odd jobs, Jarvis was an accountant. Henry lived alone, Jarvis had a family, wife and a son. Lived in a nice house in Boulder City, while Henry hung out in that downtown rathole. The only thing they had in common was appearance. Fiftyish white males, overweight."

"What about the others?"

"George Kim, the third vic, was half-Asian—other than that all five . . . Henry, Jarvis, Kim, Clyde Gibson and Vincent Drake . . . were overweight white men around forty-five, fifty. Although each had some things in common with one or two of the others, nothing other than physical appearance could be seen as a common denominator."

"Nothing?" Nick asked, hardly believing it.

Brass shrugged elaborately. "Kim worked at the Lucky Seven, Drake worked as a supervisor at the city garage and Gibson was a self-employed furniture maker. Some had kids, some didn't. Some were married, some weren't. The only other thing that changed was CASt's frequency—month between the first two, barely a week between the last two. The guy was definitely picking up speed—really getting into it. Then . . . he stopped cold."

"Okay," Catherine said, trying to regroup mentally. "What about the suspects?"

Brass blew out air. "There were hundreds at the beginning. Serial confessors, heavyset men calling in saying their neighbors were acting suspiciously, all kinds of dipsticks. When we got through weeding 'em out, we were down to three—loser named Dallas

Hanson, scumbag named Phillip Carlson, and this complete psychopath, Jerome Dayton."

Catherine said, "Fill us in."

"When I say Dayton was a psychopath, I don't mean 'eccentric,' I mean clinical. His dad, Thomas Dayton, was a big-time contractor who built a lot of the county buildings and several casinos that went up in the late eighties and early nineties—remember that guy?"

"Oh yes," Catherine said.

Nick was nodding in recognition, too.

Brass continued: "And Jerome was my personal favorite candidate for the killings, only he ended up in a private hospital where he's been since late 1995. I woulda bet a year's pay he was the killer, but Drake died *after* Dayton went into the hospital."

Nodding thoughtfully, Catherine asked, "What about the others?"

"Vince liked this loser Dallas Hanson. He was a cowboy from Oklahoma. He and his quote-unquote old lady bought a used-but-abused mobile home on the far northwest side. When she thought Dallas was screwing around on her, she threw his ass out. He ended up taking an apartment in the same building downtown where Todd Henry lived. Then he showed up on a security tape from the Lucky Seven where George Kim worked."

"Promising," Nick said.

Catherine asked, "What physical evidence did you have against Hanson?"

Shaking his head, the detective said, "The only thing was a fingerprint of his that turned up on a cup in Henry's apartment. Hanson claimed that he'd had a neighborly drink with the soon-to-be-dead man on the day Henry disappeared, but that was it."

Nick asked, "No alibi?"

"He claimed he'd been passed out drunk in his room after his drink with Henry. No witnesses, of course."

"He have a record?" Catherine asked.

"Minor," Brass said. "Got caught up in a couple of barroom dustups back in Oklahoma and had done some county time here for a misdemeanor assault . . . but nothing to show CASt-like leanings."

"How about DNA evidence?" Nick asked. "You had that semen at the scene. . . ."

Brass shook his head. "We didn't get a match, but our methodology in those days wasn't where we are now."

Catherine pressed: "What about Phillip Carlson?"

"*That* guy was a stone freak, a gay basher. He'd pose as a hooker, then when he got his john alone, he'd beat the hell out of him and rob the guy."

"Charming," Nick said.

"Oh how we wanted it to be *that* asshole. . . . Hell, he even confessed. But then it turned out he was a chronic confessor, at least when it came to any murder that had any gay overtones. Shrink said Carlson was gay or bi himself, trying to repress those tendencies, and the only thing he hated more than the average homosexual he victimized was himself."

"Sounds like a strong candidate," Catherine said.

"Sure," Brass said. "Only he just wasn't in the right places at the right times . . . or I should say wrong places. He was at the Lucky Seven, too, caught him on video. Problem was—we had him on camera within an hour of the time George Kim was murdered. That made the schedule awfully tight for Carlson, Kim living way the hell and gone across the city from the Lucky Seven. It wasn't impossible Carlson could've made the trip, but highly unlikely."

Nick asked, "Was Carlson clear on any of the others?"

"Same kind of deal with the Henry murder," Brass said, exasperation and resignation melding in his tone. "He'd been seen downtown that day, but nowhere *near* the time of Henry's death . . . and when Henry was getting the life choked out of him, Carlson was at Lake Mead with witnesses."

"Good witnesses?" Catherine asked.

Brass grunted a bitter chuckle. "Would you believe, biker gang?"

Nick smirked humorlessly and said, "Not ideal witnesses, but harder than hell to break down their stories, I bet."

"You bet right, Nick—none of 'em budged. 'Our code is our word!' "

"Oh-kay," Catherine said, and slapped her thighs. "We'll start working it again."

Brass seemed damn near on the edge of tears. "We worked that case hard, Vince and me—can't *believe* we missed anything . . ."

"I'm sure you guys did your best," she said. "But times, and technology, have changed. . . . Did you guys happen to keep any of the semen?"

Brass brightened. "Hell! I forgot all about that. I mean, it has been a long time . . ."

"Spill," Nick said.

Brass, reenergized, said, "Vince, thinkin' ahead, had it frozen, just in case. We were in early days with DNA, and we hoped the science would improve. Vince thought it would be best to be prepared, though—every unsolved murder case is an open file."

"Good," Catherine said. "Very good."

Suddenly Brass was smiling. "You know, I hadn't thought about that in . . . I dunno, ten years, maybe. Yeah, check the evidence freezer! Should be there somewhere."

They were just about to break up the confab on this high note when North Las Vegas detective Bill Damon came scowling into the conference room.

"What the hell?" he asked, the vague question directed at Brass.

"What the hell what, Bill?"

Damon came over to loom over the seated detective, then got right in the smaller man's face, saying,

"Atwater thinks me and my guys are leaking information to the media!"

Brass kept his calm, rising. "No, Bill—from what I understand, our sheriff doesn't know *where* the leak is coming from. Just that there is one."

Sneering, Damon gestured to Nick and Catherine. "Well, I say it came from here—right here!"

Nick, teeth showing but not really smiling, said, "Well, it didn't, Bill—maybe the sheriff has it right."

Brass gave the CSI a hard firm look that said the detective would handle this.

"Now look, Bill," Brass said, his voice quiet, easygoing, "the sheriff's not accusing you, or anyone else in your department—*or* ours—of being the leak. He just wants to know who the leak is, at this point. Can you blame him? And, personally—I don't think it's you."

Damon's body language shifted slightly, the detective somewhat appeased.

Catherine knew better than to mention that she had been the one to suspect Damon and Logan this morning, wondering herself if it wasn't one or both of them. The two NLVPD cops had seemed vaguely resentful of Brass absconding with their investigation.

Having gone to all of the trouble of working himself into a lather, Damon stayed angry enough to say, "And what about sharing information? I haven't heard anything from you people for, what? Three days?"

Brass held up a gentle palm. "I was just going to call you. The lab results have started coming back today, and we've got some info, finally."

Nodding a little, finally satisfied (at least slightly), Damon said, "Good. Well, good. . . . So, so tell me."

"I will," Brass said, "in the car."

Surprised, the younger detective parroted, "In the car?"

"Yeah—we're going to go talk to the TV reporter who called Sheriff Atwater, asking about CASt."

Catherine could see the young cop was feeling better about where this was going.

"Which reporter?" Damon asked.

"Jill Ganine," Brass said. "Over at KLAS?"

Everything seemed to have calmed down. Damon and Nick exchanged embarrassed smiles and sorrys, and Brass and the NLVPD detective had each taken a step toward the door when Grissom came back in, Greg Sanders trailing behind in that bright-eyed way of his.

The CSI supervisor, however, did not appear bright-eyed: His expression was grave, even troubled, as he looked down at a sheet of paper in his hand.

"Who died?" Catherine asked.

Grissom's voice was flat: "CODIS matched the semen from Marvin Sandred's back."

Catherine shrugged a little. "And that's good news, right?"

"Normally I would say, yes. But CODIS says the DNA belongs to a guy named Rudy Orloff."

Brass looked at Damon. "I know that name from somewhere—do you?"

Damon shook his head.

"I know that name," Brass repeated.

Grissom said, "Says here Orloff's got a history of male prostitution."

"Ooooh yeah," Brass said. "I remember him. We pulled him in for questioning on the Pierce case, remember, Gil? *That* skinny little scumbag doesn't have the stomach to kill anybody, let alone—"

"Evidently," Grissom said, "he developed the requisite stomach a year ago in Reno. He stabbed a john, nearly a fatal wound. Since then, he's been in Ely, doing life with the chance for parole for attempted murder."

Catherine felt something like a stomach punch. "Our best suspect has been in a maximum-security prison? For the last year?"

Grissom waved the paper. "Actually, just for about the last two months—the Reno cops didn't catch him right away; then there was the trial, a quick appeal, and finally, he was taken to Ely. Where, presumably, he still was when Marvin Sandred was slain."

They all looked at each other for a long, stunned second. If their best suspect was in prison, how had his semen ended up on the back of a murdered man in North Las Vegas?

Probably not great trajectory, Catherine thought wryly.

"What next?" Brass said, his voice filled with

exhaustion and exasperation. "What the hell *next?*"

Greg stepped forward with a weakly hopeful expression. "Maybe the epidermal cells will help us. Why don't I get back to work on them?"

"Why don't you, Greg?" Grissom said, without looking.

And Greg did.

Brass was shaking his head now, a vein throbbing in his forehead. Catherine was afraid he might stroke out right in front of them.

"It's hard to have the worst luck in Vegas," the detective said, "but we're special—we did it. The semen at the scene comes from a guy in prison, the skin cells on the rope will probably end up belonging to Bugsy Siegel."

Catherine was about to offer her own cynical comment, when her cell phone had the good sense to ring. As she withdrew it from her pocket, Nick's, Grissom's, Brass's, and Damon's cell phones all started chirping as well, a tiny technological chorale.

Suddenly thrust into the middle of six unsolved murders, over the course of a decade, Catherine Willows had only one thought as she punched the button on her phone, and it was even not her own voice, but that of Jim Brass, saying . . .

. . . *What the hell* next?

FOUR

The second murder did not require the full team's attention.

Catherine and Nick remained behind at CSI HQ, to get digging into the old cases. Grissom, Sara, and Warrick took the ride out to the suburb of Coronado Ranch.

Unlike the crime scene at the Sandred house, where he'd worked the front yard, Warrick Brown spent his time indoors. The house on Buried Treasure Court belonged to Enrique Diaz—the recently deceased Enrique Diaz, that is—a successful TV producer for the Tourist Channel, a cable television network dedicated to travel, with a particular bent toward its home base of Las Vegas, which lent itself to local production.

The house was well-to-do but not ostentatious, revealing success without rubbing your nose in it.

Stucco with a tile roof (like every other house in the neighborhood), the Diaz home was a long, lean two-story with an immaculate lawn despite the water shortage.

While Brass and Damon went off to canvass the neighbors, Grissom, Sara, and Warrick worked the scene. Sara took the outside, Grissom the inside but for the living room, which Warrick concentrated upon—where the murder had gone down.

Warrick had seen the Sandred crime scene first-hand, despite working the lawn, and also knew intimately the photos from the first victim's house; so he saw at once that this crime looked strikingly similar—difference being the surroundings were decidedly more upscale than Sandred's seedy bungalow.

Twice the size of Sandred's front room, this one gave off a strong Mexican vibe—serapes of red, green, and yellow stripes tossed on the furniture, carefully casual; a potted cactus in a sunny corner looking healthy; family photos in funky rough-wood frames dotting the walls and end tables. A matching rough-wood crucifix above the front door seemed more decorative than religious, and the floor consisted of inlaid Mexican tile, a far cry from the cheap carpeting on which the previous victim had earned numerous rug burns during the course of dying. The south wall was mostly windows and—dark as the crime might be that the CSIs were investigating—the death site itself seemed to swim in sunlight. A plasma television hung on one wall while a huge sofa, twin recliners, and a wing chair, all covered in the same beige leather, stood mute sentry over the corpse.

Centerstage, heavy-set Diaz—his dark curly hair held in place by wet-look hair product—lay nude, stomach-down, right hand outstretched, the index finger severed, the other hand tucked under his body. The murder weapon—a length of rope that Warrick estimated would measure a foot and a half or so—remained wound around the victim's neck, the reverse-eight noose pulled tight.

Again the killer had left a pool of semen on the victim's back above the buttocks. The producer's eyes bulged, his tongue lolling out of his mouth, as if mocking Warrick, an effect grotesquely heightened by the sloppily applied garish red lipstick.

And again, the lack of blood spatter made Warrick believe the vic's finger had been separated only after the heart had stopped beating.

The cooly objective Warrick allowed himself a moment of subjectivity, by way of a disgusted half-smirk. He'd worked a lot of murder scenes, but the various and sometimes bizarre ways people got themselves killed was not nearly as surprising as the way their killers chose to live. . . .

While Diaz was Hispanic, he was extremely light-skinned and could easily have passed for Caucasian, though these surroundings indicated pride in heritage. White victims had been the original CASt's preference, and Sandred had fit that bill as well; whether Diaz had been mistaken for Caucasian, or had simply been "close enough" for the killer, remained to be seen.

Maybe this was a copycat who hadn't picked up on that aspect of the original crimes, and who wasn't aware that most serial killers stayed with one ethnic group, usually their own. . . .

Of course, that wasn't a hard and fast rule; homicidal maniacs had a way of making their own rules, and rewriting them as they went, on murderous whim. Still, anything as structured as the CASt murders, which seemed to follow some sick ritual within the perpetrator's psychology, indicated a deadly attention to detail that should prove helpful to crime scene analysis.

Certainly the similarities between this and the Sandred murder were striking, and Warrick had little doubt they were dealing with the same killer—either new or old CASt.

And, anyway, despite Grissom's surprising announcement of his own hunch that the killer was just getting started—which had already been born out by the body in this room—Warrick knew his supervisor would not tolerate assumptions, even in a situation like this. Warrick would follow the evidence to see where it led. Period.

Getting out his camera, Warrick started snapping pictures. He wasn't even through the first roll of film when Grissom seemed to materialize at his side.

"First pass," the CSI supervisor said, "rest of the house looks clean."

"Nothing jumped out?"

"Nothing except how undisturbed the place is—and how much like the Sandred scene it is, in that respect."

"Ah."

"I'll go over it more closely, but my guess is the murderer never went into any of the other rooms."

"A guess, Gris? What next? A vision?"

"A third corpse, if we don't do our jobs better than we have so far."

"I hear that." Warrick clicked another photo, then shook his head. "This guy is definitely out there. You realize the kinda gear he left behind? Televison alone is worth a couple G's."

"Sometimes a killer's pathology won't allow him to steal, even though he's committed murder. It would somehow desecrate the sacredness of the act."

"Yeah, yeah I know," Warrick said, "but the guy has to be *really* nuts to leave a nice TV like that behind."

They exchanged small, wry smiles, and went to work their separate ways.

After finishing the photos, Warrick took a sample of the semen. Then he carefully removed the rope, and turned the body over.

That was when Warrick saw something clutched in the fingers of the stiffening hand—something that had been out of sight beneath the body.

"Hey, Gris! . . . You better come get a load of this."

Moments later, at Warrick's side, Grissom was looking down at the hand. "You get a picture?"

The body was getting heavy, but Warrick made no complaint as he held it up. "Not yet."

Grissom picked up Warrick's camera and snapped off three quick photos.

"Go ahead and roll him all the way over," the supervisor said.

Warrick eased the body to the floor, pulled a forceps out of his crime-scene kit and knelt next to the victim. As he moved closer and studied the card, Warrick could see that the object was a magnetic key of the type used by virtually every hotel in town and many businesses. Typically, this one had a magnetic strip down one end, with standard directions.

Using his forceps carefully, Warrick got the card by its edge, doing his best not to disturb any fingerprints. After he eased it from the dead man's fingers, Warrick turned the card over: Five words were printed in blue letters on the white plastic . . .

. . . *Property of Las Vegas Banner.*

"Well, that's not good," Warrick said.

Holding the card up, Warrick remarked, "Usually I like finding clues, don't you?"

Grissom's eyes were tight.

Warrick expected a typically dry comment from his chief, but all he got was: "We better get Brass back over here—right away."

* * *

Nick Stokes searched the aquamarine halls of CSI for Catherine. The low-key lighting sometimes worked against the nightshift, encouraging sleepiness; but considering the harshness of what they were frequently up against, Nick didn't mind the soothing atmosphere.

When they had started looking into the old CASt cases, the first problem to crop up had been that they couldn't find addresses on two suspects (the ones not exiled to a mental hospital). Now, after hours of digging, he had an address for one, but right now it looked like Nick might be filling out a missing persons report on his coworker.

He had just pulled his cell phone off his belt when Catherine stepped out of a restroom, a heavy folder under one arm.

She saw him coming and gave him a chagrined grin and a chuckle. "Quietest place to read in the whole building."

Thinking about the men's room across the hall, Nick shook his head. With the heavy men-to-women ratio in the LVPD, he couldn't say the same.

"Find anything?" she asked.

Nick said, "How about an address for Phillip Carlson?"

"Our gay basher . . . where?"

"On Baltimore, near the Sphere."

"What are we waiting for?"

"Brass and Damon to get back, maybe? You know,

the detectives aren't crazy about having CSIs outside of the lab, running loose. . . ."

Catherine considered that, then shook her head. "Grissom put us on the old cases, and we'll look into the old cases. Anyway, Brass isn't a stickler on that policy. With the workload like it is, can you see hauling a detective off a current case while we run out the ground balls on the old ones?"

"Wow," Nick said. "You trying to convince me, or yourself?"

She smiled and shrugged. "I dunno—but I'm convinced."

"Me too," Nick grinned. "But let's call for a black-and-white to meet us there anyway."

Carlson's apartment was in a building that looked like a two-story stucco motel from the fifties that had gone to pot decades ago without anybody doing anything about it in the intervening years.

Nick, behind the wheel, said, "Nice digs our boy has for himself."

Nick parked the Tahoe on the street, hoping it would still be there when they got back; then the two CSIs made their way up the outside stairs and across the concrete walkway of the second floor.

Somewhere in the neighborhood, somebody had the bass on their car stereo turned up way too loud, and although Nick knew most of the new music on the street—prided himself on that—the distortion made it impossible for him to identify the rapper in question.

Catherine knocked on the door of apartment 2E and they waited for an answer that did not come.

Nick put his ear to the orange-paint-peeling door, but heard nothing. He stood back, shrugged at Cath, then knocked, louder this time.

And again, they waited.

Nick had just pounded on it the third time when the next door over swung open and a figure leaned out.

"What the hell do you want?" called a rail-thin white dude, a sixties flashback in a white tank-style undershirt and jeans that had faded not by fashion statement, threatening to slide down his narrow skeleton at any moment.

He was an eternal "kid" of maybe fifty, with graying, unkempt hippie-ish hair and green eyes so cloudy, it might have been raining inside his skull. He'd shaved sometime this month but not this week.

As they moved closer to apartment 2D, the aroma of marijuana wafted their way.

Gone to pot is right, Nick thought.

Nick displayed his credentials and a polite smile and said, "Stokes, Willows. We're from the Crime Lab."

The cloudy eyes widened. "Something bad go down around this place? I didn't hear about it!"

Catherine had a polite smile going, too. "Could you step out here, please?"

The skinny dude stepped out onto the walkway and Nick maneuvered himself so he was between the guy and Catherine.

The dude slowly pulled the door to 2D closed, probably hoping he could do so without them noticing.

"We're looking for Phillip Carlson," Catherine said over Nick's shoulder.

The guy reared back a little. "You found him. How can I help Vegas Five-oh? You protect, I serve."

"By answering a few questions," Catherine said.

Carlson turned his attention to her, appraising her with a kind of amused confusion, as if he couldn't make out why a good-looking woman like this would be a cop. "I got nothin' to hide, Sweetcheeks. Ask away."

"It's Willows. Could we talk somewhere more private?"

Eyes flicking uncomfortably toward his closed apartment door, he said, "We could do that."

When Carlson took no further action, Nick nodded toward 2D and said, "Private, as in there?"

Carlson shook his head so rapidly he might have been trying to clear the cobwebs. "That's not my place, man."

Nick gave him the friendly smile that wasn't really friendly. "Whose is it?"

"My lady friend. She's, uh . . . not decent."

That Nick could believe.

Carlson pointed a knobby finger. "You were at the right door, before. Let's go down to my crib."

They slid nearer the rusty metal rail, to allow Carlson room to edge by and lead the way, as an amused Nick raised an eyebrow at Catherine, whose eyes were large with skepticism.

"Sorry," Carlson said, as he unlocked the door and swung it open. "Maid's day off."

He entered the dark apartment, followed by Catherine and Nick.

The curtains were pulled tight and very little light seeped in other than through the open door. Carlson flipped a wall switch, and a two-bulb overhead fixture that apparently housed Carlson's dead-bug collection bathed the minuscule living room in odd gray-tinged illumination.

Looking around at this world-class mess, Nick figured the "crib" hadn't been cleaned since the Rat Pack had ruled the Strip. The CSI had entered the dwellings of obsessive-compulsives before, but taking in this prime example of the form, he fought the urge to pull on his latex gloves.

The only furnishings were a ratty sofa, two TV trays, and a twenty-five-inch television. The walls were bare, but everything else looked like the aftermath of an explosion at a landfill. Fast-food bags and cups littered the TV trays, the top of the television, and most of the pathways through the apartment. Beyond the living room, Nick could see a small dining table with a mountain of fast-food detritus and two chairs inside a tiny alcove that had once served as a dining room.

To Nick's left ran a short hallway that led to one or two bedrooms. The most striking feature of the dump, however, was the thigh-high piles of newspapers that lined the walls and took up much of the floor space.

Please God, Nick thought, *don't let this ever be a crime scene. . . .*

"Sit anywhere" Carlson said, plopping onto the sofa on top of various fast-food sacks.

Nick and Catherine chose to stand—not as if there really were any seating options. . . .

The apartment smelled of urine, dope, and puke. Nick had had less trouble keeping his eyes from watering at dead-body decomposition sites.

Forcing himself to focus, he asked, "Mr. Carlson, do you know a man named Marvin Sandred?"

Carlson's eyes narrowed as he riffled through the Rolodex of his alleged mind, his face otherwise as blank as the walls of his apartment. "Nope. Don't think so. That all? That was easy!"

"How about Enrique Diaz?" Catherine asked.

Something that might have been thought glimmered in Carlson's eyes. "Listen, uh . . . cooperating with the Five-oh, that was my New Year's resolution back in '99. So I'm trying to be . . . helpful."

Nick said, "We appreciate that."

"But before I say anything else, I thought it's, you know, fair for me to ask you what this is all about, anyway. . . ."

"It's part of an ongoing investigation," Nick said

meaninglessly. "It's not a trick question, Mr. Carlson—do you or don't you know someone named Enrique Diaz?"

"Greek to me—even if it is Spanish." Carlson smiled to himself, savoring his wit probably in much the way he had savored the former contents of the scattered fast-food bags. "Hey—what *kind* of investigation?"

Catherine said, "Murder."

"Whoa!" Holding up his hands, Carlson shook his head. "I didn't kill nobody."

"That's not what you've told the police over the years," Nick said. "You've confessed to what, twenty-one murders?"

"Hey, I was messed up when I was a kid, but I got help. I got medication."

Catherine's smile seemed cheerful. "Like the 'medication' we smelled next door?"

Carlson's hands went to his eyes, covering them, then slid slowly down his face, pulling the flesh in a melting effect; it did not go well with what he said: "I'm straight, I tell you. That was incense, not weed."

One look at the man's dilated pupils told Nick another story.

Nick said, "My guess is the last time you were straight, the Beatles were still together."

Carlson came up off the couch, his hands reaching up like claws, his eyes wide and wild.

Nick and Catherine both drew back in surprise at

the sudden outburst. But only for a second—Nick gave Carlson a not-so-gentle push.

"Sit back down, Charlie Manson," Nick said, "and chill out."

The hands lowered, the shoulders slumped, the eyelids slipped to half-mast; he looked like a puppet hanging by a string or two. "You just . . . you got to me, man. . . . Hurts my feelings."

Nick said, "You have my sincerest apologies. Now, sit . . . back . . . *down*."

Carlson swallowed and nodded and did as Nick said. Slumping, elbows on his knees, head in his hands, their host said, "I . . . was . . . was just trying to tell you, I'm not that guy anymore. It . . . bums me out when people, you know . . . think that. I worked hard to straighten my ass out!"

Catherine said, "Well, since you're not 'that guy' anymore, you won't mind if we have a look around."

Shooting a quick look to the hallway, Carlson said, "Uh . . . I still got some rights, don't I? Or is this more of that Patriot Act b.s.?"

"I'll stay with him, Cath," Nick said. "You call for the search warrant."

Carlson looked stricken; he raised his hands. "You guys . . . come on . . . it's not what it *looks* like."

Catherine frowned. *"What's* not what it looks like?"

"Nothing . . ." Again, Carlson glanced toward the corridor, then grinned up at the CSIs, nervously. "I just got diarrhea of the mouth, is all. . . . There's no cure for that."

Nick gave Catherine a look and she nodded.

While Catherine stayed in the living room with Carlson, Nick—gun drawn in his right hand, Mini Maglite in his left—moved down the dark hallway, sweeping the flash back and forth.

Three doors.

Open ones on the left and right, and one closed one on the left side at the end.

Nick quickly checked the two open ones—bathroom on the left, a bedroom on the right, both filthy, both empty, of people anyway; Nick had a hunch Grissom could find plenty of bugs in both to make friends with. The last door, however, was locked.

"You got a key you want to give us, Mr. Carlson?" Nick called. "Hate to have to kick this in."

Seconds later, Catherine's voice pinged off the plaster walls: "He's got the key. And he's sharing it!"

Nick went back for the thing and glared at Carlson. "Why didn't you just give it to me? You don't get points for making this harder."

Staring at the floor, mouth hanging open, Carlson said nothing.

At the bedroom door, unsure what awaited behind it, Nick palmed his flashlight, the light extending between his index and middle fingers as he used his thumb and index finger to hold the key in his left hand and unlock the door. In his right hand, the gun came up as he swung the door in and stepped into the darkened bedroom.

Heavy drapes covered a window on the left wall,

shadows dancing as Nick's Mini Mag swept over the room.

But for the beam of light, nothing moved.

He flipped the switch on the wall and another overhead dead-bug repository/light came on. The pistol slipped to his side and dangled there as Nick's amazed gaze arced around the room.

Newspaper articles, magazine articles, photos, and drawings covered the walls and even the ceiling, all sharing a common theme, in the way a teenage girl might devote her entire bedroom to some pop star. Only there was no bed, and this wasn't a shrine to a singing star or film actor . . .

. . . *this was the Church of CASt.*

A small dark wood table in the center served as an altar for the holy book—*CASt Fear,* the Perry Bell and David Paquette paperback about CASt; several scrapbooks were stacked on the table, as well. Ropes tied into reverse-eight nooses hung from the ceiling in varying heights.

When Nick came back into the living room, Catherine was standing near the hallway, eager for a report. Nick's wide eyes spoke volumes.

Carlson sat on the sofa, with the dejected expression of a thirteen-year-old whose parents had just found his porn stash.

"So, Mr. Carlson," Nick said cheerfully. "This effort you made to straighten yourself out—was that before or after you opened up the serial killer museum?"

Carlson sprang up, bolted toward the door.

Catherine whirled and Nick reacted right away, but still it was too late: Carlson had made it outside.

Nick took the lead, Catherine right behind him, as they chased the shirtless eternal hippie along the concrete walkway. The skinny figure took the stairs two at a time but by the time he made ground level, Nick was closing the distance. Carlson perhaps took speed, but he didn't have it: What the suspect had was the wind of an inveterate dope smoker, and with each step, Nick drew nearer.

Carlson had just made it across the parking lot when Nick hit him with a solid tackle.

Nick pulled down his prey, the two of them rolling across the sidewalk and into Baltimore Avenue, the pavement biting into the flesh of Nick's hands and elbows, but he hung on.

Catherine was right there, ready to deal with traffic, but the pair had wound up, fittingly enough for the suspect, in the gutter.

"Aw, maaan," Carlson moaned, under Nick, the suspect's stubbly face dripping blood where it had connected with the concrete. "Not cool! Not cool!"

"Resisting arrest," Nick said, "is not so hot, either, dude."

"I'm not under arrest! Am I . . . ?"

"Oh yeah."

Nick heard a siren wail and he realized his partner had a cell phone in hand; she'd already called in backup, and a patrol car, luckily, had been nearby.

The officers showed up moments later and loaded a hang-dog Carlson into the back.

"That's what I get for praying," Nick said gloomily.

Catherine frowned in amusement. "How so?"

"I asked the Supreme Being to spare us from that apartment turning out to be a crime scene. Now, while Carlson spends the afternoon cooling his jets in an air-conditioned cell, we'll be combing every square inch of his hellhole apartment."

"Maybe God has a sense of humor," Catherine said, laughing a little.

They were walking back toward the building.

"Oh God has a sense of humor, all right," Nick said. "Trouble is, seems about the same as Grissom's. . . ."

And they returned to the apartment, to photograph, process, and dismantle the shrine to CASt; as they did so, they would try to figure out if Carlson had actually constructed a temple to himself. . . .

Sara Sidle knocked on the frame of Gil Grissom's open office door.

The CSI supervisor sat behind his desk, glasses perched on his nose as he slowly scanned a page in a file. He looked up and said, "Hey."

"Hey," she said.

She strolled in, dropped an evidence bag containing the Las Vegas *Banner* magnetic key onto his desk and flopped into the chair across from him.

"Prints?" he asked.

"Couple of partials, but nothing that pops up on AFIS."

The Automated Fingerprint Identification System had been helpful to them on numerous cases, but the system contained only prints of bad guys that had been caught.

"So it's not easy," he said. "Are we surprised?"

She shook her head. "What's next?"

"I'll call Brass. Maybe we can identify the key through the newspaper."

"Really think the *Banner* big boys will make every employee who has one show it to us?"

Grissom considered that for a moment. "If it wasn't the *Banner* or some other media outlet, maybe. My guess is they won't do anything until they talk to their lawyers."

"And the lawyers will say?"

"That it's a Fourth Amendment issue," Grissom answered, "even though it really isn't."

"Kill all the lawyers."

Grissom said, "Actually, that quote's always taken out of context. In *Henry VI,* Shakespeare was in reality implying that lawyers are valuable to—"

"Fine, right. But the *Banner*'s lawyers won't cooperate."

"No."

"And we'll try anyway."

"Yes."

An hour later, sitting in the office of *Banner* publisher James Holowell, with Grissom and Brass, Sara heard Holowell make the same argument, minus the typically Grissom-esque interpretation of the Bard of Avon.

A big window in the publisher's office overlooked a bustling warren of reporters' desks. Holowell's office was leanly furnished, a large mahogany desk taking up more than its fair share of space, the top neat but not bare, a computer monitor sitting at an angle on one corner. The evidence bag containing the magnetic key sat in the middle of the blotter like a three-dimensional ink stain.

Grissom, Brass, and Sara sat in three chairs fanned around the desk, opposite Holowell, a barrel-chested African-American with a bald (or possibly shaved) head and tortoise-shell glasses. He wore a gray dress shirt, the cuffs rolled up one turn and a blue-and-silver Frank Lloyd Wright–patterned tie.

Thus far he had been pleasant, professional, and not very helpful.

"How many employees have these?" Brass asked, pointing to the bagged key on the publisher's desk.

Holowell shrugged. "I wouldn't really know."

"Who would?" Grissom asked.

"I don't really know that, either."

"Could you find out?"

"I suppose I could."

Brass asked, "Will you?"

"Not this second, but of course I'll look into it. I have every intention of helping you, within the parameters of my responsibility to this paper."

In other words, Sara thought, _no._

Grissom, who'd been studying the publisher, asked, "Approximately how many magnetic _Banner_ keys are out there?"

"Maybe twenty," Holowell said. "Perhaps thirty."

That sounded low to Sara. Even at that, the _Banner_—the city's third largest daily paper—had a couple hundred employees, and now at least ten percent of them were possible suspects.

"Only twenty to thirty?" Brass asked. "Best guesstimate, who would they likely be dispersed to?"

"Myself, of course, all the editors and reporters," Holowell said with a shrug. "And a couple of supervisors in the press room."

They thanked Holowell for his time and rose; handshakes had already been passed around on entry, and no one bothered to repeat the ritual.

Grissom picked up and pocketed the evidence bag off the publisher's desk, then the two CSIs and the detective stepped out into the reporters' bullpen. The bustle and mild roar of the newsroom gave them a peculiar privacy.

Sara turned to Grissom and Brass. "How about, 'Kill all the reporters?'"

"Shakespeare was silent on that subject," Grissom said.

Sara said to the detective, "Are we in a better place than we were _before_ that interview?"

Brass said, "Hell, I don't know."

"Of course we are," Grissom said. "Two steps forward, one step back, is still one step forward. When we arrived we had a pool of two hundred suspects who might have a card. Now, if the publisher can be taken at his word, we're down to thirty or less. And we may be able to get a list of names."

Sara made a face. "But the card could have been *stolen*. . . ."

Grissom nodded. "If in that case we can determine from whom it was stolen, we're at an advantage—we have a starting point."

"Okay," Sara said, seeing it.

"What we do know," Brass said, getting on board, "is . . . again, taking Holowell at his word . . . that about eighty-five to ninety percent of the employees *don't* have keys."

Grissom smiled. "Exactly, Jim . . . Sara, information is our currency, you know that. The account grows little by little, one tiny piece at a time. But it grows."

With a sucking-lemon expression, Brass said, "Sounds like my savings account."

The trio had moved only a short distance when David Paquette popped out of a side office that bordered the bullpen. He wore a blue shirt and blue-and-gold striped tie, sleeves rolled more than once; he seemed both more harried and less pristine than his publisher, the fluorescent lighting bouncing off his own balding pate.

"What brings the LVPD to the enemy camp?" he asked, kidding on the square.

"Appointment with Mr. Holowell," Grissom said.

Paquette waved for them to follow him back into his office, a third the size of Holowell's, barely bigger than a cubicle, his desk was a boxy metal job with a much smaller monitor and piles of papers.

After shutting the door, their host did not get behind the desk, nor did he invite his guests to sit down; they stood in a loose huddle.

"What did you see James about?" Paquette asked. His tone had a sense of betrayal in it.

"What do you think?" Brass said. "Police business."

Paquette snorted. "Who do you think you're tryin' to hose here? I *know* there was another murder!" He pointed an accusing finger at them, each getting a turn. "And do I hear one peep out of you guys about it? No—you aren't talking to me *or* Bell, or Brower for that matter. Did we have a deal or not?"

Grissom's forehead was tensed; this was his version of a frown. "What makes you think there's been another CASt killing?"

Paquette grunted a deep humorless laugh. "I didn't say I *thought* there was another murder, I said I *know* there was. What, are you so self-important and self-deluded, you imagine I don't have other sources in the LVPD?"

Grissom offered what may have seemed to Paquette a non sequitur: "David, do you have your keycard on you?"

"What?"

"Your *Banner* keycard."

Paquette stuffed a hand in his pants pocket, fished for a few seconds, and indeed withdrew a keycard.

"What's your interest in this?" the editor asked.

Grissom pulled the evidence bag out of his pocket but kept the contents tightly wrapped in his fist. "If I show you this piece of evidence, I need an assurance."

"What the hell *kind* of assurance?"

"That our arrangement is still intact and in force. You run nothing in the *Banner* till we give you the all clear."

"After you held out on me? What a load of—"

"Hear me out," Grissom said, evidence still concealed in his grasp. "This is something only my lab knows about—it won't be in any of the other media. And it's of particular importance to your paper."

Paquette's natural newsman inquisitiveness took over. "I'm listening."

Grissom knew he had the editor, but he tightened the screws: "And we still have a deal, agreed?"

Paquette was shaking his head, but he said, "Agreed."

Letting the bag unfurl like a flag, Grissom revealed the keycard, its Las Vegas *Banner* label plainly visible to the editor.

"Yes, there has been another murder, as you know," Grissom said. "But what you—and none of the media knows—is the victim had this item clutched in his hand."

"No way," Paquette said, eyes popping. "Whose is it?"

"We don't know," Brass said.

"That's what you were talking to my boss about!"

Grissom said, "We can't reveal our sources."

"Screw you, Grissom! This, this doesn't mean someone at the *Banner* is responsible for the murders . . ." Anger and frustration flared in his voice. ". . . It could have been stolen, and planted at the scene!"

"Gee thanks," Brass said. "Where would we be without a true-crime writer like you to develop our theories for us?"

"Screw you, too, Brass."

The detective moved closer to the editor. "You and your pal Perry were closer to the CASt case than anybody this side of the P. D. insiders or the god-damn victims. You think this keycard turning up in a victim's cold little hand is a *coincidence?"*

Paquette began to speak, but then thought better of it.

"Where *is* Perry?" Brass asked.

Paquette's eyes were on the evidence bag now, probably wondering if his collaborator had become a murderer. "He's . . . out of town for a few days. Wanted to see Patty before school started."

"Patty?" Grissom asked.

Brass and Paquette answered simultaneously. "His daughter."

"She's a sophomore at UCLA," Paquette added.

"She'll be starting the school year soon, and, hey, he's her dad—he wanted to spend some quality time with her, before her schedule got too busy."

"When was the last time you saw Perry?" Brass asked.

"Day before yesterday," the editor said.

Before Diaz's murder, Sara thought. Maybe their pool of suspects wasn't so big after all; maybe it was more a hot tub. . . .

"How can we get a hold of Mr. Bell?" Grissom asked.

"Cell phone, I guess," the editor said.

"I've got that number," Brass said.

"Listen, he wouldn't do this," Paquette said. "He just doesn't have that in him."

Brass smirked, shook his head. "You and I both know that the only reason Perry Bell still has a job here is your guilt over the success you got from the book. You swam upstream, but ol' Perry's just treading water. He's still a journeyman crime writer, riding what little fame is left from your long-ago project . . . which just happens to be about the CASt serial-killer case."

The editor seemed more embarrassed than intimidated by Brass's diatribe.

After a moment, Paquette finally said, "Suppose Perry *does* have a job because of me, how in God's name does that make him a . . . a killer?"

"Maybe it doesn't," Brass said. "But that kid Brower's doing most of the work now, and Perry's got to be feeling the breath on his neck. You stay in the same job long enough, you get to feel like a dinosaur—what better way to rejuvenate his career than to resurrect CASt's career? The killer who gave him his fifteen minutes of fame?"

The editor wasn't buying it. "Perry, some kind of cold-blooded copycat? Hell, Jim—that'd make him an even sicker S. O. B. than the *original* CASt! Listen, I know Perry, and he's got a heart of gold—you know him, over the years you've cooperated with him and he with you. Good, decent guy. I'm telling you, this is *not* him."

Brass said, "Fine. So where was he when Sandred died?"

Shrugging, Paquette said, "How should I know?"

"You're his immediate superior here at the paper."

". . . He was out of the office."

"The other murder was yesterday morning. Do you know where he was then?"

"I told you! Visiting his daughter. Being a father, and a decent human being! You and Grissom ought to try it for a change! . . . Now, I have work to do."

He hustled them out.

The door shut behind them, and the two CSIs and the homicide captain were once again out in the bustling bullpen.

"What do you think, Gil?"

"I think," Grissom said, "we have work to do, too."

FIVE

Some sleep, a shower, and a change of clothes had done nothing to improve Gil Grissom's mood. Sheriff Atwater—in a patronizing, pseudo-friendly way that made Grissom's eyes glaze over—was putting the squeeze on about the need to catch this killer before panic settled over the city and, worse, national attention started scaring tourists away.

Interesting concept, really: Atwater wanted Grissom to "get off" his "duff" and do something about this case, but at the same time thought Grissom had nothing better to do than sit at his desk on the phone listening to a by-the-numbers lecture that, had it been any more predictable, Grissom could have mouthed along with.

Grissom hung up the phone, then glared at the thing, as if the instrument were responsible for Atwater's latest harangue, and for the sheriff's speed-dial now seeming to hold but one number . . . Grissom's.

The TV stations were already pulling out file video of the old CASt murders and the CSI supervisor knew the morning editions of the papers would all have stories. The Enrique Diaz case had been tied in as well, and Grissom wondered if their two small conversations at the *Banner* had somehow added up to one big leak.

Grissom abhorred the media—not the concept of the media, he believed in the abstract idea of a free press—but its bothersome reality in his work-life annoyed him; and similarly he hated politics—not the government or even any particular political party, but the self-interested backstabbing and gladhanding of those who—like the media—pretended to be interested in and aiding his work while only hindering it.

Brass trudged in and dropped copies of the three daily papers onto Grissom's desk.

"Extry extry," the detective said dryly.

The *Sun* and *Journal–Review* both ran CASt headlines, and front page stories on the new crimes with continued coverage of the old ones on the inside. The *Banner*, to its credit, covered only the current crimes with just a perfunctory CASt mention, so as not to look wholly out of step, apparently; their headline story read: *Romanov Sold In Billion Dollar Deal.* Grissom did not resent what coverage they did give the murders, as they had a responsibility to their readers (and their stockholders).

"Looks like the *Banner*'s doing its best to honor our agreement," Grissom said, "considering."

"Yeah, for what good it's doing us," Brass said, "with all this other CASt coverage . . . and you don't even wanna turn *on* the tube. And Dave Paquette's been calling me, like, every damn half hour since we left his office yesterday."

"Why?"

"Oh, I don't know—maybe to see if we've come up with something that will save his job?"

"We have to *have* something," Grissom said, "to *share* something."

Falling into the chair opposite Grissom, Brass said, "Along those lines? Never did get a hold of Bell. I've called the college-age daughter he's supposed to be visiting, but I get the machine, and the tape is full."

"Technology has its limitations."

Brass shrugged. "One way or another, I'll track down the daughter today, and see if I can get to Perry through her."

"All right. In the meantime, don't get too comfortable in that chair. . . ."

"Gil, I've never sat in a harder chair. It's almost like you don't *want* visitors. . . ."

Grissom smiled a little. "On your feet, then—let's see how the rest of our world is faring."

Brass rose, wincing as if he could feel every aching bone and muscle. "Yeah . . . let's."

They found Catherine and Nick in the break room, looking like they'd had maybe six hours of sleep between them in the past several days. Nick leaned at the counter against the back wall, waiting for the microwave. Catherine sat at a table, a paper cup of coffee in her hands, gazing into the dark liquid as if seeking a happier future; her best prospect was the raspberry Danish on a napkin nearby.

"Anything?" Grissom asked.

"Yes and no," Catherine said, holding the cup of coffee near her lips now. She blew steam off.

"I was hoping for a little more detail," Brass said.

Nick said, "How's this for a detail? Phillip Carlson is a total freak."

Grissom said, "Freak as in possessing a physical oddity? Or as in, sexually promiscuous? Be precise, Nick."

"Freak as in he's built a freaking shrine to a certain digit-snipping, semen-sharing serial killer."

Grissom and Brass sat at the table with Catherine, as Nick came over with coffee and a warmed-up bagel-and-egg sandwich, and the two of them told their story.

"Oh," Grissom said, after five minutes. "That kind of freak."

Catherine smirked humorlessly and shook her head. "Yes, but unfortunately, not looking like the *right* freak. . . ."

Brass didn't like hearing that. "Sounds to me like he's plastering his walls with his own press clippings!"

Nick said, "He's not looking right for it, Jim, at least not these new killings."

"Because?" Grissom asked.

"DNA didn't match either crime scene."

Catherine added, "His DNA didn't match anything from any of the original CASt cases either."

"And we had plenty of DNA samples to check," Nick said, momentarily putting his food down.

Grissom asked, "How so?"

Catherine said, "We ran RUVIS over the carpet in Carlson's CASt shrine room . . ."

She referred to the gadget known as a Reflective Ultra-Violet Imaging System.

". . . and white flowers blossomed all over the place."

Grissom frowned. "He's been masturbating to this CASt material?"

Brass was shaking his head. "Damn it, it does make sense. . . . He's a chronic confessor. He identifies with the sick bastard."

"But he's not *the* sick bastard," Nick said.

"Not the one we're looking for," Catherine said.

"Is all the evidence processed?" Grissom asked.

"No," Catherine said. "We've got other lab results we're waiting on, but, Gil—it's no hunch when I say Carlson's a dead end."

Nick nodded. "We're moving on to the other two suspects—Dallas Hanson and Jerome Dayton."

"As well you should," Grissom said.

Greg Sanders came in, poured himself a cup of coffee and stood smiling in front of Grissom.

"You have something," the CSI supervisor said.

Greg's eyebrows flicked up. "Our killer? Is . . . a . . . copycat."

Grissom's mood lightened. "You *know?* This isn't a guess, educated or otherwise?"

"I *know*," Greg said.

"How?"

All business now, Greg said, "I located the DNA evidence from the original cases, the stored semen samples—thanks to Detective Champlain, now retired but still our M. V. P. Anyway, none of it matches Rudy Orloff's deposit from the victims' backs . . . *or* the DNA from the epidermal cells on the rope."

"Rudy Orloff," Brass said, and sighed. "Damn, I almost forgot about him, in all the hubbub of the Diaz killing."

"Hubbub can be distracting," Greg said.

"Greg," Grissom warned.

"Sorry."

"Greg?"

"Hmmm?"

"Good work."

Greg, heady with that praise, took his coffee cup and headed back to his lab, before he got himself in trouble.

"All right," Grissom said to the others. "Let's prioritize."

"I'll take Orloff," Brass said. "I'll make our NLVPD associate Damon feel important and bring him along. I suppose I could stop and talk to the TV reporter, Jill Ganine, on the way. Maybe we can pin down the leak."

Catherine said, trying not to smile, *"You* should talk to her, Gil. She likes you."

"I'll call her," Grissom said, in quiet agony. "Strictly phone call—if a follow-up seems necessary, then—"

Brass said, "Appreciate that, Gil."

Catherine said, "Nick and I'll find out what we can about Hanson and Dayton."

"Right," the supervisor said. "What did you do with Carlson?"

Nick grinned. "He's in a cell. Found pot in the adjacent apartment, which is also his—not dealer quantity, though. And he *did* run."

Grissom thought about that. "Hold him at least till all the lab work's back and you're sure he's cleared. Last thing we want to do is put a serial killer back on the street."

"If Carlson's in stir when the next murder goes down," Brass said, "we'll at least be able to rule him out."

They just looked at him.

Brass, appalled with himself, said, "Did I say that? Please tell me I didn't assume we'd have another murder before we could stop this guy. . . ."

"I didn't hear anything," Catherine said.

"Hear what?" Nick said, nibbling his bagel-and-egg.

Catherine said to Brass, "Did you ever get a hold of Perry Bell?"

The detective shook his head. "Tried until nearly midnight. He never answered his cell phone. I've got his daughter's number in her dorm room at UCLA."

Grissom said, "You find out what you can from this Orloff. I'll track Bell and his daughter."

"What about Paquette?" Brass asked.

Before Grissom could say anything, Brass's cell phone interrupted.

Checking caller ID as he flipped open the phone, the detective said, "Speak of the devil." He punched the button. "Brass. What's up, David?"

As Brass listened for several long moments, the detective's face seemed to lengthen, every line in it deepening; his eyes, unblinking, spoke alarm.

Finally Brass said into the phone, "I'll have someone there in ten minutes. Don't touch a damn thing . . . I know you know! . . . and hold onto *any-one* who's been anywhere nearby, put 'em in a room together, because we'll want to print them."

He listened again, as the CSIs traded grave looks.

"Ten minutes," Brass said, "count on it. And one more thing—thanks, Dave."

Brass clicked off.

His eyes met Grissom's. "He's got a letter and a package from CASt."

"Or maybe the copycat," Nick put in.

"I don't think so—the *Banner* people already read the letter, because they didn't know what they had, right away. But the gist is, the real deal is unhappy with the imitation."

Catherine sighed, shook her head.

Brass went on: "Paquette's seen the originals, remember, the letters from eleven years ago that also went to the *Banner*—and he says he thinks this is the real thing."

Grissom spoke up. "Everybody just keep working on what they're working on—I'll get Warrick and Sara down to the paper right away."

"I'd prefer Dave to be wrong, you know," Brass said. "We've got enough trouble already with the copycat—last thing we need is the undefeated sicko, coming out of retirement."

"What," Nick said, with a sour half-smile, "and try to top the new guy?"

It had been a flip remark, but its truth caught all of them like a board alongside the head. They all froze with dread at the terrible thought of that.

Even Gil Grissom.

Walking into the *Banner* lobby, following Sara, Warrick Brown decided these must have been the kind of faces that greeted crime-scene analysts who'd come to a building in response to one of those anthrax calls that had been so prevalent after 9/11.

The employees he passed on the stairs gave him glances more haunted than frightened. But it was clear, word had spread through the building: The notorious CASt had once again elected the *Banner* to be his personal messenger.

And when Warrick and Sara walked past the

closed door of publisher James Holowell, who seemed to have bunkered himself inside his office, reporters at desks in the bullpen watched the two CSIs, as if observing ghosts haunting the paper, eyes glued to the pair but strictly nonconfrontational.

A loose crowd had formed outside Paquette's office, not unlike groups Warrick had seen gather when someone walked out to the edge of the roof of a high-rise hotel. Intellectually, the crowd wanted the jumper to be saved—the bystanders had, after all, cheered for the jumper's rescue, hadn't they?

But viscerally, in the domain of the id, they longed to see the poor soul take the long plunge to oblivion. This they would never admit to themselves, that animal fascination with death lurking deep in the species.

Warrick sensed that same response in the group gathered near Paquette's office—they knew that death, the real thing, lay behind that closed door. Not a corpse, but something even more exciting: the *promise* of death . . .

. . . by that superstar of death-dealers, a serial killer.

Sara fell in behind Warrick, and kept close as they neared the office. They both carried their flight-case-style silver crime-scene kits and had their credentials flapping loose on chains around their necks. Warrick could tell that Sara felt the vibe, too, that vicarious morbid rush, coursing through the crowd.

"Paquette's first one on the right," Sara said.

With virtually every eye in the place on that office

door, Warrick wondered why Sara was stating the painfully obvious—unless she just wanted to hear someone's voice (even her own) in the overt silence gripping the room.

Warrick knocked on the door and it opened a crack. He'd met David Paquette a time or two and the slice of face revealed to him was enough.

"You're . . . Brown, Warrick Brown," the slice of Paquette said.

"There's two of us, Mr. Paquette. Sara Sidle's with me."

The door opened wider but Paquette blocked the way; he frowned a little. "Where's Jim Brass?"

"This is crime lab business. . . . Do you mind?"

Stepping back, Paquette allowed them inside, but never did open the door all the way, and once they'd scooted through, the editor shut and leaned against it, as if the crowd outside might try to rush the place. Maybe use a bench as a battering ram. Light up old rolled-up papers, as torches. . . .

Hadn't the serial killer replaced the monsters of myth and movies? Perhaps due to the unique nature of Vegas—that desert oasis of fun and sun, attracting visitors and new residents from every corner of the map—the LVPD had faced more of these modern monsters than perhaps any other single department in the USA.

Nonetheless, it was a relative handful, and even Warrick Brown—the least flapable of all the CSIs, with the possible exception of Grissom—could never get used to the wholesale carnage, the literally monstrous egos, and the extremes of what had once been called evil and now seemed to be pathology.

But those "townspeople" out there? They would keep their distance; that much Warrick knew from experience—however fascinated these civilians might be, contemplating the sick mind that had sent this package into their domain, the other side of that door was as close as they wanted to get.

Two other men were crowded into Paquette's office. One looked to be little more than a kid with stringy blonde hair and wide blue eyes, wearing jeans (in the front pockets of which his hands were wedged) and a black Slipknot T-shirt. The other one was Perry Bell's research assistant, Mark Brower, in a white dress shirt with blue pinstripes and a blue-and-red tie with navy slacks.

"I think you know Mark," Paquette said to Warrick.

"We've met," Warrick said, nodding, then shaking Brower's hand.

"And Sara's an old friend," Brower said, shaking her hand too.

From Sara's expression, that seemed to be overstating it. But that was the atmosphere—oddly tense, forced. . . .

Finally deciding the villagers were not a threat, the editor left his post at the door and approached his desk, gesturing to the blonde kid. "Jimmy, here, found the letter first. Jimmy Mydalson, works in the mailroom."

The kid nodded but left his hands in his pockets; so much for the handshake ritual here, the mailroom guy too preoccupied, flicking his eyes toward the manila envelope on Paquette's desk, as if keeping track of a coiled snake that might suddenly bite him.

"This is the item?" Sara asked, taking a step nearer the envelope.

"Part of it," Paquette said.

"Where," Sara said, with a sideways smile, "is the . . . rest of it?"

Paquette summoned a grotesque smile. "What, what's in the envelope is, uh, only part of the . . . uh . . . package. We haven't touched that. The package."

"Oooh-kay," Sara said.

"The letter, that's underneath the envelope. Right there. All three of us have touched that, and the envelope itself."

"Let's slow down," Warrick said. "Tell us what happened. Take your time."

Paquette and Brower turned to Mydalson.

The kid looked like he wanted to bolt or barf or both. Finally, he took a deep breath, pointed a shaky finger toward the package and said, "That came into the mailroom this morning. I opened it, I read it, then I ran up to Mr. Brower, ran like hell."

"Mark's not even a reporter," Sara said. "Why didn't you go to one of the editors, or someone else higher up the food chain?"

Mydalson shrugged. "I trust Mark. He's always friendly."

"Okay, Mark," Warrick said. "Over to you . . ."

The mailroom kid heaved a big relieved sigh, and turned to Brower, to listen to him pick up the story.

Which he did: "Jimmy brought me the letter, I read it, then we *both* hotfooted it up here . . . so David could see it."

Sara said, "Why not take it to your boss, Mark? You're Perry Bell's assistant, right?"

Brower shrugged. "Perry's in California, seeing his daughter. David's the editor Perry reports to, so that makes David my boss in this case . . . and I took the package to him."

Warrick said, "Did anyone else handle the letter besides you three?"

Head shakes all around.

"Okay—nobody panic, but we're gonna have to print you. Got to eliminate you to hone in our bad guy. Okay?"

Head nods all around.

The two CSIs put on latex gloves. While Warrick printed first Paquette, then Mydalson, Sara moved the envelope, carefully spreading open the letter, using a forceps to smooth it and not damage the evidence any further. The paper was bond, with small precise handwriting in blue pen in perfect rows.

She read the letter once, silently, then for Warrick's benefit, began again, aloud: " *'Captain Brass—so many years have passed, and yet you have not advanced in rank. It is as if you were frozen in time and remain unchanged. In that we are alike—I too am the same. I too am frozen in time.' "*

Warrick had finished with Mydalson and was about to do Brower.

"Guys, is this really necessary?" Brower asked. "I barely touched that thing, and I got a deadline to make."

Warrick gave the man an easy smile. "Relax, Mark—anyway, it'll just take a few seconds, and it'll help us zero in the perp's prints."

"What the hell," Brower chuckled, stepping forward. "I'll just look at it as research." He held out his right hand.

Sara returned to her reading: *" 'They say imitation is the sincerest form of flattery. But I am not flattered. I feel violated, and so I turn to you, Captain, for justice. I want you to know, Captain James Brass, that I had nothing to do with these reckless, witless crimes. As a token of my sincerity, I am parting with a treasured souvenir.' "*

Frowning in thought, Sara stopped reading and returned her attention to the manila envelope itself, which was at least eight and a half by eleven; obviously something square still took up a good portion of the bottom half of the envelope.

Warrick finished printing Brower and moved to Sara's side.

Bending to look into the open envelope, he could see a white box maybe four inches square, a festive red ribbon wrapped around it. Sara was at his side, getting a peek herself; she glanced at Warrick, who took that as a hint.

Using his thumb and middle latexed fingers, he lifted the box out of the envelope, then studied it. After taking pictures of both the box and the letter, Warrick dusted the ribbon for prints, found none, and carefully cut it.

Then, Christmas: Warrick lifted off the top.

Inside the box, on a bed of cotton, lay a mummified human finger.

Paquette and Brower recoiled, and the mailroom clerk, Mydalson, jerked a hand to his mouth and ran to the door, opened it, sprinted out, knocking onlookers aside like bowling pins—all in about two seconds.

Good luck to you, kid, Warrick thought.

The white index finger was so seriously dried out, Warrick immediately wondered if they'd be able to get a print.

While Warrick took more pictures, Sara picked up the letter's narrative:

" 'You will find that I am who I say I am—that I am indeed the one and only, the genuine article, no cheap imitation—once you identify my possession. I have had no part in the two murders committed recently in our city. The person behind these acts is a sad imposter trying to feel important through my power. I will not allow that. My reputation is at stake and must be protected. If you cannot protect my good name, I will.' " And it's signed, " 'Capture, Afflict, Strangle.' "

Warrick shook his head. He and Sara exchanged telling glances—in front of these citizens, neither would comment, but both were wondering just how CASt intended to "protect" his good name.

"He's an egotistical maniac," Paquette said.

Warrick offered up the tiniest of smiles. "That may be the most accurately that phrase has ever been put to use, Mr. Paquette."

The conversation with Jill Ganine went about the way Grissom figured it would.

"Ms. Ganine," Grissom said to the phone, the image of the attractive brunette newscaster in his mind not an unpleasant one, "with a murder case like this, when confidential information finds its way into the media, we are concerned for a multitude of reasons."

"Like, who you can trust, Gil? For God's sake, call me Jill. How many times have I interviewed you? Have I ever misrepresented anything you told me? Ever betrayed a confidence?"

"No, Jill, you haven't, and I respect that."

"Good. Then you'll respect me for not divulging a source."

Grissom sighed, but didn't let the phone hear it. "You're compromising a case that involves a vicious killer, who is still at large—"

"You mean 'CASt,' or maybe you mean a copycat?"

"Jill, the person or persons who are providing you with information may very well be suspects themselves!"

"Interesting. Can I quote you?"

"This conversation isn't going to improve, is it?"

"You know, Gil—I don't think so."

"Suppose I got a court order?"

"To improve the conversation, or to try to get me to reveal a source? Do you really think either one would work?"

"Probably not," he admitted.

"But look at it this way, Gil—you can tell Jim Brass you gave it the ol' CSI try, right? Give me a C, give me an S, give an ay-yi-yi? What does it spell?"

"Goodbye, Jill."

Perry Bell still wasn't answering his cell phone and Grissom was having trouble tracking down the reporter's daughter. He finally got through to the dorm room, only to find out from Patty's former roommate that the young woman had taken an apartment this semester. Grissom asked for the phone number, but the former roommate said she didn't have it.

"We didn't get along," the roommate said. "She got really pissed at me for barfing on her rug that time. I mean, like it was *my* fault!"

"Barfing on her rug wasn't your fault?"

"No way! I was drunk, wasn't I?"

Grissom, filing away the conversation as the sociological oddity it was, thanked the roommate.

He didn't really get anywhere until contacting Sergeant O'Riley's old LA buddy Tavo Alvarez, who called back in half an hour with what he'd learned: It seemed Patty was using her mother's maiden name,

Lang, on her UCLA registration. From there it was nothing to get her phone number.

He tried her apartment first, but the young woman didn't answer. Next, he tried her cell phone and she finally picked up on the third ring.

"Hello."

She had a sweet voice with a smile in it. Faint traffic sounds made it clear she was in a car.

"Patty Lang?"

"Yes. Who's this? I don't recognize the voice."

He identified himself and told her about trying to locate her father.

"Wish I could help, Mr. Grissom. Daddy called me, day before yesterday . . . to tell me he wouldn't be coming out after all?"

The girl's up-lilting sentence/questions reminded Grissom of Sara's cadence, a Valley Girlish lilt that he rather liked, for no objective reason.

"Did he say why he cancelled seeing you?" Grissom asked.

"Yes. He said he was about to break a big story. One as big as CASt—one that would 'put him on the map again?' "

"Did he tell you what that story was?"

She laughed once. "Do you know my father very well, Mr. Grissom?"

"Fairly well."

"Has he ever told you about a story *before* it appeared in print?"

"No. You make a good point, Patty."

Her tone turned serious. "Do you think there's something wrong? With my father, I mean? Is he in some kind of trouble, or danger?"

With a father who worked the crime beat, Patty having this reaction seemed natural to Grissom.

"We don't think so. We just wanted to talk to him about an ongoing investigation. Everyone seems to be under the impression he was in LA with you."

"Well, that had been the plan. But a 'big scoop' came up—of course, with my father, it could be ice cream!"

She laughed, and Grissom smiled, but he could hear a shade of worry in her voice.

"Is there anything else I can help you with, Mr. Grissom?"

"No," Grissom said. "Thanks for your time."

"Would you . . . do me a favor?"

"Of course, Patty."

"When you do see Daddy, tell him he better call me. You've got me kinda worried."

"Sorry. Not my intention."

"But it's that kind of world, isn't it, Mr. Grissom?"

He didn't lie to her: "Yes it is, Patty. Thank you. Good-bye."

"Bye!"

He cut the connection and sat back in his chair.

If Bell wasn't in LA—if he was working on a "big scoop" here in Vegas—why hadn't the crime writer been into the office for two days?

Or was the "story" a fabrication to give him the

opportunity to kill Enrique Diaz while the world thought he was out of town? But if Perry had been trying to assemble an alibi, why would somebody who knew his way around criminal matters create such a tissue-thin one? Call the daughter, and poof—bye-bye alibi.

The longer they were unable to locate Perry Bell, the more the questions mounted. As one of the few people on the planet who might actually *gain* from the resurgence of this vicious serial killer, Bell had no alibi for the first murder and had disappeared completely right before the second.

Then, a keycard from Bell's workplace turns up in the hand of the second victim. Had the victim managed to snag it from Bell, as a dying clue?

Grissom normally rejected such overly convenient and clever "clues" as something out of Ellery Queen or Agatha Christie. He was reminded of the old movie cliche—it's quiet out there . . . *too* quiet. . . .

Perry Bell was looking like a good suspect.

Too good.

The ride through the Delamar Mountains up 93 had been even more boring than Brass had anticipated.

As scenery, mountains did not really do it for him; the fascination some people had for rock formations missed him. And for company, Damon was only half a notch above the mountains. The NLVPD detective had two subjects: shop and professional wrestling.

Brass had about as much interest in what the North Las Vegas boys were up to as he did about a sport that had a script. . . .

After what seemed like only one lifetime, they pulled up to the main gate of Ely State Prison. Eight buildings, broken down into four connected pairs, made up the maximum security penitentiary. Twelve-foot-high chain-link fence topped with concertina wire formed the perimeter, along with four three-story concrete guard towers at each corner.

A guard with a clipboard came out of the air-conditioned shack next to the gate, his walk that distinctive combination of authority and indifference that characterized the breed. He wore dark glasses and a campaign hat pulled down low.

Brass rolled down the window as the guard approached.

"May I help you?" the guard asked, though the subtext was: *Why did you bring me out into this heat?*

Brass and Damon both showed their IDs.

"We're here to see a prisoner," Damon said.

The guard had a *no kidding* expression.

Brass said, "We're on the list."

The guard was already checking the clipboard. "Yeah, here you are. You guys know the drill?"

"I do," Brass said.

The guard ambled off.

Damon asked, "What is the drill?"

"Well, it starts with hurry-up-and-wait."

They boiled in the sun for close to five minutes

before the guard finally came out of the shack again and waved them forward. As he did, the gate seemed to magically open, like Oz (whether Frank L. Baum's or HBO's version remained to be seen) and Brass guided the car on through.

The rest of the process took the better part of half an hour before the detectives were sitting at a metal picnic table in a small concrete-block room. Their guns locked in metal drawers near the guard's office, the two plainclothes police officers sat silently, sun streaming through the barred window to make abstractions on the table, as they waited for their guest.

After a somewhat shorter time than the ride to Ely, a key thunked in the lock and the door swung open. The young man who strolled in, followed by a guard, hardly looked like a killer; but Brass knew—too well—that killers came in many packages.

This one was a skinny, blond kid with wide-set, wide-open blue eyes, more pretty than handsome. His orange jumpsuit was immaculately pressed and—even though his hands were cuffed before him—Rudy Orloff moved with an easy grace, almost dancerlike . . . floating on air.

Without an invitation, Orloff sat opposite them at the picnic table.

His smile showed even, white teeth. "I remember you," he said to Brass. "But I don't remember your name. You and those CSI showboats rousted me on some murder, couple years back." Then he gazed at Damon, insolently. "You're cute, but I don't know you. . . . Not really fair, is it? You know who *I* am."

Brass and Damon both showed their IDs.

"Must be important, trading Vegas for Ely," Orloff said, "even for an afternoon. You may have noticed—this place is the devil's armpit."

Brass said, "Rudy, we came all this way just to see you. Talk to you."

"What a great big goddamn honor! Now who do you think I killed that I didn't kill?"

"Your DNA," Damon said, "was found at the scene of two murders."

Orloff didn't miss a beat. "My DNA. What, hair? Skin?"

Brass said, "Semen."

With an evil grin, Orloff said, "You boys are twisted, aren't you?"

"Heel, Sparky," Brass said. "Your spunk showed up on the bodies of two men murdered in Vegas—*last week.*"

The prisoner reared back; his smile was more confused than insolent, this time. "Say what?"

Brass told him again.

Orloff now seemed amused, if interested. "With me in stir for most of the last year, how do you suppose I managed to accomplish that? Prison library fax? Good aim?"

Brass said, "We've already checked—you haven't been released for a funeral, or on work release, or anything else. Your ass has not been outside the prison yard."

"You *are* a detective, Captain Brass. What's *your* idea how it happened?"

The detectives said nothing for a long moment, then Brass said, "We were hoping you might enlighten us."

"Why should I help *you?*"

"I'll talk to the warden and write up a report that oughta put some gold stars on your good-behavior chart."

"Well . . . that's a start. . . ."

Damon said, "This guy we're after is evil."

Orloff backed away, hands up like Al Jolson singing "Mammy." "Wow, evil! There's an oldie but goodie."

Brass said, "We're talking a serial killer. Remember CASt?"

"He's making a comeback? And here I was hoping for a *Seinfeld* reunion."

Brass's mouth smiled; his eyes didn't. "Your come—how come?"

Orloff shrugged. "All I know for sure is—I didn't kill your two dead men. Beyond that, hell . . . I'd just be speculating."

"Please do," Brass said.

The wise remark seemed to strike Orloff as a compliment, and he sat forward, folding his hands, and in a conspiratorial, one-expert-to-another fashion, asked, "You're *sure* it's my DNA?"

"CODIS matched it."

"Someone froze it, then."

"Gee, we hadn't thought of that. Did you sell your sperm to a clinic?"

"No. Or my blood, either, though there were times I tried. See, they make you pee in a cup, and I couldn't piss the physical."

"So comes the question," Brass said, "who would think freezing Rudy Orloff's semen sounds like fun?"

The kid sat back, not sullen—thinking.

Brass tried to prime the pump: "Look, we know you've been inside for a while. What we don't know is, when's the last time you were in Vegas?"

"Eighteen months ago, more or less. About right."

"You turned tricks. Anything kinky?"

Orloff grunted a laugh. "What, guys paying guys for sex? What kink could ever come up in _that_ situation?"

"Anybody who . . . paid for . . . take out?"

Orloff smiled, crossed his arms. "You mean a collector?"

"Is there such a thing?"

Again Orloff sat forward and while he was pretty, his grin wasn't. "You name the bend, somebody out there's made that way."

"I believe you. Back to Vegas . . ."

The prisoner shrugged, resumed his leaning-back, folded-arms position. "I met a bunch of party people when I was there. But my memory's cloudy. Maybe if there was something in it for me, the sun might come out."

Brass tapped Damon on the shoulder and they both rose.

"What?"

"We're out of here," Brass said.

"What, you don't want to *haggle?*" Orloff asked, brows beettled. He was damn near pouting. "I thought you came to play!"

"We came to work," Brass said. "Anyway, I don't think you've got anything to sell."

"Sit down, sit down—don't get all huffy. If I give you something, would it be worth something in return?"

They sat.

Brass asked, "Like what?"

"Solitary confinement."

Damon asked, "You *want* solitary?"

"Listen, I been working on good behavior. I'm in on attempted murder, not murder, guys. There's light at the end of this tunnel, and helping you guys builds my file up, in a good way. But we get the TV here, we get the papers. If these animals find out I helped the *heat* . . . even if it is some messed-up serial killer—they'll think it's open season. I'll never survive, if I don't find a way out."

Brass nodded. "You give me something I can use, I'll get you solitary."

"And while I'm in solitary, you get me transferred out of here, too."

Brass reared back. "Rudy—I don't know if I can make that happen."

"There's plenty of places cushier than this. I have trouble breathing this thin mountain air."

Brass wondered if Orloff had made some enemies in here that he was trying to evade; maybe that would be helpful to the cause. . . .

"I'll do what I can," Brass said.

Orloff studied him for a long time. "I believe you. I choose to believe you. But remember, if you need me as a witness, I gotta be alive! Corpses can't do shit on the witness stand."

"Understood."

"Okay. Okay, there were two guys. I don't know either of their names."

"Oh, great start, Rudy," Brass said.

"Hey, we weren't in the kind of place where you give names," Orloff said. "At least not right ones. Or do you want me to tell you, go look for Smith and Jones? . . . Anyway, there were these two guys. One was older."

"How old?"

Orloff shrugged. "Fifty maybe—that neighborhood."

"What did he look like?"

"Bald, glasses, dressed like he hadn't been shopping since he saw *Saturday Night Fever.*"

"Bald?"

"Yeah, he had, you know . . . wispy stuff, but that was it. He wore lots of polyester. You know—nice jacket, who shot the couch?"

"Okay," Brass said. "He was a . . . collector?"

"Yeah. He used to love to watch me strangle the chicken. He'd hold the cup for me to do it in, and then . . . he'd take it home. What he did with it in the privacy of his pad was not my concern—the C note he gave me was. The other guy did the same thing, only he got a little more . . . involved. Helped me."

Brass said, "Tell me about this other guy."

"Thirtyish, dark hair. I liked him—nice build, kind eyes."

"Color?"

"Brown, I think. Kinda brown. You could dive in and get lost in those puppies."

"Scars or tattoos?"

Orloff shook his head. "Not that I could see. Neither one got naked—this was a kind of voyeuristic deal, mostly. I whack, john watches, here's your cup of fun, here's your hat, what's your hurry?"

Damon said, "These guys weren't . . . together?"

"No. They just had similar kinks. It's . . . unusual, but not unheard of."

Brass thought, *Just write in with your question to Ask Dr. Orloff in the next issue of Bizarre Pen Pals Monthly.*

Brass asked, "Anything else you can think of, Rudy?"

"Two come catchers isn't enough?"

Brass stood, waved to the guard. Then to the prisoner he said, "I'll get right on this—you'll be in solitary within twenty-four hours. Thanks, Rudy—this is valuable."

Orloff, minus any attitude, said, "Thanks. You want to tell me what it was I said that helped?"

"No."

They were back in the car before Damon finally asked. "I give up, what *did* he say?"

Brass started the car and backed out of the parking spot. "The two guys he described could have been almost anyone."

"Yeah," Damon said.

"Or . . . the older one could be Perry Bell, minus the rug."

"The what?" Damon said, then he got it. "Damn! I've never *seen* Perry without that toup—I damn near forgot he was bald underneath."

"Yeah, well he may also be a killer underneath. I'm phoning ahead to Vegas to get a faxed photo of Bell shown to our little helper, Rudy Orloff. If he makes Perry Bell, we have our man . . . or anyway, our copycat."

SIX

Catherine Willows and Nick Stokes had worked all night to track down Dallas Hanson, going from one dead address to another, until finally, in the light of day, they honed in on a homeless shelter in North Las Vegas.

With Nick behind the wheel of the Tahoe, fighting hump-day morning rush hour, Catherine said, "Odd, isn't it?"

"What is?" Nick asked. He had a cup of fast-food coffee in one hand; they'd just had the kind of five-minute breakfast mother never made.

"The way this job combines the mundane with the extraordinary."

"You *are* tired. . . ."

"No, really. I mean, are we cruising to another dead end, like Carlson? Or a confrontation with a homicidal maniac?"

"I get your point," he said. "But I really didn't find that serial-killer shrine particularly mundane."

She laughed once. "Maybe I'm jaded, at that."

Nick sipped his coffee, eyes on the road, as he said, gently, "Is it hard? Knowing that right now your daughter's getting ready for school, and you're not there with her?"

"For an unmarried guy with a little-black-book of a speed dial," she said with an affectionate grin, "you're deep, Mr. Stokes. Sensitive, even."

He flashed a Nicholson grin and gave her a Presley-esque "Thank you. Thank you vurry much. . . ."

". . . The answer is yes." She'd had to call from the fast-food joint to have the sitter cover with Lindsey. "One of these days . . . I gotta get on dayshift."

They rode in silence for a while, then Nick asked, "You really think we're gonna find a serial killer at a homeless shelter?"

"It does go against the grain."

"Now if his vics were homeless, transient types, that'd be different."

"Like Jack the Ripper," Catherine said. "Or Cleveland's Mad Butcher."

"But CASt's M.O. is middle-to-upper-middle-class white males."

"I know, I know. But we check this one out—and we take no chances."

"No argument, Cath."

They both knew that many serial killers preferred

the privacy of their own out-of-the-way residences for their specialized activities. And Dallas Hanson would have zero privacy at the Find Salvation Mission and Shelter.

Then again, CASt wasn't like most other serial killers. He operated within the residences of his victims. He didn't pick up hitchhikers like Bundy did, or seduce young men into his home like Gacy had. Just because Hanson lived in a shelter didn't mean he wasn't a legitimate suspect.

In fact, hiding among the anonymous unfortunates of a city made imminent sense, from a madman's point of view. . . .

Catherine hoped the rest of the team—and she didn't just mean her fellow CSIs, but Brass, Doc Robbins, and even Damon and the assorted detectives aiding the effort—were making some progress out there, on the current crimes. This case was spiraling out of control, and Sheriff Rory Atwater—a more savvy political beast than even former sheriff Brian Mobley—would be breathing down their necks every second.

Although she respected the new sheriff, she couldn't quite bring herself to like him—that might change, but she was put off by his style: He was a slicker politician than Mobley, who had bobbled his mayoral campaign badly. She had every reason to believe the new sheriff wouldn't hesitate to leave the CSIs, Brass, and company hanging out to dry to better his own career.

"You think we should go straight from here to the third guy?" Nick asked.

Catherine shrugged. "Let's not get ahead of ourselves. But if Hanson's a washout, we could think about going to see Dayton. We're approved for overtime on this thing. Are you up to it?"

"Up to it, up for it . . . you name it."

"Amazing what one cup of coffee can do for a strapping lad like you."

Nick just shrugged and grinned. But in a moment the grin had faded, as he said, "Do you really think we have a shot at solving a ten-, eleven-year-old series of murders? I mean, they do CASt on those unsolved-mystery-type shows. He's on the list with Judge Crater and JonBenét."

She thought about that briefly, then said, "Yeah, I do think we have a real shot. We're better equipped than Brass and Champlain were, when the original murders went down."

"Yeah, and lots of cold cases are getting cracked by new technology—but Cath, other than those DNA samples Champlain was smart enough to store, we got nothing but a cold, cold trail."

"I see your point, but then, remember, Nick, on the other hand—we're very, very good."

He chuckled. "Yeah. Yeah, I almost forgot. . . ."

On Miller Avenue, Nick parked the Tahoe at the curb in front of a low-slung stucco, which was a single story but for the west end, where a second story rose into a church-like steeple; the one-story portion had a window with the bold black-outlined-red words FIND SALVATION MISSION AND SHELTER, and the two-story portion had room for a mural of an idealized praying Jesus, amateur enough to have been done by one of the mission's tenants, sincere enough to give Catherine a momentary heart tug.

They walked through the front door into what might have been the lobby of a rundown hotel: a scattering of overstuffed hand-me-down chairs and sofas around a large open room, tables covered with magazines so old they might have been collectible, in less dog-eared shape; the occasional Bible mingled with the mags. Sunshine slanted in, film noir–style, thanks to partly drawn blinds on the front window, providing light and shadow. Off to the right yawned a wide wooden staircase with oak railings that would be about the only thing worth salvaging if a wrecking ball were ever scheduled here.

A thin, sixty-something silver-haired man, whose week-or-so-worth of stubble threatened to become a beard, was sunk deep in an armchair; immersed in the sports section of the morning paper, he wore a very faded, possibly original vintage *Star Wars* T-shirt and faded-to-white jeans, which were accidently in style, and apparently had not noticed their entry. Behind a hotel-like check-in desk, opposite the front door, a thin youngish woman with mousy brown hair and black-frame glasses looked up from a religious magazine she had been reading; her oval face, bearing no trace of makeup, was not unattractive. She wore a clean, crisp white men's dress shirt and black slacks; her manner was professional, and the simple gold-cross necklace spoke volumes.

"May I help you?" she asked pleasantly.

Catherine had a necklace, too, and lifted the ID badge on its chain for the woman to get a better look. "Catherine Willows, Nick Stokes."

"Oh," the woman said. "Crime Lab? Well, we haven't had any crimes here in a long time. Haven't reported anything . . . untoward."

"Normally a detective would come around," Catherine said, "but the department is stretched a little thin right now, and we're on an important case."

"I see." Her hands were folded, appropriately enough, in a prayerlike fashion. "Well, the mission's policy is twofold. We of course help the authorities in any way we can. But we also respect the privacy and dignity of our guests."

"We're not here to arrest anyone," Catherine said. "We're doing background work, following up on an old case that may have a bearing on a new one."

Nick shrugged, smiled his easy smile, and said, "We just want to chat with one of your guests. Fill in some blanks."

Catherine's tap dance, and Nick's charm, merged to do the trick.

"Who would you like to chat with?"

Catherine said, "Dallas Hanson."

The woman's eyes flicked toward where the old-timer had been sitting with his sports page; however, when Catherine glanced back, the old man was gone.

"Where did Obi-Wan Kenobi go?" Catherine asked Nick.

He shrugged. "I don't know—we had our backs to him. Maybe he transported outta here."

"Wrong show," Catherine said. Turning back to the woman, she asked sternly, "Was that Dallas Hanson?"

"Some of our guests have—"

Catherine cut her off. "Privacy and dignity, I know. But this is a murder investigation. Was that him, or not?"

The woman sucked in breath through her nostrils, and tried to stand firm as the authority figure in charge of this desk; but in three seconds, she had withered under Catherine's stare. "No. No, that wasn't him."

The CSIs moved away from the woman's post.

"Outside," Catherine said to Nick, with a gesture toward the door. "If Obi-Wan's warning someone in here, we might have an early checkout, out a window."

"What about those stairs?"

"Mine."

Nick's expression said he didn't love her plan; but

she was the senior officer, and he tore through the lobby and out the door.

Catherine ran to the stairs, taking them two at a time, easing her head out when she got to the second floor.

Nothing.

Nothing but an open door about halfway down, on the left, the side of the hall whose rooms might have windows facing the back alley. Assuming this was the right room, Catherine hoped Nick was on his way around. Tough for one man to cover all four sides of a building. . . .

She let the heel of her hand slide down until it touched the butt of her pistol, reassuring herself of its presence. Then she started down the corridor, the pungent smell of disinfectant tweaking her nostrils.

At the open door she ducked in and found the silver-haired near-codger from the lobby hovering over another man, who lay in the cot along the left-hand wall in the cell-like room. A small, square, endlessly scuffed wooden table and two mismatched kitchen chairs were by the only window, and a squat bureau took up a fair piece of the right-hand wall.

To the man in the bed, the silver-haired man said, "You *sure* this is what you want, Dal?"

The bedridden man must have nodded, because the silver-haired man shrugged and said, "Your call, buddy," and stepped aside.

That gave Catherine her first look at the sunken-cheeked scarecrow on the cot. His hair was graying too, if less rapidly than his friend, and he had shaved recently, maybe even yesterday. But his skin was as gray as his hair, and his eyes were a plea for mercy—not from Catherine, but God.

"Dallas Hanson?" Catherine asked.

The man on the cot nodded. It took some effort.

"I'd like to talk to you."

He had sunken cheeks, high cheekbones, and a prominent forehead that made his narrow face look like a skewed metal framework full of sharp angles with skin thinly stretched over it.

"Pretty woman like you?" he said pleasantly, his voice surprisingly deep. "Sure. Don't get much company of your . . . caliber."

He looked small and bony beneath the blankets.

She got her radio out and pushed a button and said, "Nick, our man's not running. We're in . . ." She looked at the door, which was white and recently painted; a plastic card in a slot said: 218. She told Nick.

Nick said he was on his way.

She glanced at the silver-haired man, who looked embarrassed. "Gonna help your friend take the back way out, huh?"

"No law against stopping by a buddy's room," the old guy said, his voice midrange, quavery. "Or is this a fascist state already?"

"This is a murder investigation. Do you really think standing in its way is a good idea?"

He didn't answer, just put his head down, eyes not meeting hers, and started for the door.

As he passed, Catherine said, "A lot of people could have gotten hurt because of you."

The man paused, then looked at her; his eyes were bloodshot, rheumy. "Everybody in here, lady, is hurting already. You got a badge and real nice clothes. We got each other."

Catherine began to say something, then thought about what the woman at the desk had said about the privacy and dignity of the "guests"; and said nothing as the old boy, chin on his chest, walked out.

"Don't blame Bruce," Hanson said. He had worked himself up on his elbows, and he had a yellow smile going. "Most of us have had trouble with the law at one time or another—we kind of watch out for each other."

"I understand."

"Do you?"

"Yeah. I do. Would you like to sit up?"

"I would love to sit up." He tossed off the blankets and Catherine got a good look at the blackened toothpicks he called legs. "But the cancer makes it pretty much impossible . . . without help."

She was giving it to him when Nick entered and got his own good look at their suspect.

"This is my associate," Catherine said, showing her credentials to Hanson, now propped up with a pillow behind him. "I'm Catherine and this is Nick. We're from the Crime Lab. We wanted to talk to you about—"

"CASt," Hanson said.

Nick frowned, hands on hips. "You know that?"

"Cancer's eatin' my body, boy, not my brain. I can still read the papers, and we got a couple TVs in this Jesus factory. Now that someone's resurrected ol' CASt, I figured Sin City's finest would come sniffin' around again."

"When was the last time you were out of that bed?" Catherine asked.

"Other than meals and to go to the john? I think it was my last chemo treatment. Three weeks ago maybe?"

"How do you get to chemo?"

"Lori, she's the girl downstairs, she took me. Look, I haven't been able to do anything on my own for six months, and I've got another six left if I'm lucky . . . make that unlucky. I don't have the time or energy for an ambitious hobby like killin' people."

Catherine nodded. "What about eleven years ago?"

Hanson shook his head. "I was innocent then, and I'm innocent now. That cop, Champlain, he was after my ass. He didn't have anything to go on except some circumstantial crap. I didn't kill Todd Henry or any of the others. That hardass cop just needed to nail somebody, probably gettin' pressure from upstairs, and he figured he'd serve me up."

Nick said, "Mr. Hanson, if you read the papers, you know there's speculation that the new CASt killings are the work of a copycat."

"Oh. So I'm still a suspect in the *original* crimes? What a crock!"

Holding up a buccal swab, Catherine asked, "How would you like *not* to be?"

Looking skeptically at the swab, Hanson asked, "How?"

"DNA."

"You want to clear me or set me up?" Hanson asked, only a trace of sarcasm in his voice.

She found his eyes and held them with hers. "I don't want to do anything but find the truth."

"I don't know . . ."

Nick said, "Respectfully, sir, let me point out that with what you're facing, with this illness? You might want to consider cooperating."

"Why in hell's that?"

Nick shrugged. "Right now your legacy, your place in posterity, is as a suspected infamous serial killer. You don't have to leave that blot on your memory."

Hanson grunted, "Huh. You make a hell of a point, son. I got a couple kids out there, somewhere. Maybe even some grandkids. I don't take pleasure in my descendants thinkin' I was some kinda homicidal lunatic. Okay, *sold*—what do I gotta do?"

"Open your mouth," she said. "You don't even have to say, 'Aaah. . . .' "

Gil Grissom was still at his desk when his cell phone rang. Picking it up, he pressed the talk button. "Grissom."

"It's me," Brass said.

"Where?"

"Headed back to the city."

Grissom could hear the car's engine. No siren, but Brass was clearly not taking his time. "Learn anything?"

"Good chance Perry Bell's our copycat."

"Tell me why."

Brass outlined his theory, including a recap of the Orloff interview; it took a while.

"That all sounds good," Grissom said. "But where's the evidence?"

Testily, Brass said, "I thought it was your job to find the evidence."

"No—that would be your job. I *process* evidence."

" . . . Sorry."

"No problem. I located Bell's daughter."

"Good! See, you *do* find evidence!"

"In a way. I certainly got information."

Grissom filled Brass in on what Patty Lang had told him.

Brass asked, "Do we have enough for a search warrant?"

"Borderline. But I'll work on tracking down Bell before you get back."

"Bless your little evidence-processing heart."

"I'll see where everybody else is, right now. I've got Warrick and Sara working that *Banner* package, Catherine and Nick out in the field, chasing the original suspects. By the time you get here, we might be at warrant stage."

Grissom spent the next two hours searching for Perry Bell.

He called the reporter's friends and coworkers, put out an APB for the man's car, and sent a squad car to Bell's home. A uniformed officer went to Bell's house, got no answer at the front or back door, found curtains drawn on windows, looked in a garage window to see Bell's vehicle gone, and—on reporting back to Grissom—got posted out front till further notice.

No probable cause to break in. If Bell was inside, they would have to catch him when he came out. Anyway, if he was indeed the copycat, the threat of him having a potential victim in there was minimal— the copycat had struck twice so far, but (staying to the original CASt) always in the victim's home.

If Bell was outside the house, that was a different problem entirely. The reporter could be anywhere, doing anything, and unless they caught a break, Grissom and his crew wouldn't have any idea of what Bell had been up to until . . . well, possibly until the CSIs were summoned to the next crime scene.

A third troubling possibility occurred to Grissom: Bell might be innocent. The crime-beat columnist could, as the man had told his daughter, be out working on a big story; and that story wasn't even necessarily the CASt one. But if so, where *was* the reporter? Why couldn't anyone find him?

Deciding he'd done all the detective work possible from his desk, Grissom got out of there, and his first stop was the morgue, where Dr. Robbins was finishing up the autopsy on Enrique Diaz.

With a mildly puzzled frown, Grissom asked, "Two days to get to Diaz?"

Robbins shot a barely patient look toward Grissom, then continued his work. "I know you're focused on this serial killer, but in those two days, besides the late Mr. Diaz, nearly two dozen people have died under questionable circumstances in this city."

Grissom hadn't meant to antagonize Robbins; maybe this was one of those "people skills" instances everybody was always after him about.

The CSI asked, "Find anything?"

"Very preliminary. Diaz died of strangulation caused by the ligature you found around his neck. Everything else matches the Sandred murder . . . no carpet burns this time. Otherwise, identical."

"Nothing new?"

Robbins picked up a small envelope from a metal table beside the slab. "I did find these."

Grissom accepted the envelope and carefully lifted the flap. Strands of something dark lay in the bottom of the envelope, but he couldn't quite make them out. Closing the envelope, he asked, "And what do we have here?"

"Synthetic hairs . . . my guess? They're from a bad hairpiece."

"Bad?"

"Cheap . . . but Greg will tell you more than I can."

Interest piqued, Grissom asked, "Synthetic hairs from the killer?"

"Could be," Robbins said.

"You have doubts?"

The coroner shrugged. "Well, more like misgivings."

Grissom said, "Locard says two objects cannot come into contact without some kind of exchange."

Robbins stepped away from the body and looked around the morgue, as if unsure he and Grissom were alone—perhaps a corpse or two might be faking it.

"Gil, you and I both know Perry Bell. He's a nice enough guy; probably the most honest, helpful guy in the media, where our work is concerned. Certainly harmless."

"No argument."

"Synthetic hairs are going to send you in his direction as a suspect."

"Yes. We're already looking in that direction, Al."

Robbins was shaking his head. "Staging serial murders, to help himself make a career comeback? That would take a kind of genius, and a sociopath's world view. Gil, honestly—does that sound like Perry Bell to you?"

"No, it doesn't. But I remain a student of human psychology, not an expert. And right now, my concern is whether the evidence points to Perry Bell. Which it does. My next concern is to make sure that no one else is put in danger."

Robbins rested a hand on Grissom's arm. "I understand. But don't just listen to your head on this one. You have a good heart, Gil. Don't be afraid to listen to *it*, too."

"That's . . . generous, Al. But I listen to the evidence."

"No. You interpret it. And in any case where crimes are being staged, the evidence is as suspect as the suspects."

Grissom thought about that momentarily, and said, "I don't know about listening to my heart, Doc—but I won't ever make the mistake of not listening to you."

The two men exchanged smiles, and got back to their respective work.

The circumstantial evidence against Perry Bell was growing with every passing second, and Grissom felt he had enough to go to a judge for a search warrant. Though he couldn't directly tie Bell to the murders, what he did have pointed to the writer: synthetic hair that he might be able to match to Bell's hairpiece; the magnetic keycard from the *Banner;* and the semen that came from a "collector" whose description matched Bell's. Add to that the reporter being out of touch with friends, coworkers, and family since before the second murder, with no alibi for the first one, and the makings for a warrant were there.

No, not one of these things fell under the heading of compelling evidence; but as a whole they were puzzle pieces that added up to an image that, so far, resembled Perry Bell.

Judge Goshen's courtroom was busy, as usual, and, as usual, Goshen had to be completely convinced before he granted the warrant. The good thing about a warrant from this judge was that it would hold up under inspection if/when a case came to trial; the bad thing was, you damn near had to argue the case as if *at* trial. . . .

Plus, like everybody else in the criminal justice system around town, Judge Goshen knew and liked Perry Bell. In the end, however, Grissom prevailed, although it took the CSI every bit of two hours to come out of the judge's chambers with that precious sheaf of papers.

Once outside, he called Brass's cell. "You close?"

"Yeah. What have you got?"

Grissom filled Brass in, and the two agreed to meet at Bell's home in half an hour. The CSI wanted to take Warrick and Sara with him, so he drove from the courthouse back to headquarters where he found the pair busy going over the CASt package they had gotten from the *Banner* earlier. At one table, Sara hunkered over the box itself while across the way, Warrick bent over the mummified finger.

Grissom approached Warrick first. "Point to anything?"

Granting his boss a smile, Warrick said, "Anywhere I want, actually. . . ."

And held up his right hand to reveal the skin of the finger sheathing his own latex glove–encased forefinger. "I rehydrated the skin as much as I could, removed it from the digit, and then slipped it on."

"And got a nice clear print, I bet."

"Oh yeah. The finger belongs to the last original victim, Vincent Drake, the supervisor in the city garage."

Grissom felt his stomach tighten. "So the message *is* from CASt."

"Hard to read it any other way."

"Our first killer is still out there somewhere. Which means we need to find *him* before the copycat goads the real CASt into trying to compete. Stay with it and call me if you get anything else."

Warrick nodded grimly.

Grissom went to Sara's side, and she needed no prompt to report.

"The box is a generic white gift box available at any drugstore or gift shop or half a dozen other outlets in your average mall. Ditto on the ribbon—generic red, available anywhere. Envelope is common, but it's being fumed for prints now. "

"What about the fabric?"

"Still working on that."

Grissom nodded. "Sara, put that on hold. Grab your kit—I need you with me."

She flashed her a grin; she loved the lab, but the field was her passion. "Where to?"

"We're serving a search warrant at Perry Bell's house."

Her smile faded. "Almost hope we're wrong about him. Almost kinda like the guy. Feel sorry for him."

"If he's our killer," Grissom said, "save the empathy for the victims."

Bell had a nice two-story stucco home on Beacon Point, just off Gilmore and not far from El Capitan Way. The Durango Hills Golf Course, a favorite of Bell's, sprawled just a few blocks south.

Winding up with the house when his wife moved to LA after their divorce, Bell had kept the place in good repair, removing the lawn in favor of the more drought-friendly Xeriscape desert plants that were replacing grass in many Vegas middle-class neighborhoods.

The squad car remained posted out front, the uniformed officer leaning against the front fender, his back to the house as he smoked a cigarette. When the Tahoe parked behind him, the officer stubbed the butt out under his shoe and walked briskly up to the driver's side window.

"House hasn't made a move," he said good-naturedly.

Grissom recognized Carl Carrack from numerous crime scenes and knew the ten-year vet to be a sharp, good patrolman. Maybe thirty-five, Carrack stood just under six feet and carried a well-distributed two hundred pounds on a compact frame.

"Anybody at all been around?" Grissom asked.

"No neighbors, no salesmen, not even a paper boy."

Grissom and Sara were still unloading when Brass's Taurus pulled up behind them.

Brass and Damon joined them at the rear of the SUV.

Brass looked toward the house. "Do we know if Bell is in there?"

"Doesn't appear so. Carrack's been here for the last two hours, reports no movement."

"And no word of Bell otherwise?"

Grissom shook his head. "Nobody's radioed in to that effect."

Damon asked, "What about the APB on his car?"

"Nothing yet," Grissom said. "He may be holed up writing, inside, or at a motel on a bender or . . . Why don't we stop speculating and break in?"

The front door was recessed, and hidden from the neighbors on the north by the protruding two-car garage, in the shadow of which Grissom pulled on latex gloves. So did Sara. The cops did not.

Then—Brass at his side, Damon and Carrack behind them, Sara bringing up the rear—Grissom knocked on the green steel door.

"You want to try the bell?" Damon asked.

Grissom shook his head. "No. Might disturb fingerprints."

The NLVPD detective frowned. "Why, is this a crime scene?"

"Do we know it isn't?"

Damon had no answer for Grissom, and the house had no answer for Grissom's knock.

The second time the CSI knocked harder, trying the knob as he did, finding the door locked, not surprisingly.

After a brief wait, Carrack and Grissom hit the door with a ram. The lock burst, the frame splintered, the door swung open and leaned drunkenly to one side. The foyer opened into a living room at right, a staircase along the left wall. Straight ahead, down a short hall, Grissom could see into the kitchen.

Brass was the first one through, but he did not get far.

The detective pointed to something dark on the floor and said, "Blood! Everybody freeze."

The house was dark and Grissom had to pull out his Maglite to shine it on the floor next to Brass to get a clear look: a small dot of dark blood on the hardwood floor.

Grissom said, "Good catch, Jim—looks dried."

Brass got his gun out with his right hand and turned on a small flashlight with his left. "Just the same, we're going to clear the house before you guys come in."

"Nobody's been in or out, Captain," Carrack insisted. "I swear."

"Let's clear the house, shall we?" Brass said to the patrolman, gun in both hands, snout up. "Plenty of time for you to cover your ass, later. . . ."

Damon pulled his pistol as did Carrack, and soon the two of them were moving up the stairs, eyeing the second floor suspiciously.

Grissom and Sara stepped tentatively inside.

"Stay," Brass said them, then eased into the living room, and out of sight.

Grissom examined the blood under his flashlight beam again, moving closer, kneeling.

"This blood is indeed dried," he said.

Sara said, "Whatever happened here . . . ? Happened some time ago. . . ."

From upstairs came Carrack's and Damon's voices, alternating as they went from room to room, a word batted back and forth like a tennis ball:

"Clear!"

"Clear!"

"Clear!"

"Clear!"

Brass emerged from the rear of the kitchen. "From the living room you run into the dining room at the back, then the kitchen on the left—all clear."

Top of the stairs, Damon said, "Upstairs, clear!"

Grissom moved the light from the original dot of blood toward the kitchen. He found another, then another, and so on, the trail—not of breadcrumbs, like Hansel and Gretel, but blood drops—leading back into the kitchen and off to the left.

"What's in that direction?" Grissom asked Brass.

"Closed door," Brass said. "Probably leads to a mudroom, and the garage."

"Let's have a look."

Brass looked unhappy. "Maybe I should take one of the guys with guns with me first . . ."

"It'll be fine," Grissom said.

"One condition," Brass said.

Grissom knew what that condition was: He transferred his flash to his left hand and got out his handgun; behind him, Sara did the same.

The kitchen was a big galley with the dining room visible through a doorless entry to the right. Going the other way, Grissom opened the door into a small room that held a washer, a dryer, and a small table for folding laundry on the opposite wall between two doors.

The far door, Grissom figured, would lead to the garage.

Carrack had looked through the garage window earlier, so they were fairly certain that was empty. The blood trail stopped at the nearer door, on the left.

Grissom hesitated to open the door.

Few things bothered him more than the possibility of being personally responsible for destroying evidence; but if someone was behind the door, and still alive, that concern was overridden.

Prints be damned, Gil Grissom's latex-gloved hand settled on the knob, and he opened the door to peer in at a tiny landing above a dozen descending plywood stairs, a two-by-four bannister on the right side. Without hesitation, Grissom flipped a switch that turned on a light overhead as well as several in the basement below.

Behind him, Brass said, "Damn it, Gil, that hasn't been cleared!"

Grissom turned to Sara and said, "Stay here."

Then, ignoring the detective's admonition, Grissom—gun in one hand, flash in the other—started down. . . .

Very few homes in Vegas even had basements, and the CSI was surprised that Bell's house would be one of those that did. As he took the creaking steps a slow, careful one at a time, the CSI could see more blood on the stairs—not just drops—and a small puddle off to the left on the floor.

At the bottom, having already taken care not to step in any blood, Grissom took in a much bigger pool, running out from under the stairs like something leeching up from the earth.

But the earth wasn't the source of this coagulating fluid.

Shining his light back there, Gil Grissom ruled out Perry Bell as a suspect.

SEVEN

After positioning Officer Carrack and Detective Damon on the first floor, Jim Brass came down into the basement, his cop senses—honed by twenty-five years on the job—tingling, and (like Grissom) careful not to disturb blood evidence. His radar wasn't registering danger—this was the "something's wrong" tingle. Though his gun was in one hand, Brass strongly sensed he was not entering a fire zone, rather the aftermath of something . . . wrong.

On this case, with its ritualistic crime-scene fetishism, the detective knew before even reaching the last step, what he would see. . . .

Brass came around the stairs and shone his flashlight into the open area beneath. The beam hit the large puddle of blood and followed its flow to the missing right index finger and then over the plump nude dead body. Seemingly with a will of its own, the flash found the face of Perry Bell.

That was when Brass realized he'd been at least a little mistaken—he had thought he had a fix on exactly what the crime scene would look like; but after the carefully staged murders of Sandred and Diaz, this tableau came as a shock . . .

. . . of recognition: *The real CASt was back.*

The reporter's lips were painted with lipstick that mingled with blood dried on his face from a broken nose. Beaten almost beyond recognition, Bell had suffered more than any other victim, past or present, of CASt (or the CASt copycat). Semen was splashed on his lower back. Blood was everywhere in the basement, not like the neat amputations of the copycat, but spattered and sprayed.

"God-*damn*-it!" Brass exploded.

He wound up to throw the flashlight, but caught himself just before he let it fly. Instead, he turned it off, and jammed it into his pocket.

"I didn't work the original crime scenes, Jim," Grissom said evenly. "But I take it . . . this is the real deal."

Shaking his head, breathing hard, Brass let out a few choice epithets, then said, "Well at least we know he's still out there—and in our jurisdiction. He didn't move away or get run over or . . . shit, Gil, this . . ."

Grissom, awkwardly, touched Brass's arm with a latexed hand. "Do the work, Jim. Shake off everything else."

Brass nodded, swallowed. "This is even more brutal than the crime scenes from years ago. It's like CASt nurtured a . . . special rage for Perry. Who was, after all, the reporter whose book chronicled the original spree. Making money off CASt, saying 'bad' things about him."

Grissom shrugged. "Everybody's a critic."

Brass had his cell phone in hand before he realized he'd even reached for it. He brought it up to his ear, his fingers somehow having figured out to hit the speed dial. "This is Captain Jim Brass—who's this?"

The voice on the other end was cool and female. *"Laurel Thompson, Captain."*

That sent a quick spike of relief through him. Nothing rattled Laurel—she was one of the best dispatchers in the city.

"Laurel, I need you to send a patrol car to the *Banner*. The officers're to take David Paquette into custody on the CASt case. If he's not there, send a car to his house."

"Yes, sir. Murder charge?"

Meeting and holding Grissom's eyes, Brass struggled with the urge to say yes.

The trouble was, he had no real proof, though logic seemed to say that if Bell wasn't the copycat, then Paquette had to be. Silently he willed Grissom to find some evidence to bust the editor; to speak that sentiment aloud, however, would only invite Grissom's disfavor.

To the dispatcher, Brass said, "Have them take him into protective custody."

"Pardon?"

"Laurel, tell the officers Paquette's a material witness, and that I'm concerned for his safety. . . . In the meantime, I'll call David and tell him what's going on myself."

"Car'll be dispatched immediately. Ten-four, Captain."

"Thanks, Laurel."

He clicked off.

"Material witness?" Grissom asked.

"Do we have enough to collar him?"

"No."

"Point is, get him off the streets until we know one way or the other. If Bell's not the copycat, Paquette is the next best guess."

"Here's a small suggestion," Grissom said. "Let's not guess."

"Then find me some goddamn evidence!" Brass snapped.

"Actually," Grissom said, "that shouldn't be hard. . . ."

Grissom moved in for a closer look.

The differences between this crime scene and those generated by the copycat were subtle but plentiful.

Grissom, kneeling near the mutilated hand, said, "The finger was severed while the victim was still alive."

To Brass, this was obvious. Bell's heart had definitely been pumping when his finger got cut off.

"Tell me about it," Brass said. "More blood here than the other two scenes combined."

"The lipstick appears to be a darker shade than the one applied to Sandred and Diaz," Grissom said. "But I can't be sure without lab comparison if it is truly darker, or if the limited light, and this preponderance of blood, is playing tricks on my perception."

"I'd say darker," Brass said.

Grissom continued, gesturing to the corpse: "The broken nose was likely sustained when Bell opened the door for his killer. Doc Robbins will provide the details, but this beating is clearly more vicious than anything either CASt or the copycat has done before. For reasons unknown—despite what we might speculate about his feelings for the author of *CASt Fear*—CASt felt compelled to torture Bell more than the others."

Brass just chewed his lower lip.

Grissom turned toward Brass. "Can you see it, Jim? In your mind?"

Bell is home alone. He's in his study, going over his old files on CASt, excited that the ancient case has given his career a new lease on life. The doorbell rings and he comes downstairs. By the second ring he's gotten to the door to open it.

The front door is recessed, in a shady area, and it's hard for the neighbors to see what's happening. It's similarly difficult for Bell to see who's on his doorstep. Either the killer strikes immediately, or Bell knows the killer and invites him in, and then the killer strikes as soon as he's inside.

Capture.

Either way, Bell catches a blow in the face—a heavy blow, breaking the reporter's nose and causing blood flow that will eventually lead the police to the basement.

Blood dripping from his nose, Bell is dragged by the killer down to the basement. Bell is stripped.

Affliction.

The noose is slipped around his neck and pressure is slowly applied. As the noose is tightened, Bell starts to slip away. He's brought abruptly back by the first punch to his face, immediately followed by another and another, the blows raining down. He tries to roll into a fetal position, to avoid the savage attack, but the killer jerks on the rope, the noose tightens again and Bell is forced to comply.

The killer lifting Bell's head by the rope, turning the face to just the right angle, then delivering another powerful punch to the reporter's face. Eventually, he passes out, the pain simply too much. He awakens after he doesn't know how much time to the sensation of something closing around his index finger.

The killer has Bell's finger between the blades of a metal clipper. The steel feels cold against his skin until the killer tightens and the pain begins. The cold is replaced first by the warm rush of blood, then the blinding heat of pain as the killer snips off the finger. Bell watches what had once been his finger bounce on the floor before he closes his eyes, nerves screaming, but it does no good. The pain is like nothing he's ever felt before and he momentarily forgets the rope around his neck, but a quick jerk by the killer reminds him and again the noose tightens around his neck.

Strangulation.

He fights, but it's no use. There's no air. His chest burns, aches as his lungs battle for every last molecule of oxygen.

Then there is none, every fiber of his being on fire. Slowly, surprisingly, the pain begins to subside, the burning eases and a warm thick liquid blackness covers him. Bell is floating now in this thick black sea, the warmth calming him as it ebbs and flows each second, becoming elongated, enjoyable as he relents. The blackness is not just outside him now, it has entered him and Bell floats away, trouble and pain gone forever.

Everything gone forever.

Sara joined them. Her eyes tensed as she took it all in. "This . . . looks the same but different."

Still kneeling near the body, Grissom looked up, pleased with her, and said, "Yes."

"We'll need to pull his phone records," Brass said, a stray thought coming to him.

Grissom nodded. "We may be able to figure out whether the killer forced him to make the call to his daughter, cancelling his trip, or if he really did cancel to work on the story."

"Maybe the story was working on him."

Standing, Grissom said, "The killer spent a considerable time with Bell, to do this kind of damage. Once Al gives us time of death, we can cross-check it to the phone records and see how close the call to his daughter came to the attack."

"That was my thought."

Grissom said to Sara, "Check his bedroom—see if he was packing."

"Okay. Then . . . fingerprints?"

Nodding, Grissom said, "Anything on the first floor the killer might have touched—banister coming down these stairs, for example."

"I'll try the front door, too."

"Tell Carrack and Damon to stay put," he said, "and not to touch anything else. Let's not contaminate the crime scene any more than we already have."

Brass was on his cell phone again, making the call to David Paquette.

The editor picked up on the second ring.

"David, Jim Brass. I'm sending a car to pick you up."

"Why in the world?"

"We're placing you in protective custody as a material witness."

"The hell you are! I've got a paper to put out."

"This is a serious matter, David. Overrides any work concerns."

"Give me one good reason why."

"Perry Bell's dead."

Paquette said nothing, but halting breathing told

Brass just how hard the news had hit the editor . . . unless that was a pose.

"Another CASt victim," Brass said.

"Oh, my lord in heaven . . ."

For a moment Brass wondered if Paquette had started to cry. The editor and Bell had been friends, collaborators. And the murder related directly to the project they had done together that had put them both on the map.

Brass said, "Look, Dave—don't give the officers any trouble; let them take you into custody. We can protect you. And maybe you can help us."

"Oh . . . okay."

"It's going to be all right."

"I . . . I don't think so, Jim. We're . . . we're supposed to cover the news. Not . . . not *be* the news."

"Well, cooperate with us and we'll keep you out of the headlines."

Brass broke the connection.

"You do really think he did this?" Grissom asked.

Shaking his head, Brass said, "His reaction has me wondering—I think he was weeping, Gil."

"They were friends."

"What do I think? I think I'm not going to think anything from now on about this goddamned case, until you tell me to."

"Thinking is allowed. It's the guesswork we need to steer clear of."

Brass's cell phone rang.

He answered; it was Sergeant O'Riley. He listened, thanked the sergeant, and said to Grissom, "Just got word that Orloff at Ely State Prison says the photo of Bell we faxed over is *not* one of the two 'collectors' he dealt with. . . . Sounds like he wasn't the copycat. . . ."

"Give us some time to work the crime scene," Grissom said. "We'll get something."

Even for Vegas, their luck was lousy.

Everywhere they turned, the CASt case threw them a curve. Somehow, the killer was getting to them across the years—a madman who had stopped his vicious spree when Nick Stokes was still in college—had somehow found a way to travel through time to thwart their investigation today.

After their washout visit with Dallas Hanson at the mission, Nick and Catherine had stopped back at the lab long enough to drop off Hanson's swab and get the DNA test going. Nick believed it would turn out the same as Phillip Carlson's had—no match— but the job was about evidence, not belief.

Now, they were headed out on Blue Diamond Road toward Pahrump and the Sundown Continuing Care Facility. A sister facility of Sunny Day in Henderson—where Warrick and Catherine had recently stopped an angel-of-death killer—Sundown was more of a lockdown facility than its sibling across the valley.

Behind the wheel, Nick asked, "So what have we missed?"

"Nothing that I can think of," Catherine said. She went silent, and actually did think; then she added, "We've worked the evidence. Possible Brass and Champlain were on only wrong trails, years ago, and the real CASt isn't on the original suspect list."

"Yeah, but Brass and Champlain are first-rate guys—"

"Sure they are. But we've done it before, too—can happen easy enough, you start believing your theories before the evidence is in."

"Happens," Nick admitted. "But if CASt isn't one of these three suspects, then what have we contributed?"

"We've ruled them out," Catherine said. "That's important, too."

Nick's nod was grudging.

Following Amargosa Road out into the Last Chance Range, Nick couldn't help but mirthlessly smile at the hospital's location. *"Last chance" is right,* he thought. Most of the patients at Sundown were dangerous either to themselves or others, and consequently spent most of their time under complete lockdown—served meals in rooms that were really cells, only getting out for exercise once a day, one-at-a-time, in a tiny yard to walk laps for fifteen minutes.

Nick pulled into the parking lot, home to maybe a dozen cars, most of which were parked at the far end, near the employees' entrance of the wide, one-story building. The facility was larger than it seemed from the front. This Nick knew, having once flown over in a helicopter, getting a view of the huge pentagon; and on a previous visit, Nick had seen the interior of the building, which had gone on forever, with endless wings, like something out of a bizarre bad dream.

If you weren't mentally ill when you came here, it would be easy to get with the program. . . .

They climbed down from the SUV and walked toward the front entrance.

"When I have my breakdown," Catherine said, "promise to shoot me if they send me here."

"No problem—same in my case?"

"Deal," she said.

The glass double doors were chicken-wire woven. Nick tried to open one and it didn't budge.

Catherine pointed to a sign on the door that read: PLEASE USE SPEAKERBOX TO REQUEST ENTRY.

Nick said to her, "Okay, so your attention to detail is better than mine."

Catherine went to the box next to the door and pushed the button.

Several moments dragged by, and Catherine was frowning at Nick, as if asking for permission to try again, when a female voice asked, "May I help you?"

"Catherine Willows and Nick Stokes to see Dr. Jennifer Royer. We're from the LVPD Crime Lab."

"Do you have an appointment?"

"No. But I left a message on her machine."

" . . . Just a moment."

Another long pause followed, Nick and Catherine looking at each other, wondering if they had been ditched.

Finally, the woman's voice came back over the speaker: "I'll buzz you in. Please have your credentials ready."

The buzz that followed reminded Nick of the handshake gag you could buy at various casino magic shops. He opened the door for Catherine and they passed through. Behind him, Nick heard the thunk of an electronic lock.

"And we *asked* to come in here?" Nick said.

A wide-eyed Catherine said, "This is not a happy place. . . ."

The lobby was clean, walls a soft mint green, floors a lighter green tile, with the only decorative touch a starkly framed architectural drawing of the facility itself.

A thick patina of sadness seemed to cover everything, like emotional dust; despite the double glass doors letting sunshine seep in through the wiremesh, the lobby remained shrouded in faint gray light, in part due to fluorescent tubes under discolored plastic tiles in the ceiling. A darker green sofa and a few matching unpadded chairs were scattered against the far walls, with a low-slung table littered with *Psychology Today* magazines. The scent of pine cleaner clung to the air, doing little to dissipate an aroma of sickness and death that seemed to emanate from the walls, the air ducts, even the furnishings.

These impressions were subjective to say the least, but Nick could see from Catherine's quietly appalled expression that she shared them.

She confirmed this by whispering to him: "You're not a guest here, not even a resident—you're a hostage."

A heavyset woman in white was framed in the reception window. She had bottle red hair and a hard, dark glow about her, as if her displeasure with her lot in life had turned radioactive.

"May I help you?" she asked. It seemed more a warning than an invitation.

This was the intercom voice.

Catherine said, "We're the LVPD personnel to see Dr. Jennifer Royer?"

They stepped forward and held out the IDs on the necklaces.

The reception nurse leaned forward, read them. Looked up, blandly skeptical. "Do you have anything else?"

Dutifully, they showed the gatekeeper their wallet IDs, as well.

She gave them a smile that seemed to say, *Congratulations for meeting the admission standards, but don't get cocky: You still have to get* out. . . .

Or maybe Nick was just feeling a little paranoid.

"Down the hall on the left," the nurse said, not looking at them any more, "third door."

The third door on the left was open and Nick knocked on the frame.

A woman of about forty, her red hair—not from a bottle, short but not mannish—looked up, seated behind a desk cluttered with files. She apparently did not avail herself of the Vegas sunshine much, though with her fair Irish complexion, that might have been self-protection. She had a narrow face with a long straight nose, blue almond-shaped eyes and a wide mouth—unusual but attractive features, the intelligence behind them apparent.

"Ah," she said, her voice carrying the hint of a Southern accent, "you're the Crime Lab people. I got your message, but haven't had the chance to return it. Glad you went ahead and came out anyway. . . . Sit, sit."

Two metal-frame chairs were waiting opposite the desk, and the CSIs took them.

The office was small and neat, except for the desktop, indicative of a perpetually busy occupant. The desk itself was metal as were the two file cabinets that ran along the left wall. The doctor's chair looked comfortable but not overly so. Nothing elaborate at Sundown—but sufficient. And not one thing more. . . .

"I'm Catherine Willows and this is Nick Stokes."

The woman smiled and it seemed genuine, one professional to another. She had small, straight, white teeth. "I'm Dr. Jennifer Royer, the head doctor. . . . You can fill in your own joke."

"We'd like to talk to one of your patients," Catherine said.

"Congratulations," the doctor said, with just a faint trace of amusement. "That makes you part of an elite group."

Catherine frowned. "Excuse me?"

Dr. Royer's smile pursed. "The patients housed at Sundown generally don't receive visitors of any kind, not even from the LVPD."

"How about family?" Nick asked.

"That varies from case to case," Royer said. She sighed, and shook her head; her dry good humor was clearly her way of dealing with this depressing place. "Patients are sent here for diverse reasons, at least in the sense that there are countless but myriad ways the words are written down. But in reality? There's really only one reason our patients are within these walls: Someone, or perhaps everyone, wants them locked up."

"Warehoused," Catherine said.

The doctor—her frankness refreshing if surprising—nodded and said, "Exactly—shoved out of sight."

"But once they're here, you try to help them."

Royer's smile froze—it was almost a grimace now. "We try."

Nick asked, "How's your success rate?"

With a self-deprecating shrug, the doctor said,

"We prefer not to share that information—this is, after all, a private facility."

Nick exchanged glances with Catherine—a success rate so low, it wasn't available to the public?

Catherine said, "Surely a significant percentage of your patients leave, and return to a normal life."

"Some do. Most of them go out in a way that I'm sure your crime lab is familiar with . . . Now how exactly may I be of help to Las Vegas law enforcement?"

Shifting in the hard chair, Catherine said, "As we indicated, we'd like to talk to one of your patients."

"Which one?"

"Jerome Dayton."

Dr. Royer didn't hesitate. "No Jerome Dayton here."

Catherine winced, perhaps thinking she'd misheard. "I'm . . . sorry?"

Shaking her head now, Dr. Royer said, "No one here by that name."

Nick said, "You're absolutely sure of that?"

"I should be—I'm the attending physician for every patient at Sundown."

Catherine glanced at Nick, who could see his partner was getting irritated. To Royer she said, "We had information Dayton was a patient here."

"Well, he's not a patient now."

Nick noted the ambiguity of that and pounced. "But he *was?* Jerome Dayton was one of your patients?"

The smile was long gone. Dr. Royer's face had turned stony. "There are just around one hundred guests here at Sundown and none of them is named Jerome Dayton."

"Did he go out in one of those body bags you mentioned?"

The doctor thought for just a second, then said, "I don't think I can be of any help to you. Very sorry."

Catherine pressed: "Could you check your records?"

"No." The finality in the previously pleasant doctor's voice was unmistakable. "That would be a violation of the patient's right-to-privacy."

"But if he's *not* a patient . . ."

"The privacy of former patients is also a concern."

Shaking her head, smiling in a forced manner that had little to do with the usual reasons for smiling, Catherine said, "Dr. Royer, this is a murder investigation. We just got word of our third murder in a little over one week."

The stony face remained such.

Nick said, "Jerome Dayton was a major suspect in the CASt case . . . perhaps you remember it? And if he's *not* a patient in this hospital . . . then he's a key suspect in the series of murders occurring in Las Vegas *right now.*"

Dr. Royer did not seem terribly impressed by Nick's impassioned statement. She merely said, "That doesn't give either the Las Vegas police or, for that matter, myself any authority in a matter of violating this patient's rights."

Catherine nodded icily. "You have a point. So we'll get a court order."

The doctor shrugged, then jotted a number on a business card and handed it to Catherine.

"That's our fax number" she said. "Have the court order sent here. In the meantime, let's see if we can track down Mr. Dayton's records."

Catherine blinked, and her expression would have been no different had Dr. Royer slapped her. "You're . . . going to help us?"

"Call for your court order," she said crisply, "and we'll look while we wait."

"I don't understand. . . ."

"Of course you do. You're both professionals. I can see that. Well, so am I . . . and I'm a stickler for the rights of our patients, Ms. Willows."

Catherine seemed almost embarrassed as she said, "Of course you are."

"Is there any reason to think you won't get your court order?"

"No. That will be easily obtained."

"All right," the doctor said. "Then if this man *is* a killer, there isn't a second to waste."

While Catherine made the cell phone call, Nick watched Dr. Royer search through one of the file cabinets. Apparently Sundown hadn't converted their older records to computer files as yet—not surprising.

By the time Catherine had made her call, the doctor was already sitting down again, going over the contents of a file folder, her expression thoughtful.

"As soon as the judge signs the order," Catherine said, "it'll be faxed over."

"May be a waste of time," Dr. Royer said, eyes still on the file.

"Why?" Nick asked.

The doctor looked up and said, matter-of-factly, "I don't see how Jerome Dayton could be your killer."

"Why?" Catherine asked.

Royer nodded at the file before her. "Jerome Dayton became a patient here about ten years ago. Long before I accepted my post at Sundown, by the way."

Catherine said, "Well, that tallies with what we know about Dayton—he would have been admitted ten years ago."

"Yes. He was admitted as a paranoid schizophrenic."

"Meaning," Nick said, "he heard voices?"

"That's only one of the symptoms," Royer said. "Hallucinations, both auditory and visual, can be symptoms of schizophrenia. But the patient can also suffer from delusions of persecution."

"Was that the case," Catherine asked, "with Jerome Dayton?"

"Yes, he did have such delusions."

Royer slowly scanned the file further. She read to herself for five minutes, flipping through pages.

Nick and Catherine waited patiently. Ten minutes

more had passed before the dour nurse returned with the fax and placed it on Royer's desk. The nurse disappeared, Royer glanced at the fax, nodded, and returned to her reading.

Several minutes later she said, "It appears Jerome thought his father was emasculating him, forcing him to have sex."

Catherine said, "Do we know these were in fact delusions?"

Nick picked up the thread: "Were there examinations to look for signs of sexual abuse?"

"According to this file," Dr. Royer said, "there were indeed such examinations, and nothing was found to support the young man's claims. The father, Thomas, was, of course, one of the biggest contractors in the city at the time."

Nick frowned. "Since when is there a cure for schizophrenia?"

"Four out of five patients respond well to certain medication," Dr. Royer said. "In Jerome's case, Haldol helped him turn a corner. He was, according to the file, going through counseling and group therapy while he was here."

Catherine's expression was troubled. "So, he was under control . . . if not cured."

"Yes."

"And he was released?"

"He was," Royer said.

Nick shook his head, disbelievingly. "When *was* this?"

"Seven years ago."

Nick sat forward. "He was cured in *three years?*"

Royer looked at the CSI over the file. "I've already said, he was not 'cured.' He was, however, on medication, and had his illness under control. According to the file, he made incredible strides once my predecessor diagnosed his problem. Jerome was even taking day trips and weekends with his parents."

Catherine asked, "Is that normal?"

The doctor smiled, the first time since the subject had changed to Jerome Dayton. " 'Normal' is not a scientific term, Ms. Willows. And since you're a scientist yourself, you can guess how seldom the word 'normal' comes up around a facility like this. . . . No, such day trips are not 'normal,' but it's not unheard of either. Remember, Jerome was admitted voluntarily; he cooperated when his parents admitted him."

Catherine, alarmed, asked, "Could he have signed *himself* out?"

"That's possible, though the file doesn't specifically indicate as much. . . . Sometimes diagnosis and medication are all a patient needs to get on the road to recovery, Ms. Willows, and they get better at a remarkable rate. Sometimes spending time with family—day trips and weekends—can be beneficial to the healing process."

"Seven years," Nick said, shaking his head again. "I can't believe no one knew this guy was back on the *street.*"

Royer shrugged. "If he was a suspect in the CASt case, those murders stopped what, eleven years ago?"

"Ten," Catherine said. "He was admitted just before the last murder."

"That's why I don't see how he can be your man," Royer said. "He's been out for seven years, and there have been no killings."

"Until recently," Catherine said.

"Granted," the doctor said, nodding, "until recently. But you're the criminalists—you tell me: Do serial killers normally take a seven-year hiatus?"

Catherine shook her head. "No. But as scientists, doctor, we don't use the word 'normally' much in our work, either. . . . Do you know where we can find Jerome Dayton?"

Royer thumbed through the file. "Ah, here it is. . . . Presumably, his parents. He was released into their custody."

"The father's dead," Nick said. "Two or three years ago. Got lots of play in the press."

"I remember that," the doctor said. "Mr. Dayton was something of a celebrity, at least locally. Then I can only assume Jerome Dayton is still with his mother."

"Can we be sure he stayed on his medication?" Catherine asked.

"Reasonably sure. For the first several years, he did counseling, group therapy, and received his drugs here. Eventually, he started obtaining his meds from our sister facility, and this file stops. You might want to get the subsequent file from them."

The doctor then carefully read the order.

"Everything looks good," Royer said. "Do you mind if I photocopy this file, before I turn it over to you?"

"Not at all," Catherine said. "No telling how long it might be in our hands."

"Right . . . I wish we could have been more help, but everything I see here points at Jerome's innocence. And as you'll see, there are no violent episodes in his history, either."

"*Known* history," Catherine amended.

The doctor echoed that, then went out to get the file copied.

"I can't believe it," Nick said to Catherine. "This clown was released seven years ago, probably the best CASt suspect of all, and no one knew he was out!"

"Well . . . maybe it doesn't matter."

"Doesn't matter?"

"Yeah, Nick. I mean, he was incarcerated *here,* when the last murder of the original CASt cycle went down."

Soon Dr. Royer returned, and gave the original file to Catherine, who said, "Thank you, Dr. Royer, for your time and effort."

"We do what we can."

When they were outside, Nick said, "You remember the date of the Drake murder?"

"Well I've got it written down," Catherine said, and took out her pocket notebook and showed him.

As he pulled out the Tahoe keys, he said, "What does the *file* say for that date?"

Catherine riffled through, found it, and then looked at Nick with wide eyes. "Oh . . . my . . . God. Jerome was on a weekend visit to his parents."

Not knowing whether to feel nauseated or triumphant—and settling on a little of both—Nick said, "Maybe we'd better go find Jerome Dayton, and see how well he's doing these days. You know, if the meds are doing the trick?"

"Why don't we," Catherine said. "We can cure him of one thing, anyway."

"Yeah?"

"He isn't paranoid. We *are* after him."

EIGHT

At a chair by a counter in a lab, Sara Sidle greeted the sheaf of test results that Greg handed in to her as if her birthday had come early.

"You'll be pleased," Greg said from the doorway.

"I'm pleased to get anything solid," Sara said. "I'm tired of processing air. . . ."

"If you do, keep an eye out for hydrogen."

She grinned at him and said, "Thanks for the tip," and he was gone.

Finally, Sara thought.

The first sheet said the lipstick used on Diaz was an exact match to the shade used on Marvin Sandred—Bright Rose by Ile De France. This tended to confirm the theory that the vics shared a killer, which was further supported by the next page stating that the rope from both murders had the exact same chemical makeup.

Next was a photo that showed a fracture match between the end of the rope that had killed Sandred, and one end of the rope that murdered Enrique Diaz.

"Doesn't get better than that," she said aloud to the empty lab.

"What doesn't?" Grissom asked, loping in.

"We know that the same person killed Sandred and Diaz."

He came over to where Sara sat and leaned in. She walked him through it.

"Our most important product," he said. "Progress." He pulled up a chair. "Now what about the manila envelope from the *Banner?*"

"Prints on it belong to the three employees— David Paquette, Mark Brower, and Jimmy Mydalson. Their prints were on the letter too. That of course just confirms what we already knew about who handled the envelope at the paper. How about you? Get anything on the handwriting?"

"Going to see Jenny now. Care to come? We might both expand our vocabulary."

Jenny Northam was a handwriting expert who'd done freelance work for CSI for years, but recently came aboard full-time. In her own digs, she had sworn like a pissed-off longshoreman with Tourette Syndrome; but here at CSI, Grissom had been encouraging restraint.

As Sara and Grissom headed for Jenny's cubbyhole, the CSI supervisor seemed lost in thought, not an unusual condition for him. Sara didn't mind the silence—she was trying to work it all out in her head.

Finally, as they approached Jenny's office, Sara stopped and said, "Bell wasn't killed by the same perp as Sandred and Diaz, was he?"

Grissom gave her a guardedly hopeful look. "This opinion rises from evidence?"

"Yes—the brutality of the beating and the amount of blood. Does Doc Robbins confirm the finger was cut off while the victim was alive?"

"He does."

"And from the photos, the semen appears spattered, random, not in what I believe you aptly described as the 'poured' fashion of the other two."

Nodding, Grissom said, "All well-observed, Sara, but still circumstantial—we need better results from physical evidence before we start drawing conclusions. For example, if the semen at the Bell scene does not match the planted Orloff DNA at the other two."

"And I presume Greg is working on that."

"Yes. But DNA takes time."

"Too bad this isn't a TV show," she said. "We could have the results after commercial. . . ."

Before long they reached the ajar door of the Crime Lab's handwriting expert, Jenny Northam.

Grissom knocked, then entered without waiting for a response.

Jenny was on the other side of the small lab, rolling around on her wheeled office chair like a drunken race car driver with a stuck accelerator. Petite, barely five feet and maybe one hundred pounds, the dark-haired Jenny ruled over various expensive equipment, which took up three of the walls and most of the large light-table in the middle, the infield of Jenny's makeshift racetrack.

"Any luck?" Grissom asked without preamble.

"Freakin' A," Jenny said, her voice too deep to come out of that tiny body. "Or do you prefer 'frickin' A'?"

"Either is better than the alternative," Grissom said, "but I prefer results."

"Results I got out the wazoo," Jenny said.

Sara covered her smile with a hand. Jenny was doing her best to fit in at the sometimes politically correct CSI workplace, but there were still occasional lapses.

Jenny was saying, "I compared the *Banner* letter to the ones from the original CASt investigation."

"Yes?" Grissom asked.

"The paper's different, though both are common bond, and the writing's in ballpoint. Small, precise but childlike—what you'd see from some damn prodigy."

Sara said, "I was the first to read the letter, and I

was struck by the perfection of the handwritten spacing, the evenness of the lines."

"Damn straight! But it's unlined paper! There's a kind of . . . genius behind them."

Grissom said, "Surely you're overstating."

"Well I'm not overstating when I say this is as good a match as I've ever seen. This will hold up in any court, and a blind monkey could make this match."

"Just the same, Jenny," Grissom said, "I'm content to stick with you."

The handwriting expert was thinking about that as Grissom strode out, Sara falling in alongside him.

"You knew it was a match," Sara said.

"If not," Grissom said, "it would've been an expert forgery . . . and how many people had enough access to the original notes to pull *that* off?"

They went back to Grissom's office where they found Warrick waiting.

"I got Bell's phone records," he said.

Grissom said, "Al says the lack of rigor mortis shows Bell had been dead approximately forty-eight hours."

Warrick nodded. "Within an hour of when he made the call to his daughter."

"If he was *forced* to make the call," Sara said, "his nose was probably already broken. Didn't she notice that he sounded funny?"

Warrick said, "If Perry was talking to his daughter,

knowing CASt was about to kill him . . . did he manage to give her a clue of some kind?"

Grissom said to Sara, "Give her a call and find out."

The supervisor took his pocket notebook out, flipped a couple of pages, tore one out and handed it to her.

"There," he said.

"Grissom," Sara said, leaning in. "I don't think it's appropriate, a CSI being the one who tells this poor kid that her—"

"She knows. Brass already made that call."

And Grissom went out.

Sara looked at Warrick, who had a wry half-smile going. "I can do it," he said, "if you're uneasy about it."

"No. Thanks, but no, I can do this. I *should* do this. . . ."

Going back to the lab, Sara got out her phone and dialed the number.

Patty Lang picked up on the first ring; the voice was tired—and was that anger as well? "Hello?"

"Ms. Lang?"

"Yes."

"This is Sara Sidle. I'm a CSI with the Las Vegas Crime Lab. I'm very sorry to bother you at a time like this."

"No, you're not bothering," Patty said, an edge in her voice. "You're working on my father's murder, aren't you? Well, that's what I want to hear."

Sara swallowed. "I'd like you to know I'm sorry for your loss. We all liked your dad around here. Not every reporter has a fan club around the police department, you know. But your dad was one of the good guys."

"Thanks for saying that. What can I do to help you find the son-of-a-bitch who killed my father?"

"Did your father sound normal on the phone, when he cancelled his visit?"

"I don't know if I understand the question. What do you mean by 'normal'?"

"His voice," Sara asked, "his mood. Was there anything about the call that seemed different than usual?"

Patty Lang took a moment before answering. At last, she said, "This isn't as easy to answer as it should be. You see, Ms. Sidle, I spoke to my father *many* times when he didn't sound 'normal.' He might be excited about a story he was working on, or depressed about the rut he was in or about losing Mom. And it wasn't unusual for him to call me after he'd had a few too many cocktails, either."

"Did he sound like he'd been drinking this time?"

"No," Patty said. "Not . . . exactly. But he was a little . . . odd, now that I think about it. Stiff. Even . . . stilted."

"As if he'd been prompted about what to say?"

"That's a strange thing to . . . Do you think his killer was there with him?"

Sara saw no reason not to be frank. "We think the person responsible saw that your father was about to leave on a trip, and figured out that you were expecting him."

"And forced him to call and cancel the trip?"

"Yes."

"But, why . . . ?"

"To delay the discovery of his body, Ms. Lang. To make our job more difficult."

"You mean, I'd have been alarmed when Daddy didn't show up, and you might have gone looking for him, earlier than you did."

"Yes."

"Ms. Sidle, I've read my father's book about this . . . this bastard. I have a good idea of how he must have suffered before he died. And I'm . . . I'm only dealing with that thought right now by knowing that Daddy's at rest now . . . and that this creature will be caught."

"If anyone can stop CASt, it's us."

"That . . . that is very good to hear. But . . . oh my God. Now I understand. . . ."

"Understand what, Ms. Lang?"

But the young woman was crying.

Sara swallowed; held onto the phone and waited.

Finally the voice returned: "When he said good-bye to me . . . at the end of the call? He called me Pat-Pat. That . . . that was my nickname, when I was a little girl. I thought it was so strange he'd call me that, after all these years."

"I see."

"Do you? Ms. Sidle, he was saying good-bye to me . . . forever."

The woman began to cry again and Sara said a few comforting things before they finally were able to say their own good-byes.

Catherine Willows sat at her desk, phone to her ear, hoping she didn't get Brass's machine.

Then Brass came on the line, and she blurted, "It's me."

"How did you and Nick do out at that facility? What is it . . . Sundown?"

"We found out Jerome Dayton is no longer a guest at that particular hotel."

"What?"

"Hasn't been for a while. Say, seven years?"

The long silence told her that this was news to Brass.

She continued: "Seems he got therapy and medication and returned to society, all better."

"Good for him," Brass said coldly. "I suppose his father got him out?"

"That would be a big bingo—Jerome was released into his parents' custody."

"Hell . . . Well, Tom Dayton had a lot of pull in this city. I'd like to say I'm surprised."

Catherine said, "Of course, as you know, his father's dead now. I assume Jerome's living with his mother."

"Not unless he's gone Norman Bates on us," Brass said. "She died six or seven months ago. Got some play in the papers. You didn't see it?"

Something cold ran through Catherine. "You mean . . . Jerome's got no supervision?"

"It doesn't sound like it." Brass's voice changed from outrage that Dayton could be on the street without him even knowing, to something more hopeful. "Cath, that means we have a suspect for the copycat. A good damn suspect. . . ."

"Maybe. Or maybe you need to go back further." She drew a deep breath. "Jim—there's something else you need to know."

"I'm in no mood for twenty questions, Catherine."

"From the very moment Dayton was institutionalized, he was given day passes, weekend passes, to spend time with his folks."

"God *damn* it! Are you telling me he was—"

"Away from Sundown the day the last CASt kill went down . . . yes. He was in town when Vincent Drake was murdered."

Silence on the line. For a moment she thought Brass had hung up, or maybe hurled the phone across the room.

She asked, "Jim?"

"I'm here."

"Did Dayton have siblings?"

"No. Only child."

"Then he would have inherited everything. Like, say, the family home?"

Brass didn't miss a beat: "That's on Proud Eagle Lane."

A hint of a smile found its way across Catherine's face. "Of course it is. Where the hell is Proud Eagle Lane?"

"Inside the TPC at the Canyons golf course."

"Ah. I know the area. Round of golf costs more than a week's pay for a lowly CSI."

"Cath, imagine what kind of home might face onto a course like that."

"Jim, I'd like to find out."

"Good. Then grab Nick and meet me there—but don't bring your clubs. We'll play another game."

"What about a warrant?"

"There isn't a judge in the county that'll listen to us at this point." Brass's voice lightened, or pretended to. "Let's just go see how Jerry Dayton's doing, out on his own. Can be tough on a 'kid,' y'know—losing his mom and dad."

Catherine found Nick talking to Greg Sanders in the lab, gave her partner a nod from the doorway, and he joined her in the corridor.

"Strike two," he said by way of greeting.

"On?"

"DNA. Dallas Hanson is not the copycat, nor is he the original CASt."

"We knew that."

"We *thought* that. Greg proved it."

She reported her conversation with Brass.

"Hey, great," Nick grinned. "I been thinkin' about gettin' a membership to TPC. Maybe buy a home where I can walk right outta my back door onto the links."

"Sounds like a plan. You could start as a caddy."

They exchanged smiles and headed for the parking lot, spring in their step. Finally, maybe, catching a break on this damn case. . . .

The guard shack that blocked their entry into TPC at the Canyons was not quite as big as Catherine's first apartment, if more nicely appointed. The air conditioner hummed quietly and the guard who came out to meet them wore pants with a crease you could slice bread with and a perfectly pressed shirt with a highly shined badge and absolutely no sign of perspiration. He was tall, muscular, and chisel-chin handsome, looking more like a golf pro than a security guard.

His mouth smiled but his eyes were hard and cold. "Beautiful day, huh? And how can I help you?"

Nick showed his credentials and introduced himself and Catherine.

As at Sundown, the guard asked to see further credentials and Nick looked privately toward Catherine, crossing his eyes, and she laughed as they both handed over their wallet IDs.

"Everything in order," the guard said. "Sorry to be a stickler—we have some very important people out here at TPC, club members and residents. Where is it you need to go?"

Nick gave him the Dayton address.

"Maybe I should call ahead for you," the guard said.

Brass seemed to appear from nowhere, standing next to the Tahoe and holding forward his own ID wallet. The guard took an involuntary step backward.

Brass said, "Don't call ahead."

"Well, uh . . . Captain Brass? I'm afraid that's our policy."

"It's not ours."

Glancing in the door rearview mirror, Catherine saw Brass's Taurus parked in the drive behind them.

The guard said, "Sir, we're not just a country club. We're a gated community, and our residents—"

"Call ahead, I come back and arrest you for obstruction. Is that policy clear enough?"

Nodding numbly, the guard retreated to his shack and his air conditioning, and raised the gate so they could enter the TPC at the Canyons.

Everything here shouted affluence—the houses, the lawns, the cars, even the mailboxes, everything bigger, nicer, costlier, showier. They passed the clubhouse, where the golf carts stickered for about as much as Catherine's car. Nick pulled over, allowed Brass to pass them, and they followed the detective's Taurus through the compound until they ended up on Proud Eagle Lane.

The expression "a man's home is his castle" is usually an exaggeration, but in Jerome Dayton's case, those words were the literal truth: The sprawling two-story stucco was twice as large as Catherine had seen in any other housing development in Vegas, a town that had more than its share of wealth and celebrity. Painted a light coral, the huge residence stood out among the other, slightly smaller mansions, which were uniformly a sand color.

With Brass in the lead, the trio approached the door. The detective had been working hard for days now to keep the anger and frustration in check, to view these CASt killings as homicides and not personal affronts. But now he felt angry, frustrated, with himself, as if it had been his responsibility to know that Jerry Dayton had been released from Sundown.

But such facilities were not required to inform law enforcement about the risks they were sending out into the world. And the Dayton family had somehow kept their son in check—to say Jerome Dayton had kept a low profile over these past years was a supreme understatement. Perhaps he'd been locked away in an upper room of this castle, like the Man in the Iron Mask, a medicated if pampered prisoner in his own home.

Only what had happened, lately? After both his jailers—that is, his parents—had shuffled off the ol' mortal coil?

The lunatic would be in charge of the asylum.

Of course, it might be a coincidence that Dayton had been on a weekend pass when Vincent Drake was murdered, but Brass—like Grissom—held no truck with coincidence.

Coincidence was God's way of telling a detective that he had screwed up, probably missing something,

something important. That, as much as anything, was why Captain James Brass was so royally pissed off when he marched up the sloping, winding sidewalk to the massive double doors of the Dayton home.

Ignoring the bell, the detective pounded on the oak door with his fist. When no one answered immediately, he pounded again. He could feel Nick and Catherine behind him and he could also feel their mounting tension.

Were they wondering if he was losing it?

Well, maybe he was—and god *damn* it, maybe he had a right. Eight men were dead over the last eleven years, and what had Brass ever managed to do about it? It had been his job, his and Vince Champlain's, to catch CASt nearly a decade ago, and they had booted it big time.

Now the sick evil son of a bitch was running wild again; only, finally, Brass might be on the literal doorstep of the solution. . . .

He was preparing to pound a third time when the door on his left suddenly opened, and framed there, leaning on the jamb, stood a tall, thin, dark-haired, hawkish-faced man with piercing green eyes, attired in a blue button-down shirt and black jeans.

Jerome Dayton.

Despite the years, little about Dayton had changed—the narrow face remained largely unlined, the hair untouched by gray; the only addition that Brass caught was an earring added to Dayton's left lobe, a "D" crafted out of small diamonds.

His eyes narrowing, upper lip curling in contempt, Dayton said, "Brass," the single word an epithet.

"Been a while, Jerry," Brass said, coolly, even as something burned in his stomach.

"How did you people get past the gate?" Dayton's voice was as glacial as the glare he tossed at Catherine and Nick, then fixed upon Brass.

"You know, Jerry," Brass said, "I'm flattered you remember me. Your lawyer liked to keep us apart, as I recall."

"Who are your flunkies?"

"These are crime scene analysts from the Crime Lab—Catherine Willows and Nick Stokes. I've been telling them all about you. We're anxious to sit and talk about . . . old times. And new."

Dayton said, "Not without my lawyer sitting in," and started to close the door in the detective's face.

Brass forced himself into the doorway, blocking the young man's attempt.

Dayton's eyes turned to slits; his sneer of a smile formed slowly but effectively as he took a long, deep breath. Then he exhaled and said, "And my lawyer, I think, is just who I should to talk to—in the case of a harassment suit."

Brass put on his patented rumpled smile. "Come on now, Jerry—you must see the papers, the TV. Certainly you know why we're here. You're going to have to talk to us at some point. We're just eliminating the old names from our list, and you can get that out of the way and—"

"Old *suspects,* you mean." The hawkish, sneering face looked at each of them, pausing for a derisive chuckle, again landing on Brass. "You think I don't know what you want? You're here about *Cee Ay Ess Tee.* Wasn't ruining my life *once* enough for you?"

Giving the man a tight smile, Brass said, "That earring's sure handsome, Jerry. Never knew you to go in for the bling bling."

Dayton's smile widened, lips parting to reveal perfect white wolfish teeth. "It was my mother's—a ring I had made into this. Normally I'm not ostentatious . . . you know that, Captain. But I loved my mother."

"How about your father?"

Dayton frowned. "This conversation is over."

Catherine eased forward a little. "Mr. Dayton, the crimes you were suspected of aren't what we're investigating. We're not after the real CASt—many believe him dead, or at least living far away from Las Vegas."

"Really," Dayton said, vaguely interested.

"We're after this new killer—this copycat."

Nick said, "Yeah—kind of the new, improved CASt?"

"But obviously," Catherine said, "we have to revisit and review the old files. It's really quite routine."

Brass realized what Catherine and Nick were up to: If Dayton was the real CASt, they'd been needling him pretty good. . . .

Dayton was studying Catherine, stroking his chin with his right hand. A swollen, ugly purple bruise painted most of the back of it.

With a nod toward the man's hand, Brass said, "Quite a purple badge of honor you got yourself there, Jer."

Dayton lowered the hand, shrugged. "Shut it in the car door." He shrugged. "I get distracted sometimes. Do stupid things. Don't you, Captain?"

"Been known to. But why don't you let us do you a solid—I'll have one of the CSIs take a picture of that mitt of yours, we can be witnesses, and you can use it when you sue the car manufacturer."

"Lame," he said, shaking his head. "So lame. Are we done?"

Nick said, "We could be, if you'd let us take a DNA sample."

Catherine said, "Clear you once and for all."

The armor-piercing gaze shifted toward Catherine. "My name wouldn't *need* clearing, if Detective Brassballs here hadn't made a hobby out of me, when I was just a damn defenseless kid. This jerk harassed my family, during the original CASt case, and now he's trying to do it again. I'm almost glad my parents are gone, so they don't have to endure this humiliation a second time."

"Speaking of which," Brass said, "who *is* your caregiver now, Jerry? You are still on medication, I presume. . . ."

"I'm a big boy, Captain. I take of myself, and yes, I am on medication, and have been since you railroaded me into that institution."

"If you feel railroaded," Catherine said, "why keep taking the meds?"

His chin, which was almost pointed, lifted. "I don't deny that I have certain medical problems. I have a chemical imbalance that manifests itself, on occasion, as what you cretins would call mental illness. I monitor my own condition now."

Nick asked, "How's that going?"

"Very well. It's working. I take my meds on schedule, every day—I even have a little pillbox with the days printed on, like the senior citizens."

"Nothing to be ashamed of," Nick said.

The green eyes flared and so did the hawkish nostrils. "Who in *hell* is *ashamed?*"

Holding up hands, half-smiling, Nick said, "Whoa—little touchy, aren't we?"

Their reluctant host swallowed. Summoning dignity, he said, "I have lost both my parents. They were never the same after the CASt debacle. I watched them both die, slowly, a process that began long before they actually ceased to breathe."

Dayton's glare returned to Brass.

"It started," the man said, "when they had to put me in that place, that . . . that *home.* Well, I'll tell you how much progress I've made, Captain, battling my illness. I used to blame *you* for their deaths." He pointed a purple finger at Brass. "But now I know . . . you were only doing your job. Trying to do your best for the community, however misguided and misinformed you were. . . . My psychiatrist almost got me convinced that it wasn't your fault."

Brass said, "So you're not mad at me, anymore, Jerry?"

Dayton shrugged. "Well . . . therapy is an ongoing process."

"Speaking of which, what's your doctor's name?"

"I don't have to share that with you."

If Brass's grin had been any tighter, his face would have split. "How about I get a court order, Jerry, and we try this again?"

"Want a name? I'll give you a name."

"Thank you." Brass got his notebook out, pen poised to write.

"Carlisle Deams—D-E-A-M-S. My attorney."

Brass put the notebook away.

Grinning his wide white grin, Dayton said, "And I guarantee you, Captain, he'll be at the courthouse before you. While you attempt to get your nontestimonial court order to get my DNA, my attorney will be filing an injunction to stop you from harassing me further."

"When'd you learn so much about the system, Jerry?"

"I started studying up in Sundown. I had plenty of time—and incentive."

Brass studied the man. "How about I get a patrol car to park outside here, until we get back with our nontestimonial court order?"

A flip phone came out of Dayton's pants pocket. He hit a button. While he waited for someone to answer, he said, "Captain, Captain . . . you make this too, *too* easy. . . ."

Brass spun on his heel and pushed through a faintly startled Catherine and Nick and stalked off. They followed quietly.

As he went down the driveway, Brass could hear Dayton say, "Carlisle? Jerry Dayton." After a pause, he said, "Fine, fine. I'm just calling to remind you why I keep you on a such a healthy retainer. . . ."

Brass, pleased he'd managed not to pop the guy, walked around the Tahoe and got out of earshot. To his surprise, Nick and Catherine were right behind him.

Nick said, "He doesn't *seem* delusional."

Catherine said, "He's smart."

Brass just shook his head. "I don't want to talk about it—we'll pick it up back at the lab, okay?"

He stomped off, got into his car and managed not to peel out as he gunned the gas and sped away. He was only a block away when he called dispatch and ordered a patrol car to come sit on Jerry Dayton's front door.

If Jerry Dayton thought Brass had been kidding, the guy really *was* delusional. . . .

* * *

Warrick Brown found Grissom and Sara in the former's office, going over crime-scene photos from the Bell murder. Flopping down in a chair in front of Grissom's desk, he let out a long sigh.

"Good news," Warrick said, "bad news. Choose."

Grissom said, "Good?"

"Finally matched the fingerprints on the *Banner* keycard."

"They belong to Perry Bell."

All the air went out of Warrick's balloon. "How the heck did you know?"

"Same way I know the bad news is no one else's prints are on the card."

Warrick sat up straighter now. It drove him nuts when Grissom did this and the CSI supervisor did it a lot—to all of them. "Greg already gave you the report?"

Grissom shook his head.

That was the other thing that made Warrick mental: Grissom never told him how he knew these things.

Warrick went to the doorway, turned and pointed an accusatory finger at his boss. "If you're *guessing* again . . ."

Grissom cast a boyish smile Warrick's way. "No reason to get nasty."

Warrick trudged back to the lab, and immediately dug in to work on the remainder of the prints. His goal was to know who was who, and where they were, in proximity to the crimes. And he wanted to know before *Grissom* knew. . . .

He dumped all the prints into the computer and let the software sort out what matched what. While he waited, he caught up on reports, starting with one Greg had sent that said the dried blood in the Bell home all came from Bell himself.

Another report showed that the synthetic hairs removed from Enrique Diaz matched the toupee of the late Perry Bell. If the late Bell really was the copycat— which was strongly suggested by his ersatz hair being on Diaz's body and his *Banner* keycard being found at the scene—did that mean they were now only looking for one killer?

Had CASt served as vigilante, showed the copycat who the *real* Bad Boy in Town was, and capped the cat?

Warrick wasn't sure what to think.

Thankfully, he had little time to worry about it. His phone rang and Grissom told him to grab his kit—an officer had found Perry Bell's missing car.

The parking garage for the Big Apple Casino and Hotel hid behind the main building, which was on the corner of Tropicana and Las Vegas Boulevard. The six-story concrete parking structure was the perfect place to ditch a ride. A cop on a routine drive-through had spotted the local wheels parked on the sixth level, almost by itself.

When the officer ran the car, Brass's APB came

up, and the officer called in that he had found Bell's car.

The 2003 blue Cadillac hunkered in a corner, a lonely visitor to the Big Apple. While Grissom worked the trunk, Sara hit the backseat, and Warrick labored up front.

Warrick found several hairs lodged in the seams of the headrest, which he carefully caught with tweezers, then bagged. He dusted the ignition, the dash, the steering wheel, and the glove compartment for fingerprints, vacuumed the floor for stray fibers and detritus, then used the electrostatic print lifter to get footprints from the gas and brake pedals.

When he had finished all that, Warrick went over the seats (as they said in the Vegas lounges) one more time. Just on the front edge of the driver's seat, out of sight (unless you were on hands and knees), he found a maroon spot, the diameter of a pencil.

First he photographed it, then carefully scraped what appeared to be dried blood into an evidence envelope. He hoped the blood wasn't Bell's.

When he showed Grissom what he had found, the supervisor said, "Nice catch."

Warrick grinned at what, coming from Grissom, was an effusive response. "Just doing the job."

"Get back to the lab and keep up the good work. Find us something that can help us track down Perry Bell's murderer."

"You got it, Gris."

As they loaded their equipment back into the Tahoe, Sara cast a tiny crooked smile on him. "Suck-up," she said.

Warrick just grinned.

NINE

Back at the Crime Lab, Warrick Brown catalogued the evidence from Perry Bell's car, sent it off to the appropriate labs, then dug in to try matching the footprints from Bell's brake pedal with the print he'd obtained in Marvin Sandred's yard.

Nothing.

He checked the pedal print against Bell's shoes.

Nothing.

He checked Bell's shoes against the print from Sandred's yard.

Nothing.

Longer it don't, he told himself, *sooner it's gotta.*

Hadn't Grissom himself said, *"The essence of good police forensics is perseverance?"* On the other hand, Warrick's supervisor was unlikely to accept what was known as "the gambler's fallacy," that piece of folk wisdom Warrick picked up before kicking his gambling habit: The longer you didn't win, the sooner you had to start.

For gamblers, a fallacy. For this CSI, a theory.

Sara came in, waving a report; she seemed chipper, which considering the double shifts they'd been pulling was either a miracle or hysteria.

"Got the results on the hairs you found in the headrest of Bell's car," she said, easing up next to where he sat.

He looked up, arching an eyebrow that asked for more info.

She gave it: "All but one strand matched Bell's toupee."

"What about the other hairy little devil?"

She offered a shrug. "A stranger."

"Could belong to our killer."

"We'll be closer to knowing when Greg gets through with that straggling strand—root was still attached."

"Nice."

She nodded brightly. "Greg's running a DNA test to match it to the blood spot you got off the seat."

"Which also may match our killer. Well—can you believe it? Getting somewhere." He shifted on his chair, frowned in thought. "Sara, is Greg also checking that DNA against the original CASt crimes?"

"Yes—but he won't have results for a while." She gave him a pleasant shrug of a smile and said,

"Meanwhile, I'm back at it—just thought you'd wanna know."

"I appreciate it," he said, meaning it, knowing how easy it was for each CSI to get immersed in work and not take the time to bring the others up to speed. Tunnel vision, working in a vacuum, was an obvious but too frequent FUBAR in any CSI lab.

He got back to his own work, entering fingerprints from the Cadillac into AFIS. While those ran, he dropped by to see Greg Sanders himself—never hurt to apply a little pressure.

Greg leaned back in a desk chair, feet up on a table, *Rolling Stone* magazine open on his lap, listening to his iPod.

Warrick with both hands waved at the tech, as if bringing in an ailing plane for a landing, finally got his attention, and Greg smiled and tossed the magazine on the table, put his feet on the floor and detached himself from the iPod.

"And you want to give all this up," Warrick said, with an open-hand gesture, "to go out in the field with us?"

Arms folded, rocking back in the chair, Greg said, "Here's the thing, Warrick—when you excel in a profession and reach the top of your game, you need to walk away and try something else. . . . You know, before you stagnate."

"Right," Warrick nodded, leaning against a counter. "So is that what you're doing right now? Stagnating?"

"I'm *working*. Hard at it."

"Maybe you should take five. Wouldn't want you to sprain anything."

Greg cocked his head, raised his eyebrows. "What I'm doing is running your DNA tests."

"And what have you found?"

"Nothing yet. Perfection takes time."

"So I hear."

"Still replicating the DNA."

Warrick nodded, started out. "So I'll check back in an hour or so."

"Sure—drop by. We'll trade barbs and witticisms some more."

Warrick paused in the doorway. "Two hours, then?"

"Make it tomorrow—end of shift. Even that's pushing it."

Warrick smirked mirthlessly. "Well, what do you have for me today? Anything?"

"How about, the rope that strangled Perry Bell is different than the ones used at the previous two murders? Do anything for you?"

Drifting back in, Warrick said, "Yeah—consider me officially perked up. . . . Different how?"

"For one thing—it's older."

Warrick frowned. *"Older* rope?"

"Probably a good ten years. Same deal with the lipstick: It's Ile De France brand, all right; but it's a shade called Limerick Rose, which is what the original CASt used, back in the good old days."

"I thought that stuff was off the market."

Greg nodded. "At least seven years. Copycat's been using *Bright* Rose—a newer product, but similar shade."

Frowning, trying to wrap his head around this, Warrick said, "Are you telling me that lipstick from ten years ago is still usable?"

The tech shrugged. "All in the packaging. And if someone took care of it—kept it in climate-controlled conditions—almost anything's possible."

"Why would anyone do that?"

"Why would anyone strip, torture, and strangle a victim, apply lipstick to the mouth and put a DNA cherry on the sundae?"

"I got a better one. . . . Why would *two* people do that?"

"That kind of question, I can't answer. What I can give you is: old rope and old lipstick, on the new killing . . . You think ol' Mackie's back in town? The original CASt, I mean?"

Warrick's shrug was elaborate. "It's looking that way. Can you imagine a scenario where the copycat suddenly shifts to *old* rope and *ancient* lipstick?"

"Just tell me this isn't Freddy versus Jason."

"Greg—it just might be."

The tech grinned. "You could always call in Ash to take 'em on."

"Huh?"

"*Evil Dead?* Chainsaw? . . . Warrick, you have absolutely no sense of great cinema."

"Riiight," Warrick said, and slipped out.

Back in the fingerprint lab, Warrick checked the results of the first batch of prints he'd put in. Paquette, Brower, and Mydalson's prints were, of course, on the CASt envelope from the *Banner.* Bell's prints were all over his house and on the keycard. No fingerprints inside the Diaz residence, other than those of the owner; same was true of Sandred's place. No surprises, there.

But then the computer slapped Warrick right in the face.

Fingerprints, from the doorbells of the two houses, matched.

And the truly shocking thing was the identity of who those fingerprints belonged to. . . .

Warrick grabbed the report from the printer and hustled off to tell Grissom. The CSI didn't know what thrilled him more: the idea that the case was finally breaking; or that for once he had something that Grissom couldn't already know.

Gil Grissom and Jim Brass sat opposite David Paquette at the interview room table. The editor's gray suit looked rumpled and much the worse for wear; so did the editor, his red-rimmed eyes indicating sleep was a luxury he hadn't availed himself of since being taken into protective custody.

"What makes you think Perry wasn't a victim of the copycat?" Paquette was asking. "Why do you peg the *real* CASt for Perry's murder?"

Brass and Grissom exchanged looks; the latter nodded and handed a file to the former, who got up and handed it to Paquette.

Brass said, "I know crime scene photos are second-nature to an old police beat reporter like you . . . but these are rough. The first set is Sandred, then Diaz . . . and then Perry Bell. I know Perry was a good friend. . . ."

Paquette opened the file, hunkered over the photos, his face turning as white as dead skin over a blister as he paged through. During the final set, he shook his head and said, "Perry . . . oh, God, Perry . . ."

The editor shut the file, passed it down to Brass, who took it and returned to his chair next to the CSI.

"I . . . I see what you mean," Paquette said. "The first two are . . . obviously staged. The final one . . . final one is all too fam . . . familiar."

The editor leaned on an elbow and covered his face with a hand. He wept.

Brass rose again, pushed a box of Kleenex toward him, and he and Grissom waited for several minutes.

The editor used two tissues, drying his eyes, blowing his nose, then he gathered himself and said, "What makes you think this . . . this maniac might be after me, too?"

Grissom said, "You were the coauthor of *CASt Fear*—with Perry a target, his collaborator seems likely a second one."

Brass made a casual gesture. "Of course, it's possible *Perry* was the copycat."

Paquette's bloodshot eyes popped wide. "Are you serious? You can't be serious. Perry? Perry Bell?"

Grissom said, "Perry was a good reporter past his prime, apparently with a drinking problem. Putting CASt back on the front page would revive his glory days. Desperate men do desperate things."

"Gil," Paquette said, "you knew Perry. He was a sweetheart. He just didn't have the sick twist of mind necessary, not to mention the stones, to carry off those first two killings."

Brass said, "John Wayne Gacy visited children in hospitals and did a clown routine. He was active with the Chamber of Commerce."

"Not Perry. No way."

"Dave, I tend to agree with you. I think Gil does, too. But it's an easy road to take."

The editor blinked. "What do you mean?"

"I mean, that the real CASt—seeing that a copycat is stealing his thunder—might logically assume that you and or Perry were responsible."

"Perry the copycat? *Me?* Why, in hell?"

Grissom said, "With the exception of a small handful of police, you and Perry know more than anyone about the original crimes . . . including the digit removal and the semen signature."

Paquette had nothing to say to that. He rubbed his stubbly chin. "Then . . . you really think I'm next, on his list?"

Before either man could answer, Warrick slipped into the interview room.

Grissom gave him a sharp glance—this was a breach of not just procedure but etiquette—but Warrick leaned in and said, "I know, I know, I'm sorry . . . but this won't wait." He shot a look at Paquette, then handed his supervisor the printout.

Grissom read it fast, then passed the sheet to Brass, who also quickly absorbed its contents. Warrick slipped out.

Brass looked up at Paquette. "Tell me about Mark Brower."

"What *about* Mark?" Paquette asked.

"Is there any way he might have had access to the hold-back details on the original case?"

"Not that I know of—he wasn't even around during the first cycle of murders, or for that matter, when Perry and I were writing the book."

Grissom said, "Could Mark casually . . . wheedle something like that out of Bell . . . like when Perry was in his cups?"

Paquette thought about that. "Possibly. Perry reprinted the book—there was talk of revising it, which ultimately didn't happen, because it was a self-publishing deal, and expensive."

Grissom considered that momentarily, then asked, "So Perry and Mark, when the possibility of doing a revision was on the table, might have talked about the details that were omitted first time around?"

"I don't know that for a fact, Gil. But it's possible, yes. You're not looking at *Mark* as a suspect?"

Brass said, "Aren't we?"

"He's one of my best employees. He's a stand-up guy."

Grissom titled his head; an eyebrow raised. "Really. Maybe you can explain how his fingerprints got on Marvin Sandred's doorbell?"

Brass added, *"And* Enrique Diaz's doorbell?"

Paquette smiled disbelievingly and shook his head. "Oh that's just crazy . . . I don't buy that for a minute. . . ."

"At least consider the sale," Brass said, and he handed the report across to the editor.

Leaning over, holding the sheet in both hands, close to his face, his expression shifting from incredulous to outraged, David Paquette read of the match between the prints on both doorbells and the ones Warrick took at the *Banner* office.

"Goddamn that little bastard!" Paquette said, shaking the sheet. "That psychotic little son of a bitch!"

Grissom and Brass traded glances, both thinking that the editor's warm assessment of Brower had not taken long to turn.

Brass said, "What do you make of it?"

Grissom said, "What would inspire Mark Brower to play CASt copycat?"

"Are you kidding?" the editor said. "It's painfully obvious! Mark figured to resurrect CASt, and frame Perry for it."

Brass said, "To what end?"

"Think about it! He immediately takes over the column, and he's in a perfect position to write the follow-up book himself . . . as the crime reporter who actually worked at Perry 'CASt Copycat' Bell's side."

Quietly aghast, Grissom said, "For something as fleeting . . . as meaningless, as fame? Brower would go to these . . . bizarre, malignant lengths?"

Paquette said, "You're not naive, Gil. Of course he would."

Brass's mouth twitched with disgust. To Grissom he muttered, "No wonder you prefer insects."

Paquette said, "I'd, uh . . . just as soon stay in protective custody, if you don't mind."

"Our pleasure," Brass said, just as his cell phone trilled. He left the room to answer it in private.

Grissom said, "Perry Bell's crime-beat column was at a dead end. Why would Mark Brower see it as a career opportunity worth killing for?"

Paquette was shaking his head, his smile a glazed thing. "Bell was at the end of his career, his life. For Brower, it's a stepping stone, but think of the context: It's a different world than back when Perry and I wrote *CASt Fear*. Now there's way more of a chance for movies, TV, and on top of the book sale, he'd have speaking fees, talk shows would pick this up, he'd maybe even wind up on Leno or Letterman. Mark Brower . . . if this plan worked . . . would've been a star."

"He may still be," Grissom said softly, "after we arrest him."

"Damn right," the editor said. "Look at Richard Ramirez, David Berkowitz, Aileen Wuornos. Between movies, documentaries, TV shows, books, hell—they have more exposure than some mega-stars."

Grissom—wondering if he'd somehow entered a *Twilight Zone* of infamy—glanced toward the door just as Brass came back in, his face a pissed-off mask.

"What now?" Grissom asked.

Rage barely in check, Brass said, "Patrol car I assigned to keep an eye on Dayton? They lost him. He came out of the house, drove off and our men got stopped at the gate long enough for Dayton to shake them. *Shit!*"

Paquette folded his hands; looked at the table.

Something about Paquette's manner—his attempt to turn invisible—triggered Brass. He turned on the editor. "You—you *knew* he was out! Didn't you, Dave?"

The editor shrugged once, stared at his hands.

"You fucking *knew!*" Brass yelled, his voice echoing off the walls.

Paquette turned away, then blurted, "All right! Yes." He threw his hands in the air. "Yes, damn it, I knew!"

Brass drew a deep breath; exhaled; said, "Did *Perry Bell* know a major CASt suspect was on the streets?"

". . . No."

"Brower?"

"Not to my knowledge. Who knows with that bastard."

"How long have *you* known Dayton was out?"

Paquette hung his head. "I knew . . . knew not long after he got out. Maybe a month."

Grissom said, "Seven years."

The editor nodded.

"And it never occurred to you to tell us?"

"I didn't see it as your business."

Brass slapped his hand on the table and Paquette jumped.

The detective said, "Not even when *murders* started in again?"

"We all thought it was a copycat." The editor shrugged. "Look, the murders had stopped. Dayton got out of the nuthouse, and nothing bad happened. Anyway, you remember our book. You read it, right?"

Grissom said, "I just reread it. You didn't think Dayton was a valid suspect. You devoted a chapter to him and how the police were on the wrong track."

Brass leaned on his hands. "Oh . . . why, Dave, I almost forgot. You said Vince and I were on the . . . what was the phrase? 'Verge of persecuting Jerome Dayton, an innocent afflicted with mental problems?'"

Paquette sat up, his face red. "Damn it, Brass,

Dayton was innocent! You know that. Hell, he was already committed out to Sundown, when Drake got killed."

Grissom had never seen Brass deliver a more terrible smile than the ghastly thing he cast upon David Paquette. "Really, Dave? You investigative journalists really dig, don't you? Only you failed to dig up one small fact: *Jerome Dayton was on a weekend pass when Drake was killed.*"

". . . what? Oh, no. Oh, hell no . . ."

"Hell yes, Dave."

Shaking now, Paquette fell back in his chair, tears glistening again. "Honest to Christ, Jim—I thought he was innocent."

Brass said nothing.

Grissom said, "Where's Brower right now, Dave? Is he at work?"

The editor sighed, shrugged. "Normally . . . but if he's working on a story, he could be out anywhere."

"Reporting news, you suppose?" Brass asked sarcastically. "Or making it?"

Brass sent an ashen Paquette back to protective custody.

As he and Grissom walked down the corridor, Brass got on his cell and dispatched Detective Sam Vega to try to locate Brower at the *Banner;* then he called for two patrol cars.

Grissom said, "You're picking up Brower?"

"Gonna try to. If he's our copycat, that makes his

house par for the CSI course. Wanna round up Sara and Warrick and come with?"

"Try and stop me."

Mark Brower lived in Paradise, on Boca Grande, just off Hacienda Avenue. *Boca Grande,* Brass thought, "Big Mouth" . . . who the hell would name a street that?

The tiny bungalow with an attached one-car garage was what a Realtor would call cozy, talking up the proximity of Tomiyasu Elementary School, and a prospective buyer would call small. From the street, the place appeared empty, curtains drawn, doors closed. The postage-stamp lawn hadn't been mowed for some time—not that it mattered, brown as it had turned.

Brass blocked the driveway with the Taurus, while Warrick left the CSI Tahoe in front, he and Grissom getting out to join Brass next to his vehicle. The two squad cars were parked nearby, uniformed officers hustling over to huddle up with the others.

"Around back, you two," Brass told the officers, but before he got any further, his cell phone rang.

"Brass."

"Vega. Brower's not at the paper, and nobody here has seen him since around lunchtime yesterday."

Brass cursed, once. "All right, Sam—thanks. We'll hope he's in the house." He cut off the call and reported to the others.

"Next best chance is here," Warrick said.

The two patrolmen—Carl Carrack again and another vet, Ray Jalisco—had headed around opposite sides of the bungalow. Jalisco radioed that he'd looked through the window of the garage: Brower's car was gone.

Brass acknowledged that and waited for the two men to get around back and report in before he, Warrick, Sara, and Grissom approached the house.

Sara and Grissom hung back near the garage, to serve as backup, while Brass and Warrick went for the door. Warrick took the side near the knob, while Brass went wide to the far side.

Once in place, Brass knocked loudly on the door. "Mark Brower, open up! Police!"

The order was met with silence.

"Anything?" Brass asked into his walkie-talkie.

Carrack's voice came instantly. "Nothing, Cap— tumbleweed blowin' through, back here."

Brass pounded on the door again.

They waited.

Nothing happened.

Raising his chin and nodding toward the door, Warrick signaled Brass that he was going to try the knob.

Brass nodded permission; his pistol was in both hands, barrel pointed skyward. Leaning forward, Warrick had his gun in his left hand, to use his right to turn the knob.

To the surprise of both men, the door was unlocked.

The CSI gave the door a shove and it swung in out of Brass's way, and the detective entered the house, gun dropping down to chest level, both hands still gripping it.

Though the room was dark—only marginal light spilled through the open door and filtered around the drapes—Brass could nonetheless see the place was a shambles.

Oh, hell, he thought. *Another damn crime scene . . .*

Having come through on the detective's heels, Warrick hesitated just long enough to hit the light switch next to the door, prints be damned in a potentially dangerous situation like this.

An overhead light revealed a tight little living room of overturned and broken furniture, magazines, newspapers, framed pictures, and knickknacks, all scattered as if dropped from above, TV set on its side, frame cracked, picture tube shattered.

Brass listened, listened, listened, but heard no sound save a clock or two ticking. The living room led straight into a dining room, where three of four chairs at a round oak table were overturned. The fourth chair lay in splinters, possibly having been used as a weapon. The detective and the CSI remained silent as they moved across the living room, guns at the ready. Just inside the dining room, a hallway peeled off to the left, and another door at the back of the room led into the kitchen.

They tried not to disturb evidence, but first priority was clearing the house, and—if they ran across

him—taking Brower into custody. Signaling to Warrick to watch the hallway, Brass moved to the
kitchen. Warrick backed along with him, careful
where he stepped, but keeping his eyes mostly on the
hallway, having no desire to be attacked from that
direction.

The kitchen—light streaming in through windows
over the sink—was even messier than the other
rooms; it was almost as if a tornado had swept
through without touching walls or roof. Brass also
noticed blood spatter here and there on the floor,
and on the counters—more indicative of a brawl
than the chopped-off fingers of this case. And it was
easy to note the smell of food going bad in the refrigerator, standing ajar.

To the right was a closed door, the garage proba-
bly; to the left, a door that led to a bedroom, maybe.
Jalisco had looked through the garage window, so
Brass went to the unknown entry first.

With Warrick guarding his back, Brass found a
neat spare bedroom, a single bed against one wall, a
desk with a computer against the other wall, near
the only window. He checked the closet, but found
only some hanging clothes and a case of computer
paper.

"Clear," Brass said for Warrick's benefit, backing
out.

They proceeded with the garage, finding it de-
serted, as well. They went back to the dining room
and into the hall, checking two bedrooms, the bath-

room and all the closets. Mark Brower was not here, but it was abundantly clear that someone—two someones—had very much *been* here.

Back outside, Brass huddled again with the CSIs, saying, "There was a hell of a fight in there, but nobody's in the house now . . . and from the smell in the kitchen, there hasn't been anyone for some time."

"You think CASt found out Brower is the copycat?" Warrick asked.

Brass shrugged. "I dunno, but something went down here . . . either that, or this guy's a worse housekeeper than me. We'll keep searching for him. I'll talk to DMV and find out about his car, get an APB out."

Turning to Warrick and Sara, Grissom said, "We're here, we'll work the scene. Maybe there's something. Sara, bedrooms and bathroom. Warrick, dining room and living room. I'll be in to help you, soon as I do the kitchen."

Brass returned to his car as Grissom got his kit out of the Tahoe. As the three crime-scene analysts neared the house, Grissom said, "Warrick, you've already been in the house. Go through and open the garage door, so I can get to the kitchen that way."

"Will do."

Enough feet had tracked through the crime scene already, and Sara had no choice but to enter through the front door to get to her assignment. Still, no reason for Grissom to add his prints to the pile.

A minute or so later the garage door motored up slowly and Grissom ducked inside. The garage was clean—a bicycle hanging upside down on the right wall, a small workbench in back, a lawnmower at left next to a plastic garbage can. A fresh oil stain about the size of a softball marked the cement where a car usually sat.

Moving through to the kitchen, Grissom got his first look at the destruction inside.

A small table, just big enough for two, normally in a bay window, had been shoved off in a corner, one chair on its side, the other, its back broken off, near the door to the garage, broken back wedged under the refrigerator. The mess included mounds of spices and powders on both the floor and the counters, having spilled from several open cupboards; and a broken bottle of jelly looked like a purple fragmentation bomb had gone off.

The tiled kitchen floor provided prime opportunity for footprints, and inspired Grissom to get out the electrostatic print lifter. He rolled out the mylar sheet, applied the two electric leads and touched them to the sheet, taking five long mylar sheets to get the kitchen done.

Next, he photographed the room from various angles, before going through the kitchen on his hands and knees, investigating the various pieces of things that had ended up on the floor during the skirmish. He bagged shards of broken glass that might contain fingerprints, did the same with bits of broken furniture and the toaster. He took samples of blood, and carefully collected threads of fabric and various powders that were probably only spices.

Finished, he took one last look around. He had covered the floors, the counters, the small table, and chairs and even looked in the open cupboards and been careful to dust for prints. The CSI was packed up and ready to leave when he glanced over at the double well sink. He *had* looked in there, hadn't he? Retracing his investigation, Grissom realized that when he had gotten to that part of the kitchen, he'd been focused on several blood smears on the countertop, and the hope that one might hold a fingerprint.

Pulling his Mini Maglite out of his pocket, Grissom returned to the sink. The garbage disposal side had a plastic cover fitted tightly over the drain. The sink itself was empty. The one place where all the mess should have gone, it was completely avoided, just another anomaly in a lifetime of crime scene anomalies.

The well on the right held a microwave container of chicken noodle soup that had obviously been spilled there from the drainboard next to the sink. The strainer basket had wound up across the room, against a wall, possibly used as a weapon hurled by one opponent at another. Grissom had bagged that already.

Looking down into the mass of noodles leaking into the slotted drain, Grissom thought he saw something shiny wink at him.

Carefully moving the noodles aside, the CSI got his forceps and shone the beam of his flash on the object as he gingerly guided the tips of the tool around the object.

The last thing he wanted was for the thing to fall through the slotted drain, into the trap. He would take the drain apart if he had to, but would prefer not. Slowly, carefully, he got the object into the center and clamped down on the forceps, locking the object in the tool's grip. Lifting it out, Grissom saw that he held a tiny diamond encrusted "D."

Flipping it over, he saw a joint on the back where something had been broken off. This was, he thought, most likely an earring. If so, why did Brower have a "D" earring?

Bagging it, Grissom placed the earring in his kit. Jerome Dayton might be a probable candidate for the "D," but this seemed an unlikely piece of jewelry for a man.

He'd check with Brass later. But right now, Sara and Warrick needed help with the rest of the house.

TEN

Outside the Brower house, Jim Brass paced.

For the first time, in a case that stretched back to the beginning of his Vegas career, he sensed that the end might be in sight. The Brower house had been a blind alley in that neither the copycat suspect nor the real CASt had been found within; but the signs of struggle indicated that both had been present.

Would CASt once again slip away? Would this case still be consuming him if he worked on it another ten years? Every time they'd gotten close, the rug seemed to get pulled out from under . . .

And so Jim Brass paced, at once angry and gleeful, frustrated and gratified, apprehensive and hopeful. As the CSIs loaded their equipment, the detective finally planted himself on the sidewalk next to their SUV.

He watched as Grissom lifted an evidence bag out of his kit; then the thoughtful CSI approached him.

"You know Brower," Grissom said. "Does he have anyone in his life whose name starts with 'D'? Someone who might wear this?"

Brass looked at the bag: The glittering diamond earring was broken, but the detective recognized it at once.

Grissom was saying, "The only names I could come up with, in the CASt context, were David Paquette and Jerome Dayton. But this seems to be a *woman's* bauble."

"It once was," Brass said. "It belonged to Dayton's mother—sonny boy had it made into an earring . . . and I saw him wearing it, *today.*"

The two men's eyes locked for a beat, and a pair of very faint smiles formed, and curt nods were exchanged . . .

. . . and then they were moving, Grissom slamming the rear doors on the Tahoe, Brass running for his Taurus, yelling to Carrack and Jalisco to follow him, leaving one squad behind to maintain the crime scene.

To Warrick and Sara, Grissom called, "Get in—CASt may be taking his curtain call!"

The parade of vehicles—Brass in front, followed by the CSI SUV and a patrol car—tore across the city, sirens screaming, Hacienda to Sandhill, then north to Tropicana, and back east to hook up with

I-515. Calling for backup, Brass found himself flying up the on ramp at eighty, and nearing one hundred as he sped north.

Around Pecos Road and Stewart Avenue, the interstate curved to the west, and Brass wove through traffic as he raced toward Dayton's palatial digs. By now two more patrol cars had fallen in behind Grissom's Tahoe, joining the motorcade. Brass blew down the off ramp at Town Center Drive, still going over fifty, and sailed across Town Center before swinging into the TPC at the Canyons, the guard having the good sense to raise the flimsy barrier when he heard the sirens and realized the onslaught was not slowing down, let alone stopping at his shack.

As they approached the club's residential section, Brass cut his siren and Grissom behind him followed suit, the patrol cars, too. Brass squealed the vehicle to a halt in front of Dayton's driveway, where the garage doors were down, though a familiar black SUV roosted out front of the castlelike house.

As Brass raced across the lawn, not bothering with the winding sidewalk, Sara and Warrick practically jumped out of the Tahoe to fall in behind him. Grissom moved off on his own, edging toward the driveway. Already standing on the porch were Catherine and Nick, glancing back with puzzled expressions.

Rushing to the steps, Brass stopped and looked up at them, figuring they'd heard his call for backup on the radio. "How'd you guys beat me here?"

"We didn't know you were on the way," Catherine said, lifting her eyebrows. "We're here to serve the warrant for Dayton's DNA."

"You got a warrant?" Brass asked, amazed.

Catherine said, "Yeah, Judge Landry."

Brass, frowning, was shaking his head. "All we had was the bruised hand . . ."

"And the news that Dayton was on a weekend pass when Vincent Drake got killed."

Nick said, "Dayton's old man helped keep the judge off the federal bench, y'know . . . and that Dayton family lawyer, Carlisle Deams, took part."

Brass found himself grinning. "Shrewd choice of judges, Cath."

Her smile was wicked. "Gil may hate politics, Jim, but it can cut both ways."

"I been knocking and ringing the bell," Nick said, jerking a thumb at the double doors. "Our boy doesn't seem to be home. What brought you on the run?"

"We found signs of a big struggle at Brower's house," Brass said, "and Grissom just snagged Dayton's earring, processing the scene."

"What," Catherine said, "that diamond D?"

"Dee one and dee same," Brass said.

Nick hit the bell again, but no one seemed to be coming; while they waited, Brass called for Carrack and Jalisco to bring the ram.

From the street, Grissom called out, "Trail of fresh

oil! Looks like Mark Brower's car hasn't been fixed yet."

Carrack and Jalisco hit the doors with the ram, right where they met, blowing them open with a satisfying crunch.

Then Grissom was in their midst, a referee with a flag on the play; he was slipping on latex gloves.

With quiet authority, the CSI supervisor said to Brass, "I want gloves on everybody—this may be a crime scene. We do not want to compromise anything that could put a serial killer away."

Brass said, "Same page," and gloves were snapped on before the entire group entered the house, guns drawn—even the notoriously gun-hating Gil Grissom.

Beyond a surprisingly small entry loomed a high-ceilinged living room, appointed in stark white with expensive yet oddly bland furnishings. An open doorway to the right revealed a huge kitchen, while a hallway to the left led to two stairways, one up, one down; a door on the left presumably opened into the attached garage, while at the end of the hall was a bathroom smaller than a ballroom, another hallway peeling off at right.

Sara and Nick moved into the kitchen. Jalisco and Catherine went upstairs; Warrick and Carrack took the living room, leaving Brass and Grissom to head downstairs into the basement.

* * *

As Sara Sidle followed Nick into the kitchen, he ducked slightly as he swept his pistol around the room; Sara stayed high, fanning in the opposite direction.

The large modern kitchen was empty—it seemed scrupulously scrubbed to Sara, even compared to her own much tinier but still tidy one. With all the gleaming polished chrome and steel, she was reminded more of an operating room than a kitchen—which was not a particularly comforting thought.

A pass-through on the left provided a window into the empty dining room. Next to that was a doorway between the two rooms.

The only thing out of place was a pink-tinged towel in the sink. Sara could hear Nick's breathing next to her, short quick bursts, the tension getting to him, too.

She nodded toward the towel. "Blood?"

"Could be," he said, his voice low. Then into his radio, he said, "Kitchen clear."

Going back the way they had come, Sara led Nick down the hall, toward the garage door.

Upstairs, Jalisco slipped into a bedroom to the left while Catherine Willows watched the two doors to the right—wouldn't do to have a demented serial killer spring at them from behind.

Or was there any other kind of serial killer, than demented?

"Guest room," Jalisco said. "Clear."

Catherine crossed past the stairwell to the first door on the right, heart pounding but her hands cool around the pistol grip. She always felt nervous in these situations—a little edge was a good thing—but never scared. Of all the nightshift CSIs, she had fired her weapon on the job most often, and had several kills to (what she did not like to think of as) her "credit." Trained well, and trusting of that training, she still felt completely in control—even though, like any cop in such a situation, she had no idea what might lay around the next corner or behind the nearest door . . .

. . . like the one on the right, which was open.

She stepped in quickly, swept the large bathroom with her handgun.

Everything was white, walls, towels, fixtures, rug, and of the highest quality, but nothing in this blizzard seemed out of place. She brushed back the white shower curtain to make sure no one was in the tub, then called to Jalisco: "Clear."

The last room upstairs, another bedroom, had been converted into an office. An L-shaped desk took up half the room, a huge desktop computer tucked underneath, an equally big monitor perched above.

Jalisco checked the closet while Catherine looked around the room. Walls were bare and white, desk was pale gray, the computer a pale gray as well, very little sign of use—a few books, the usual dictionary and thesaurus and so on, neatly between bookends, and a box of paper. The atmosphere was vaguely impersonal, even institutional, as if Dayton had become so used to Sundown, he'd brought that feel home with him.

Jalisco leaned back out the closet and said, "Clear."

The uniformed officer pushed the button on his walkie and reported in. "Clear upstairs."

Warrick Brown and Carrack circled like dancers with guns around the huge living room with its cathedral ceiling. Warrick spotted a formal dining room off to the right; at left, Carrack checked a fireplace that—instead of having a solid closed back—opened onto a bedroom. Moving to his right, around one end of a white leather couch, Warrick satisfied himself that the living room was empty.

He couldn't remember the last time he had been in such a monochromatic chamber: carpeting, furniture, walls, ceiling, everything was white, with the sole exception of the black face of the wall-hanging plasma screen and the blacks with red LEDs of shelved (and elaborate) stereo equipment.

The blankness of these surroundings chilled Warrick, and he did not chill easily. Could the Dayton family have lived this way? Or—as his instinct told him—had Jerome remodeled after their deaths, to make this castle his own?

That was when Warrick noticed something that

wasn't there: family pictures. Nowhere in the entry room or this living room, typical places for framed family photos, either on a wall or gathered on a table, was there any sign of the father and mother who had raised this only child.

For all the money in this room, the leather, the expensive video/stereo gear, Warrick had seen hotel suites with more personality.

Either Jerome Dayton had no personality, or he kept it well concealed . . . even at home.

"Clear," Carrack reported.

The pair moved on.

Brass barreled down the stairs, Grissom struggling to keep up.

This was a finished basement, the stairs emptying into a small space with doors on the right and left. Brass turned the knob of the door on the left and Grissom waited as the detective entered, finding himself in a family room with thick brown carpeting and brown sectional furniture under a row of windows that looked out over the backyard.

A 32-inch TV on a pedestal sat against the wall on the right; the wall to the left of the door was filled with paperback-packed bookcases, while the far left wall held another door.

Hell, Brass thought, *this place has more rooms than some hotels on the Strip. . . .*

And each one had to be cleared.

* * *

Sara opened the door to the garage and hit the light switch with the heel of her latexed palm—a fingerprint-preserving habit of hers.

Two cars were parked within: a new late-model white Lexus; and an older blue Dodge so filthy it was a wonder no prankish finger had written WASH ME in the grime. She and Nick moved carefully through, looking behind boxes and under a tool bench, making sure no one was hiding.

Finally Nick knelt to peer under the Dodge.

"Oil leak, all right," he said.

He rose and opened the passenger door, called back, "Keys in dash," then flicked the glove compartment open. He pulled out the registration and read aloud: "Mark Brower."

Sara pushed the talk button on her radio. "Garage clear. We have Brower's car, a very dirty Dodge."

Brass nodded when he heard Sara's voice come over the radio.

He checked over his shoulder, to see if Grissom had followed him into the family room, which he had; then Brass moved to the door at the back, grabbed a breath, hefted his pistol, and turned the knob.

Warrick and Carrack had gone down the hall, passing the door to the garage, taking a right into the bedroom that had been visible through the shared fireplace.

No one was in here, at least on first look.

This was obviously the master bedroom, and the stark white decorating theme persisted with a dresser, bureau, and four-poster bed.

Carrack checked the walk-in closet while Warrick entered another huge bathroom. Didn't take him long to find a pink-tinged wash cloth in the shower stall. Even without lab results, the CSI knew he was looking at a blood stain.

"Warrick!" Carrack called from the walk-in closet.

At the patrolman's side, Warrick followed Carrack's pointing finger to a pile of clothes next to the hamper: jeans with several dark spots on the legs and a blue T-shirt with a dark splotch on the front, which also appeared to be blood.

Into his walkie, Carrack said, "Bedroom clear."

Following up, Warrick said into his radio, "Gris—we have blood-stained clothing up here. Copy that?"

"*Copy,*" came Grissom's voice.

In the basement, following Warrick's news of blood-stained clothing, Brass switched off his walkie-talkie.

Much as he liked keeping the flow of information alive between teams, he did not want the cross-talk giving away his and Grissom's position.

Beyond the family room, he found himself in a bedroom.

But not just a bedroom, and not another room in this largely featureless house, painting itself an innocent white.

"Gil," Brass said. "You're gonna love this. . . ."

The "bedroom" was more like a dungeon; oh, there was indeed a bed in it, a simple black bed with black silk sheets, centered in the middle of the room; but there were no windows in here, and as both men got out their flashlights and flicked them on, the darkness of the room was only heightened by illumination.

The walls were painted a flat black; the carpet was black indoor–outdoor. Shackles hung from the ceiling at the four corners of the bed, and an amazing array of rough-trade instruments hung on the wall to the left, the tools of a sadist's workshop. Though the blackness made them difficult to discern, knobs gave away doors at left and right on the wall opposite.

Brass felt Grissom move up beside him.

"Door number one," Brass whispered, "or door number two?"

"Lady or the tiger?" the CSI supervisor replied with a terrible little smile.

But Brass never had to choose.

The door at left opened and a blood-drenched Jerry Dayton stepped into the room. Nude except for a flimsy pair of jockeys, the young man froze when he saw the pistols leveled at him, then raised his left hand against the glare of the flashlights.

His right hand remained behind his slightly turned body.

"Show me your hands, Jerry," Brass said tightly.

"Lower the light," Dayton countered. "I can't see a damn thing!"

Neither flashlight moved.

"Show me your goddamn *hands,*" Brass said, taking a half-step toward his suspect.

The hand came up, but as it did, Dayton flung something . . .

. . . something warm and mushy that struck Brass in the cheek, the detective firing, the sound like a thunderclap in the enclosed space, Dayton ducking to his left, the object he'd tossed flopping to the floor.

Grissom's beam found what had hit his friend in the face, putting a small spotlight on a severed human forefinger that seemed to point back at the CSI; its ragged bloody end leeched red.

At the same time, Brass's beam caught Dayton darting through the door on the right, leaving it open.

Brass yelled, "Freeze!"

But the suspect was gone.

"Dayton is yours," Grissom said, and slipped past him to go in the lefthand door.

Alone now, Brass shone the flashlight through the ajar door at right, then went after the suspect.

Even before the blood-streaked, near-naked figure had emerged into the black room, Gil Grissom had heard someone moaning.

Though his weapon was in hand, Grissom hadn't fired when Dayton literally flipped a finger at Brass, the CSI hesitating for fear of striking his friend, who flinched into his line of fire.

"Grissom! Grissom!" The voice was Sara's in the walkie-talkie. "We heard a shot—are you all right? What's going on?"

"Stay put," Grissom said into the walkie. "Brass is in pursuit of Dayton—keep all possible exits blocked!"

He clicked off.

Grissom's ears still rang from the gun as he moved out of the black bedroom, but he could make out the moaning, despite his compromised hearing.

This room was not black.

It was red.

Bare cement walls, floor, and ceiling—some pipes exposed above but blending into the overall mono-color scheme—had been painted out by a bright glossy red. The only light was a red bulb, stuck in a high socket on the left wall and, like every other room in this house, had another door at the far end. In the center of the crimson chamber—above a drain in the floor, cloaked in shadow but not clothing—Mark Brower hung from a noose just tight enough to keep him from moving, but not constrictive enough to kill him.

His hands were behind him, obviously bound but by what Grissom could not yet see. Blood poured from behind Brower to pool almost invisibly on the scarlet floor, and even Gil Grissom needed no further evidence to know that the finger flung at Brass had been unwillingly contributed by Mark Brower, mouth agape in some sort of bawling that Grissom saw but could not quite hear with his ringing ears.

His eyes wild with fear, and pleading with his potential rescuer, Brower managed, "Help me," but the words came to Grissom only as a faint, far off whisper, though the CSI's lip-reading skills made the cry crystal clear.

The red chamber was empty but for Brower, but Grissom didn't know whether Dayton's dive through that other door might not bring him back here around through a back way. As such, he didn't want to holster his weapon; but he had to help Brower, even if the common palmar digital artery was too small for the copycat to exsanguinate.

With any major trauma, however, the victim might go into shock, and Brower was definitely bound (so to speak) to injure or kill himself, if he didn't quit bouncing around with the noose around his neck. . . .

Switching his gun to his left hand, Grissom withdrew a pocket knife, got it open, and started to cut the rope just over Brower's head. The entire time, the CASt copycat kept moaning, "Help me, help me," like the human-headed fly in the old horror movie, and that was about how distant it sounded to Grissom, with his gunshot-ravaged hearing.

But the longer the CSI worked on the rope, the more the gunshot echo dissipated and the ringing in his ears dissipated too, Brower's appeals growing louder and more intense.

"Quiet," Grissom said, his own voice not much above a whisper. "We don't know where he is."

"You got a goddamn gun, Grissom!" Brower said, his features distorted with hysteria and pain. "Get me the hell out of here!"

Grissom kept at it and when he finally cut the last strand, Brower dropped to the floor, rolling into a fetal position.

"Gris!" came Warrick's voice from the walkie-talkie. "Please report! Do you need assistance?"

He pocketed his knife and pulled the walkie off his belt. "I have Brower down here. He's alive but short a finger."

"I'm coming down with Carrack and Jalisco—"

"No," Grissom interrupted, voice was low but emphatic. "Stay upstairs—it's dark down here, might wind up shooting each other. Set up a perimeter around the house, watch doors, windows, any possible exit. Brass remains in pursuit of Dayton, who is naked and bloody . . . and possibly armed and dangerous."

Nick came on then. "Gris, you sure you—"

"No," Grissom said, and shut off his radio.

Though the handcuffs served as a temporary tourniquet, Grissom thought it best to get direct pressure on Brower's wound. After returning his walkie-talkie to his belt, the CSI withdrew a standard handcuff key, and released the man . . . despite his own desire to leave him cuffed, and save time at the inevitable arrest.

"Sit up," Grissom said.

Brower just lay there, whimpering—*probably,* Grissom thought, *much as Sandred and Diaz had, when this creature exercised his performance art upon them, at their expense. . . .*

With more urgency, Grissom said, "Sit *up.*"

"Help me . . ."

Grissom did not want to touch Brower, who was, after all, evidence.

So it was not entirely a lack of compassion for the copycat that prompted Grissom to say, "No."

Reluctantly, Brower managed to sit up by himself. Grissom handed the man a handkerchief.

"What am I supposed to do with this?" Brower asked numbly.

Grissom said, "Apply direct pressure to your finger."

"*What* finger? That maniac *cut off* my goddamn finger!"

"Apply direct pressure to the wound . . . and stay here."

Still agitated, Brower asked, "Where the hell else would I go?"

"Well, if it's upstairs, you'll probably be mistaken for Dayton and shot." Which would be a nice irony, considering that was who Brower had homicidally imitated.

"I'm not going anywhere," he whimpered.

"To jail, you are," Grissom said.

Grissom moved to the back door of the room, listened intently, hoped it was the last room in this fun house, and reached for the knob.

Following Dayton, Brass—his flashlight beam leading the way—plunged into darkness.

He wanted to move faster, sure that Dayton was getting away; but he also knew others were posted upstairs, and that a little caution might go a long way toward keeping himself alive, if Dayton happened to be lying in wait somewhere. . . .

The detective swept the area with his beam.

Some kind of storage room—empty cartons stacked, shelves all around with smaller unmarked boxes; but no suspect.

Brass crossed the space, and found—yes—another damn door . . . open.

Doing his best to move silently, Brass eased through and swept the light over a workroom with bench, to his left; along the other walls, tools on pegboard, a drill press, a table saw, and a smaller bench with both a grinder and a vise. Beyond the bench on the left, at the far end of the room, naturally, waited yet another door. Smell of sawdust in his nostrils, Brass was almost past the bench when he felt a blow against his left leg, just below and to side of the knee, and then a blinding pain.

The gun and flashlight both fell from his hands, his weapon clattering to the floor somewhere at right, the flash bouncing off something before hitting the floor and spinning to a stop, the light now pointed at him.

He looked down at the knife sticking out of his pants leg, a dark circle spreading in the gray slacks. He started to lose his balance, but before he went down, Dayton rolled out from under the workbench and came up with a head butt that sent Brass tumbling backward, starbursts in his eyes, and he crashed into something hard, then fell to the floor.

He was trying to get back on his feet when a click preceded stark but limited illumination.

Very nearby, Dayton—red spattered on his face like he'd been eating barbecue, sloppily, eyes showing white all around, his wolfish white teeth exposed in an animal snarl—stood at the workbench, having just flipped on a switch for a single work light.

Brass had been looked at with displeasure by many a perp in his time, but never with such complete contempt and hatred.

"You—you meddling imbecile son of a bitch . . . you petty little civil servant scum of the earth . . . you've screwed my life over for the *last goddamn time!*"

Dayton lurched over and grabbed the handle of the knife and yanked it out of the detective's leg, like a demented dentist extracting a tooth.

Feeling white hot pain from head to toes, Brass nonetheless kicked with his good leg at the red-streaked naked figure, sending the killer sprawling back, and giving himself time to at least get to one knee before Dayton charged him again.

And when the attack came, Brass crouched low as Dayton raised the knife high.

When the blade arced down, Brass threw himself forward and left, the knife grazing his sportcoat and sending Dayton off balance, just as Brass smashed into the killer's knee with his shoulder.

Brass heard the satisfying crunch as Dayton's knee gave way and the killer toppled, twisting as he went. Then with a jungle cry, Dayton lunged at Brass, and the two of them rolled on the floor, fighting over the one knife they had between them.

Again Grissom found himself in a darkened room and flipped on the flashlight.

This room was small, rather like a fruit cellar, and indeed a set of shelves against the wall on the left recalled such a cubicle. Of the five shelves, three contained books and magazines and scrapbooks, including various editions of *CASt Fear,* including the recent one self-published by Perry Bell; Grissom allowed himself an educated guess that the other books and magazines contained chapters or articles about the murders, and the scrapbooks CASt clippings.

The next shelf held coils of rope and a dozen lipstick tubes: Limerick Rose.

And the top shelf was home to a row of small jars, the likes of which you would be unlikely to find in a typical fruit cellar, except perhaps at Ed Gein's farm.

In each jar sat a dried, shriveled index finger.

All but two, that is.

One jarred finger looked fairly fresh—very possibly, Perry Bell's.

And the fifth one from the left had no finger at all—likely the jar that had held Vincent Drake's finger before CASt sent it to the *Banner,* sacrificing it in defense of his good name.

This thought was still passing through his mind when he heard the sounds.

Grissom looked toward their source, yet another door, and what else was there to do but go through it? In such a small room it took only three quick steps, and he went in to see a yellow light on over a workbench and—their backs to him—the naked bloody Dayton and Brass struggling over a knife, locked in both their hands.

Brass had blood on him, too, perhaps not all of it Dayton's.

Grissom crossed the workroom just as Dayton, on top, hooked a left that caught Brass's chin and knocked the detective's head against the concrete floor. Brass didn't seem to be unconscious, but the fight appeared out of him, momentarily at least, and Dayton now had control of the knife. He grabbed onto Brass's left wrist and lay the hand on the cement. He was pressing the blade against the forefinger, just above the knuckle, when Grissom put the nose of the pistol against the back of Dayton's head.

"Drop the knife," Grissom said.

Dayton moved the knife to Brass's throat.

"Back away," CASt said, "or I cut it!"

"When I fire," Grissom said blandly, "your motor skills die with you."

Dayton froze.

"It's not a theory," Grissom said.

CASt cast the knife aside.

Grissom backed off slightly. "Stand up and fold your hands behind your head."

Coming up slowly, Dayton spread his arms wide, crucifixion style. Then with great care, the killer wove his fingers together behind his head, grinning defiantly at Grissom.

"Turn around," Grissom said.

Dayton did.

Then Grissom holstered the weapon and got out his handcuffs, about to secure the prisoner's hands behind him; but Dayton dipped, swept a leg around, and took the CSI's feet from under him.

Grissom went down hard on the cement.

Leg throbbing, Brass struggled to his feet, then slipped, his fingers nudging something cold . . .

. . . his pistol!

Grabbing the weapon, he wrapped his fingers around the grip and managed to get to a knee.

Dayton was punching a disoriented Grissom in the face, once, twice, then as the naked killer pulled back his fist for a third blow, Brass got his footing and once again Jerome Dayton had the mouth of a pistol kissing the back of his head.

"Case you were wondering," Brass said, "difference between me and Grissom? He did his best *not* to shoot you. . . . Jerry, Jerry, Jerry—please, please give me an excuse."

Dayton swallowed thickly.

Sanity got the better of the madman, and he put his hands up, and caused them no further trouble.

ELEVEN

As he sat in the interview room, Jim Brass was constantly aware of the bandage under his pant leg, and the stitches pulling at his skin. On either side of him were Sara and Nick, who had worked the case from its two different angles: new and old.

For the first time since the discovery of Marvin Sandred's body, Brass was not struggling with rage and/or frustration. He felt good—cool and calm, and ready to enjoy his revenge as a dish best served cold.

Across the table, a sullen, silent Jerry Dayton—in jailhouse orange and handcuffs—stared at the detective with death daggers in his eyes, and Brass felt only amused. Next to Dayton sat attorney Carlisle Deams, looking as respectable and distinguished as a college dean, a ruddy study in gray (hair, mustache, three-piece suit), frequently referring to a small pile of papers, a man who seemed unable to stop talking in his effort to assure Brass that his client wasn't talking.

The "tell," as ex-gambler Warrick might say, was the attorney's eyes: dark dead orbs that might have been a shark's.

"My client has nothing to say to you people—do you understand? Nothing."

Dayton's cuffs were in front of him—not the standard, safer behind-his-back—since he was in the presence of his lawyer.

"He was fairly chatty before," Brass said, "when he was running around wearing nothing but Mark Brower's blood, and sticking a knife in my leg."

"Well, you'll just have to be content, Captain Brass," Deams said with a nasty smile, "with your memories."

Brass provided his own mirthless smile. "My take on your client is that he has a mind of his own. This meeting is a courtesy, really."

The lawyer's dead black eyes blinked. "A courtesy?"

"Yes—to provide Jerry an opportunity to explain himself, to express his unique point of view."

Warrick said, "Mr. Dayton obviously has a certain pride in his . . . hobby. We thought he might like to help us sort out *his* work from that of this . . . interloper."

Sara said, "Of course, Mr. Dayton, if you don't

help clear things up? His efforts may be confused for yours, and vice versa."

Dayton was frowning, and the lawyer patted his client on the arm while saying to the adversaries across the table, "Very clever. But your attempts to play on my client's pride are not going to crack his resolve. He has nothing to say to you, nor are either of us interested in anything you might have to say."

Brass shrugged. "Well, then, we'll let the evidence do the talking . . . in court."

Deams chuckled dryly. "I'm more than happy to face the best the District Attorney can throw at us."

"Good." Brass beamed. "You're happy. I'm happy."

Deams smirked. "Let me tell you what you have— a charge against my client for simple assault."

Warrick said, "Not that simple—he kidnapped Mark Brower, and cut off his finger, and had him bound up in a torture chamber."

"Mark Brower came to my client's home and attacked him."

Sara gave up a smile. "Really—so Mr. Dayton cut off Brower's finger in self-defense? And put his head in a noose? That'll be fun to hear you argue in court."

Dayton frowned at his attorney, who then said to Brass and the CSIs, "Whatever you may have in the Brower matter is beside the point. You can't really think you're going to successfully prosecute my client for events that happened a decade ago?"

Brass said, "Mr. Dayton's DNA hasn't changed in

ten years—and we have his DNA from then *and* now."

"Stored under what conditions?" Deams said, waving that off as if it were nothing more than a bothersome gnat.

Warrick said, "We have voluminous physical evidence, Mr. Deams, including the fingers your client harvested from his victims, which we removed from his little basement museum."

Deams even shrugged that off. "We believe Mark Brower planted that evidence in my client's home."

"Well, then Brower must've made your client help him out," Warrick replied, "because only Jerome Dayton's fingerprints are on those jars."

The attorney gestured with open hands. "Circumstantial evidence. You have surprisingly little. Is there anything else?"

"You mean, other than your client running around bare-ass with blood all over him," Brass said, "stabbing a police officer whose presence was backed up by a warrant?"

Deams twitched something that was not exactly a smile. "My client is . . . a troubled young man. He has a medical history, which includes medication that has been quite successful in curtailing his . . . problem."

"Not lately," Brass said.

"We will show that a physician recommended my client take a drug holiday—that's a common practice for patients suffering chemical imbalance, who have been medicated for many years. It would appear that this holiday was . . . ill-advised."

"Ill-advised?" Brass said. "Maybe we should prescribe your client's doctor a lethal injection, too?"

"No such barbaric thing will happen to my client, Captain Brass. In fact, I'm quite sure this particular case will never get to trial."

"Your 'troubled' client," Brass said, "was institutionalized before, and yet he was out within three years. And now that Mommy and Daddy aren't around to keep him in a druggy haze, he's reverted to his 'barbaric' nature. No—even if you manage to convince a judge and jury that Jerry here doesn't know the difference between right and wrong . . . and I grant you he's a homicidal sociopath . . . he'll be in a state institution that'll make Sundown look like Club Med."

Dayton finally spoke—three simple words, directed at Brass: "I hate you."

"Well, that can be your new hobby, Jerry," Brass said, "in your new padded pad."

That did it.

Despite the cuffed wrists, Dayton came scrambling over the table at Brass, but Brass was ready and simply slipped aside, the killer sliding over the edge of the table, accidentally kicking his lawyer in the head before he landed face-first on the floor in an upended pile. The kick had sent Deams off balance, and he'd tumbled off his chair onto the floor as well.

A uniformed officer rushed in, but Brass waved

him away, grabbing Dayton by the scruff of the neck and picking him up like a big plastic bag full of trash; then Warrick was on the other side of the prisoner and together they dragged the dazed Dayton around and sat him down in his chair, hard.

Sara had come around to help the flustered attorney to his feet, and Deams growled a thanks at her and proceeded to slap away at his expensive gray suit as if it had gotten filthy from his trip to the carpet of the spotless interview room.

Both CSIs and the homicide captain seemed more amused than frightened or even flustered by this lame attack from a known serial killer.

"Jerry," Brass said, in a tone usually reserved for wayward children, "you really must watch that temper—someday you may do something really violent, and who *knows* what kind of trouble you'll get yourself in."

"I object," the lawyer squeaked. He had finally stopped brushing away imaginary dirt from his suit.

"You're not in court, counselor," Brass said. "Sit down!"

The attorney drew in a breath through clenched teeth; but he sat.

Deams turned to Dayton and, quietly, said, "You don't have to say anything. This interview is over when we say it's over."

Dayton was pouting; he might have been a six-year-old, stiffling tears. Stealing a glance at Brass, he said to the attorney, "I'm not afraid of him."

Deams shook his finger in Dayton's face. "You should be!"

Dayton lurched forward and bit down on the lawyer's finger, just under the middle knuckle, viciously.

Deams was screaming and both Warrick and Brass came around the table once more, the uniformed officer who'd been stationed outside sprang in again, this time with gun in hand.

With Warrick behind him, holding on to him, Dayton released his toothy grip and the attorney drew his hand away; the flesh was broken but the digit was still intact.

"You're not my father!" Dayton screamed.

The attorney, blinking fear and pain, said, "Jerry, you need to be quiet . . . just be quiet. . . ."

"You are *so* fired!"

"Jerry, please—"

"I told you what he did to me, Deams, and you didn't do anything!" Dayton strained forward as a cool Warrick held him by the shoulders. "You could have helped me! You let me go back to that house. Well, you're lucky I didn't make an example of you, too, counselor! Get out of my sight."

Holding up his good hand, Deams said, "Slow down, Jerry—you don't know what you're doing or saying. Your emotions are running away with you. You need to calm down, and look at this rationally. So *much* is at stake. . . ."

"You bleeding money out of me is at stake, you

conniving asshole!" Looking across the table at Brass, Dayton said, "Get him out of here—now!"

Sara was at the attorney's side. "Let's get that finger looked at, shall we?"

Deams swallowed, nodded, and—after gathering up his briefcase and papers in his good arm—allowed Sara to take him by the elbow; but the attorney paused near the door to say pointedly to Brass, "If you continue this interview, outside of my presence, with my client in his current mental state, I will—"

"He's not your client," Brass said.

"Yeah!" Dayton yelled childishly, suddenly pals with Brass. "I'm not your client!"

The attorney, who was holding the hand with the damaged finger out in front of him, as if hailing a cab, said, "Tomorrow he'll come to his senses. Tomorrow he'll hire me back."

"Today," Brass said, "you're not representing him. Good luck with the finger."

Sara walked the lawyer out.

Brass gave the uniformed officer a nod, and he stepped out. Now it was just Brass, Dayton, and Warrick.

Dayton's breathing—which had accelerated to that of a sprinter crossing the finish line—began to slow; his shoulders relaxed under Warrick's grip, and suddenly it was like the CSI was giving the prisoner a massage.

"I'm okay," he said, looking back at Warrick.

Warrick let go of him.

Dayton sat docilely, cuffed hands before him on the table. He slumped a little. He seemed placid now, and a little tired.

To Brass he said, "You and I . . . we may be . . . antagonists, but . . . we do understand each other. Respect each other . . . right?"

Brass and Warrick exchanged tiny significant glances.

"Sure, Jerry," Brass said.

"I'll talk to you. Tell you whatever you want to know. Start to finish, okay?"

"I'd appreciate that."

"But just you, Captain. I don't . . ." Dayton looked back at Warrick and said, "No offense, but you aren't anything to me. The captain and me, we go way back."

"No offense," Warrick said.

Brass nodded and Warrick did, too, and went out. The CSI would be on the other side of the two-way mirror and the uniformed man would still be just outside. Dayton had no more fight in him.

He just wanted to talk.

"I hate that guy," Dayton said.

"Warrick?"

"What, that tall guy? No, no—that goddamn attorney of my dad's. He's the one who got me sent out to Sundown, and that place was a nightmare."

"Really."

"Locked up, doped up, no TV after ten, monitored

everything you read—cancelled my *Hustler* subscription!"

Forcing any irony from his voice, Brass said, "Sounds like cruel and unusual punishment to me, Jerry."

"You know what the worst part was?"

"Tell me."

"Nobody there but crazy people. Everybody was a damn . . . loon! Do you know what it's like to deal with *loons* all day long?"

"I can imagine."

"I don't think you can."

"But your father and his attorney, they got you out. Why are you mad about that?"

Dayton was shaking his head, staring into nothing. "I told Deams what my father did to me, and he said he believed me, but I don't think he did. Otherwise he wouldn't have sent me back . . . there."

"Tell me about your father."

"Do I have to?"

"No. But it might help me understand you better." Brass sat forward. "We're connected, you and me, Jerry—you said so yourself. I think you understand me—I needed to stop someone who was very smart and clever, who was taking victims. It's my job to stop that kind of thing."

"Sure. I . . . I was only mad at you because . . . I don't mean to insult you, Captain."

"No, Jerry. We can be frank with each other."

"I don't do well with . . . authority figures."

"Like your dad?"

Dayton leaned his elbows on the table and put his hands on his face, looking out between his fingers, handcuffs jingling. He blew out a long breath. "Let's just say he was a hard man to please."

Brass nodded. "Yeah—I had one of those."

"Your father was mean to you?"

"Strict. And like you said, Jerry, hard to please."

"Not like *mine*, I bet!" He assumed a sterner posture, pointed across the table at Brass with the index fingers of his bound hands. " 'You're a disappointment, young man, a disappointment.' " His eyes glistened with tears. " 'We give you everything, and every opportunity, and you keep disappointing us! You're nothing but a weakling . . . a weak little girl. You know what weak little girls need, Jerry? Do you know what they need?' "

All the while the forefingers pointed and accused and waggled, and Jim Brass had no need for a court-appointed psychiatrist to explain the killer's fetish for taking his victim's forefingers as grisly souvenirs of his triumph over them.

The prisoner fell back in his chair, spent, the tears spilling, making wet ribbons down the narrow hawkish face.

"He beat you?" Brass asked. "On your . . . bare bottom?"

Dayton laughed bitterly. "Oh, is that what your 'hard' daddy did to you, Captain? You had it *easy!*

Oh, but I had to bend over, all right . . . I bent over for Daddy, so many, many times. . . ."

Brass frowned; Catherine and Nick had reported to him what the Sundown doctor had said about Dayton's stories of sexual abuse.

"Your father . . . violated you?"

"That's a nice word for it." He sat forward and screamed: *"He made me his bitch!"*

Brass shook his head.

Then he said something he never imagined to hear himself saying, much less truthfully: "Jerry, I'm sorry for what you suffered."

The killer's father, Thomas Dayton, had been a pillar of the community for decades, with nary a whiff of deviant behavior. Not that that was un-usual—some of the most important people had kinks buried beneath their decent surfaces; bigger the se-cret, deeper the cover-up.

And as Brass recalled Tom Dayton, from the few times he'd met the man—once at the mayor's annual prayer breakfast—the detective suddenly realized that this heavyset white male had been the template for every one of CASt's victims.

"Your victims," Brass said. "They *were* your father."

"Yes . . . yes. Those bastards, I made every one of them *my* bitch."

"But you stopped. When you came back home, from Sundown. Did your father stop abusing you, was that it?"

"He did stop. I was too big. And, well . . . he knew what I'd done, after all; he was afraid of me, in a way . . . at least I had that much satisfaction. But they kept me on those meds, and I was like a dog with a shock collar, y'know?"

"Is that why you stopped, Jerry? The meds?"

"Maybe. And the doctors. I mean, I never came out and talked about what I'd done, not really. But like you said, I'm smart and I'm clever. I could find things out by just talking to them, hypothetically. And I came to learn something, from the therapy."

"What was that?"

"That I couldn't make it right, I couldn't make what my father did not have happened, even if I made a thousand of him my bitches."

"Did you ever think to do it to . . . him?"

"Captain, haven't you been listening? Every *one* of them was him!"

"I mean . . . the real 'him,' Jerry. You never thought of killing him?"

"Killing Daddy?" Dayton blinked; he seemed confused. "How could I do that? He was my daddy. Didn't you love your daddy, Captain?"

"I did, Jerry. I did. But even if killing a thousand pretend daddies didn't help you heal, maybe . . . talking about it will be a start."

"To you? You're not a doctor!"

"Is that who you want to talk to, Jerry?"

Dayton snorted. "Not hardly. I can make them jump through hoops."

"Then talk to me." Brass shrugged. "Can't hurt. Look, we both know you're going away for a long time. You want it to be a hospital or a prison? Maybe I can help you choose."

"Hospitals," Dayton said with a derisive laugh. "I've already been down *that* road. . . . Do they let you subscribe to what you want to subscribe to in prison?"

"Depends on the facility. Did you say your father knew what you'd done? That you were CASt?"

"Of course he did."

"How?"

"He was . . . bawling me out about something. He'd stopped doing the . . . act . . . with me, I was too big, too old, too much stronger than he was. But he still, you know . . . told me what to do, told me what a disappointment I was. So I'd had enough of that and said, 'You better watch it, old man,' but he just laughed at me. So I told him. Showed him."

"Showed him?"

"The fingers. In the jars? I had four, I think, when I told him."

"So he knew."

"He knew, all right."

"And he and your attorney made arrangements to have you put away, where the law couldn't touch you."

"Yeah. See, the old man thought you were getting too close. That you were going to catch me. He said you were a really good, smart detective, that you were from back east where cops were tough. And that's one thing I agree with him on—you're good. So is that guy Grissom."

"Thanks. Was your father . . . upset with you, for what CASt did?"

Dayton closed his eyes. "He knew what I was doing, I think he figured out why I was doing it, but the only thing he gave a damn about was the 'potential scandal.' You know—the shame? So, he put me in that . . . that hellhole till the heat blew over."

"Then he took you out again, quietly."

Rocking gently now, Dayton said, "Yes. It was voluntary committal, so that wasn't hard."

"Did anyone besides the doctors know you were getting day and weekend passes?"

Dayton thought about it. "Deams did, for sure; I mean, he helped the old man get me out—the doctors were against it."

"But they didn't know about your hobby?"

"Please don't demean what I do by calling it a hobby, Captain. It's a statement, and a kind of . . . catharsis."

"Sorry, Jerry."

"No, the doctors didn't know I was CASt. I did tell them about what my daddy did to me, but I don't think they believed me. Who would *you* believe? One of the biggest men in town, or his sick-in-the-head kid? Anyway, they just thought I was too ill to be outside yet—you know, until they had a better handle on what was wrong with me."

Brass was putting certain disturbing pieces together. "And of course your father wanted you out as soon as possible, because he didn't want the doctors to know the reason behind your illness."

Dayton finally opened his eyes. He had a slightly startled look. "Is that why?"

Brass sighed. "Jerry, I appreciate your frankness."

"I've been straight with you, haven't I?"

"I would say so."

"Have I earned the right to ask you a question, Captain?"

"Okay."

"Were you the one?"

"The one . . . what?"

"I mean, you're smart. Really good. But I always had trouble believing you were the, you know . . . one."

Brass sat up. "I *don't* know, Jerry. Honestly."

Dayton sighed. Smiled. "Good. I wouldn't have liked that."

"Jerry, please explain what you're talking about."

Rubbing a wrist where the cuffs were chaffing, Dayton said, "Some cop knew about me. I mean, must have known, because the old man? For years he bitched about having to contribute to what he called 'the widows and orphans fund.' "

Brass's belly tightened. "What did you think that meant?"

Dayton shrugged. "Somebody, one of you people, figured out I was CASt, hell, years ago . . . and the old man paid that person off. For years I thought it was you, Captain. And I'm glad it wasn't."

Brass felt something dying, deep inside.

"Anything else I can tell you, Captain?"

"Why did you come back? And kill Perry Bell?"

"You know why. Somebody was stealing something very precious to me—my identity. My . . . like Superman! Secret identity."

"Why choose Perry?"

"Well . . . I'm not a smart detective like you. I work the other side of the fence, I guess. But I thought I had it figured out. I thought Perry was the copycat."

"But he wasn't."

"My bad," Dayton said. "Want to hear about it?"

Brass wanted to say no, but said, "Yes."

"I can't feel too terrible about the mistake," Dayton said. "After all, Perry Bell was a fat old drunk with no pride. What little he had in life, I gave him . . . because he picked up the fame I spilled, with that book of his. He didn't have the *strength* to do what I do."

As CASt emerged and Jerry Dayton receded, the killer sat straighter, his eyes bright, and for the first time since entering this interview room, Brass felt he was facing the blood-streaked fiend who had stabbed him.

"He begged for his life, of course," CASt said, voice cold, detached. "Said he was innocent, someone else must have done it. Funny thing is, he *knew* who the copycat was, but the damn drunk didn't even *know* that he knew."

"I'm not sure I understand."

"Well, he didn't suggest that the copycat might be Brower, until I helped him . . . focus."

"How did you do that?"

"How do you think? Cut his finger off. It's what I do."

". . . Why did you continue, Jerry—when you knew Bell wasn't the copycat?"

"Captain, would *you* leave a job half-done? I hated Bell for the things he said about me in his trashy book. He made it sound like I was out of my mind."

"The book helped make you famous."

"True. And perhaps that's why I took it so easy on him. . . . You found a key card at a murder site, didn't you?"

This CASt introduced as blandly as if asking the detective to pass the salt.

"Yes," Brass said.

"Bell's, of course. It wasn't until he and I were discussing my problem that he realized that Brower must have been the one who'd taken it."

Brower had been Bell's assistant; the card would have been easy enough for him to swipe.

"Why did you suspect Bell, and not his collaborator, Paquette? He cowrote *CASt Fear,* after all."

CASt shook his head. "Bell was out stirring things up with speaking gigs and trying to peddle that old crap book. Paquette was successful, he'd moved on. Anyway, I always suspected my father had paid him off, too, like that cop."

"Your father never mentioned who it was, this cop."

"No. But we both know, don't we, Captain?"

Brass said nothing.

CASt slumped in the chair and became Jerome Dayton. He looked exhausted.

Brass could hardly blame him, feeling drained himself.

"I fill in everything you need?" Dayton asked.

"You did fine, Jerry."

"You're not disappointed?"

"No. I may want to talk again. There's a lot of ground to cover, so many old cases."

"No problem. I like talking to you."

Brass said, "Good. I'm glad."

"You know what I really like about you, Captain?"

"What's that, Jerry?"

"You never point your finger at me."

"And Jerry," Brass said, "I never will."

The attending physician reluctantly granted Grissom and Catherine access to his patient. Despite a considerable loss of blood, Brower could talk without endangering himself. The doctor did limit the visitors to two, so Nick remained in the hall with the uniformed officer stationed outside the private room.

As the two CSIs entered this typical hospital room—the white walls, white ceiling, and single fluorescent tube behind plastic just above the bed—it oddly recalled to Grissom the living environs of the real CASt.

The copycat CASt lay under a white blanket, on top of which his heavily bandaged left hand lay, like a giant gauze club. Other than that, Brower seemed physically unaffected from his visit to CASt's castle.

As they'd entered, Brower had turned toward the window, the blinds slightly open to give him a third-floor view south, toward the Strip.

Catherine said, "Really think looking the other way is going to do the trick, Mark?"

The patient said nothing, staring out the window in stony silence.

Catherine walked around the bed and across his field of vision, and closed the blinds.

Brower glared at her, then turned away only to be confronted by Grissom, standing with arms folded and a placid smile.

Then the patient looked straight ahead and raised his right hand, in which the television remote resided, and turned the high-riding TV on, volume way up.

Grissom plucked the remote from the killer's hand and switched the set off. Brower's eyes never left the black screen.

"You don't have to look at us, Mark," Grissom

said. "In fact, I'm fine with that. But you do have to talk about this."

"Nothing to say."

Catherine leaned in. "Well, we have things to say."

"I don't have to listen. I'm the victim here, and you people are treating me like I did something wrong."

"You're the CASt copycat, Mark," Catherine said. "That's very wrong."

"I was investigating the original case," he said. "You should give me a reward for helping you nab the real CASt."

"Thanks," Grissom said, his inflection light. "But I'm afraid the understudy doesn't get to go back on stage and become a star. You see, Mark, we've been to your house. We found the tinsmith clippers—which test positive for blood—that you used to cut off the fingers of your victims; we've got the rope you used, lipstick, the entire makings of the road company CASt."

Brower's face fell, but then he managed to summon indignation. "What the hell good will that do without a warrant?"

"That's why we're here, Mark," Grissom said pleasantly, and lifted a hand that held the very document; he handed it toward Brower, who looked at the small sheaf of papers as if it were on fire.

"On what grounds?" he demanded.

Grissom tossed the warrant on the bed, while Catherine provided the patient with a soothing smile.

"We matched your fingerprints to the door bells of Marvin Sandred and Enrique Diaz."

Brower said, "They . . . they must have been planted. I'm a crime beat reporter! I wouldn't do anything, so . . . so . . ."

"Dumb?" Grissom asked. "Want to tell us about it?"

"No."

"All right. Then I'll tell you. . . . Paquette wouldn't fire Bell and he wouldn't promote you while Perry was still there. If Mark Brower was ever going to get his own column, make a real name for himself, Perry Bell had to go. But why not just kill Bell?"

Brower said nothing.

So Catherine answered, "What, and make him a martyr? You needed to discredit him, Mark, and at the same time provide yourself the ringside seat for a major crime story, and do your own CASt book."

Suddenly Brower spoke, softly, very softly. "I was carrying that fat drunken bastard for the last five years. It was my turn to be someone . . . my turn to be the star reporter."

"Maybe you still can be," Grissom said brightly. *"Ely Hard Times* is always looking for a good scribe."

Brower clearly didn't know what Grissom was talking about.

Catherine patted the patient's bandaged hand, ever so gently, and explained: "Prison newspaper, Mark. You can be the Death Row correspondent . . . for a while."

* * *

How long he'd been driving around, Brass had no idea; darkness had settled over the city, and he still hadn't found his way home.

Things had sorted themselves out and Grissom had assembled the evidence in a manner that gave them a pretty good handle on the facts.

Mark Brower would likely receive a lethal injection, though he had cooperated, giving Grissom and Catherine a complete confession—which actually might buy the reporter a lifetime lease on a maximum security cell out in Ely. Might.

Jerry Dayton would likely not face the ultimate punishment, at least not the one this world provided. At least six men were dead, but Dayton would spend the rest of his life in a mental hospital, the kind that didn't hand out weekend passes like free samples at a supermarket.

Though he could hardly believe it himself, Jim Brass felt sorry for Dayton, and hoped within the walls where he would live out his troubled life, the man would get some real help, a measure of peace.

Not every day that a cop took two serial killers off the streets, but what should have been an evening for celebration had found the detective driving aimlessly around Henderson, avoiding the address he'd come to town seeking. Finally, he gave up and pulled in at the guard shack at Sunny Day Continuing Care Facility.

The guard rang ahead, and when Brass got to the

building at the far end, his old partner was sitting on the front step of the building in a dark bathrobe and slippers, smoking a cigarette.

"Want one?" he asked Brass.

The detective shook his head. "I quit."

"I got a drink for you inside . . . ?"

"Quit that, too."

"What a damn bore you've become, Jim."

Brass looked through the darkness at Vince Champlain. In the meager light seeping from neighboring apartments, Vince seemed very old, almost frail. Funny to have it come this—Champlain had always seemed so strong to Brass, back when they were partners, almost a father figure; but the man who had covered his back for years now seemed weak.

Brass sat next to his old friend.

Vince took a long drag; let it out; chuckled, coughed. "Margie won't let me smoke in the apartment. Makes me come out here. Treats me like a little kid."

"We put Dayton away today."

"I heard. All over the tube. And Mark Brower? Who'da thunk it?"

"Who'da thunk it."

With a sideways glance, Champlain said, "So I suppose you talked to that lunatic Dayton yourself?"

"I did."

"Never know what those crackpots are gonna claim, do you?"

"Is that your way of denying it?"

The retired cop shrugged. "If you think you know, you think you know. What can I do about it?"

"Until just now, I figured maybe I was wrong. We weren't the only ones on the case."

"Damn near. Well." Champlain took another deep drag. Let it slowly out. Did not look at Brass. "What are you going to do about it?"

Brass looked up at the stars. "Not sure yet."

"You could forget about it. Write it off as the ravings of a loon."

Brass lowered his vision and brought it in line with his ex-partner's, and the men locked eyes.

"Sorry," Champlain said, and looked away. "Shoulda known better."

". . . Margie know?"

Champlain shook his head. "Why? . . . You gonna tell her?"

"Not my place."

"What *are* you going to do? I have a right to know."

"The rights you have are to remain silent and to have a lawyer appointed for you if you can't afford one, though with the money Tom Dayton gave you over the years, I'm pretty sure you can get a decent one. Maybe even Carlisle Deams."

The frown had anger in it, and disappointment; but also embarrassment. "So . . . you're taking me in? My own partner?"

"Maybe I'm just reminding you. I don't know how

you verified Dayton was CASt, or how you did that without the press . . . or me . . . tipping to it. But you had enough to put the squeeze on Tom Dayton, despite all his power."

"When did you get so goddamn self-righteous?" Champlain said, stubbing out his smoke under a slipper. Without hesitation, he lit another one.

"Call it that if you want, Vince. I took an oath and they gave me a badge. I don't have a wife. I have precious few friends away from my job. So I don't have much but the ability to go to sleep, justified. It's enough."

"Go to hell, Jim. Just a little goddamn money, is all."

"If that's how you get to sleep, that's your business. But people died, Vince. Vincent Drake and Perry Bell were both killed by the real CASt, after you took Tom Dayton's money to look the other way. Those murders could have been prevented. . . . *Why?* So you could retire in comfort?"

Champlain tossed his cigarette into the night, trailing sparks. He gave Brass a long hard look. "Yes."

"That simple."

"Simple choice: retire on Dayton's money and have a little something, or retire after thirty years on a pension I could barely live on myself, let alone support my wife. See, I *do* have a wife. And life."

"A life that a couple of people had to die so you could maintain?"

Champlain stared into the dark. "I'm not proud of

that. I thought the son of a bitch was just another vegetable on the funny farm, never to be heard from again."

"You were wrong."

"You think I don't know that? But it was too late to do anything about it!"

"Yeah? Or did you just ask for a bigger stipend from Daddy Dayton . . . ? What do these apartments run for, anyway? You get full health treatment here, too, right?"

"Right. What are you going to do, Jim?"

Brass thought about it. "Give me a cigarette."

Champlain did. Lighted it up. "Thought you stopped."

"I did. But you're not worth losing my sobriety over."

The detective took several long drags.

Again Champlain asked: "What are you going to *do*, Jim?"

Brass turned and looked hard at his former partner. "I'm going to sleep on it. Who knows what the night will bring? You know the cop trade, Vince— never know what's coming next, when the next confession's gonna walk in the door, or when some poor bastard's gonna decide to eat his gun. . . . What are *you* going to do?"

Then Brass pitched the sparking cigarette into the night, rose, and began to walk away.

Champlain was on his feet, but Brass couldn't see it.

But he heard the man call out: "Is *that* how you're gonna leave it? After all these years? After I watched your back?"

But Brass did not reply, just kept walking.

And Vince Champlain watched his partner's back one last time, until Brass had been swallowed by the darkness.

A Tip of the Test Tube

My assistant Matthew Clemens helped me develop the plot of *Binding Ties,* and worked up a lengthy story treatment, which included all of his considerable forensic research, from which I could work. Matthew—an accomplished true-crime writer who has collaborated with me on numerous published short stories—does most of the on-site Vegas research, and is largely responsible for any sense of the real city that might be found herein.

We would once again like to acknowledge criminalist Lieutenant Chris Kauffman CLPE—the Gil Grissom of the Bettendorf Iowa Police Department—who provided comments, insights, and information; Chris has been an important member of our CSI team since the first novel, *Double Dealer,* and remains vital to our efforts. Thank you also to another major contributor to our research, Lieutenant Paul Van Steenhuyse, Scott County Sheriff's Office; as well as

Sergeant Jeff Swanson, Scott County Sheriff's Office (for autopsy and crime scene assistance), and Lieutenant Steve Johnson CLPE, Certified Forensic Artist, Davenport, Iowa, Police Department.

Books consulted include two works by Vernon J. Gerberth: *Practical Homicide Investigation Checklist and Field Guide* (1997) and *Practical Homicide Investigation: Tactics, Procedures and Forensic Investigation* (1996). Also helpful were *Crime Scene: The Ultimate Guide to Forensic Science,* Richard Platt; and *Scene of the Crime: A Writer's Guide to Crime-Scene Investigations* (1992), Anne Wingate, Ph.D. We would also like to acknowledge *BTK* by David Lohr, www.crimelibrary.com. Any inaccuracies, however, are my own.

At Pocket Books, Ed Schlesinger, our gracious editor, provided solid support. The producers of *C.S.I.: Crime Scene Investigation* sent along scripts, background material (including show bibles) and episode tapes. In particular, I'd like to thank Corinne Marrinan, the coauthor (with Mike Flaherty) of the indispensible Pocket Books publication, *CSI: Crime Scene Investigation Companion.* As I've told Corinne, how Matt and I wish we'd had her excellent book from day one.

Anthony E. Zuiker is gratefully acknowledged as the creator of this concept and these characters; and the cast must be applauded for vivid, memorable characterizations that influence every word we write. Our thanks, too, to the various *C.S.I.* writers for their inventive and well-documented scripts, which we draw upon for backstory.

About the Author

MAX ALLAN COLLINS, a Mystery Writers of America "Edgar" nominee in both fiction and non-fiction categories, was hailed in 2004 by *Publisher's Weekly* as "a new breed of writer." He has earned an unprecedented twelve Private Eye Writers of America "Shamus" nominations for his historical thrillers, winning twice for his Nathan Heller novels, *True Detective* (1983) and *Stolen Away* (1991).

His other credits include film criticism, short fiction, songwriting, trading-card sets, and movie/TV tie-in novels, including *Air Force One, In the Line of Fire,* and the *New York Times*–bestselling *Saving Private Ryan.*

His graphic novel *Road to Perdition* is the basis of the Academy Award–winning DreamWorks 2002 film starring Tom Hanks, Paul Newman, and Jude Law, and directed by Sam Mendes. His many comics credits include the *Dick Tracy* syndicated strip (1977–1993); his own *Ms. Tree; Batman;* and *CSI: Crime Scene Investigation,* based on the hit TV series for which he has also written three video games, two jigsaw puzzles, and a *USA Today*–bestselling series of novels.

An independent filmmaker in his native Iowa, he wrote and directed *Mommy,* premiering on Lifetime in 1996, as well as a 1997 sequel, *Mommy's Day.* The screenwriter of *The Expert,* a 1995 HBO World Premiere, he wrote and directed the innovative made-for-DVD feature, *Real Time: Siege at Lucas Street Market* (2000). His latest indie feature, *Shades of Noir* (2004), is an anthology of his short films, including his award-winning documentary, *Mike Hammer's Mickey Spillane.* A DVD boxed set of his films will appear in 2005.

Collins lives in Muscatine, Iowa, with his wife, writer Barbara Collins; they frequently collaborate on fiction, sometimes under the shared byline "Barbara Allan." Their son Nathan is majoring in computer science and Japanese at the University of Iowa in nearby Iowa City.